Inevitable

Written by Kolene Taylor

Prologue

Eve walked down the street with her shopping bags in both hands. Her big white floppy hat sat cocked on the right side of her face dipping over her black Donna Karen sunglasses. Her sandy hair lay across her shoulders. Her navy jacket extended down to her knees and was set off by the matching skirt that didn't dip much further.

Stopping to admire a red chiffon evening dress displayed in the window of one of the exclusive boutiques downtown, she checked her watch. She had time. She was meeting Lola and Teresa for lunch and she knew only Lola would be on time, Teresa was notorious for being late. Luckily, the restaurant where they were meeting was just up the street.

Strolling down the avenue looking at the newest designs, Eve knew she shouldn't have walked from her office to the restaurant. Shopping was her weakness and she always gave in to temptation. Her impulsiveness got her in more trouble than debt and she promised she would make wiser decisions. Two pair of shoes later, she was now looking at this dress in the window. Staring longingly at the beautiful scarlet dress, she exercised her discipline and made the decision to walk past the entrance of the store.

"You know you would look too good in that dress."

That unforgettable voice sent chills up and down her back causing Eve to stop in her tracks. She hadn't heard that voice in two years and she couldn't believe she was hearing it now. She took a moment and gathered herself before she responded.

"Well, I'm teaching myself to resist temptations, no matter how enticing they can be."

She turned to face her past.

"Well, resisting is overrated," he said, smiling that easy smile. "I say go for it."

"Well, Elijah," she said offering a sad smile. "I did that before and it didn't quite work out like I wanted." *Damn I remember that smile.*

"Ah, you remembered my name." He answered with mock surprise. "Two years is a long time." His smile broadened. "Well, can I tell you that you look better than ever?"

"I could never forget your name," she said, taking off her glasses and revealing deep brown soulful eyes. "And I have more scars from you than even I will admit to and some that will never let me." She whispered to address the latter comment.

He cocked his head questioning. And she took in Elijah's handsome face. *Damn, this man will forever be fine.*

They stared in awkward silence.

Elijah finally spoke. "I'm still working here in the city although I do have another offer on the table. Some would say that it is an offer that I can't refuse."

That was such a random thing to say. I have never experienced him seemingly so uncomfortable, she thought. "You know those offers you can't refuse sometimes are not what they promise." She paused letting her words stand between them, and then she looked down at her watch again. "I have to go. I hope that all your endeavors work for your good."

"I do too." Elijah answered with a suggestive meaning.

Eve started adjusting the bags in her hands. "It was nice seeing you Elijah. Take care."

Eve turned around and began to walk away. She didn't hear him behind her so when he touched her chills skipped along her spine and somehow settled in her stomach. His touch had that everlasting affect. She turned and looked up into his eyes.

"Eve, I was thinking..."

Eve smiled removing his hand from her arm and placing her shades on her face. "No Elijah, don't think. That is what got us here."

What is really going on?
Chapter 1

Eve Newborn ran around her bedroom looking for her shoes. He would be there any minute and she wanted to be ready. Why was she nervous? While looking at her hair in the mirror, she grimaced. *Don't worry about it. You look fine. It's not like you're trying to impress him. It's just ice cream.* She ran her hand over her nutmeg-colored skin and through her tawny locks. *Your skin is looking the bomb, girlfriend.* She smiled at her image and pulled her hair back into a ponytail, slicking the fly away hairs with a little gel. Finally, she grabbed her shoes and headed toward the living room.

"You wearing that?" Her sister, April, held a pint of ice cream as she fired the question from the doorway of the bedroom. April was a younger version of her older sister except her hair was like coal and she had a much rounder face.

"Yeah. Why?" Eve asked looking down at her dress. It was loose fitting and comfortable. "I shouldn't?"

April shook her head. "You look fat."

"Well, what am I going to wear?" Eve panicked. She went back into her closet.

April moved into the room and plopped down on the bed. She often stayed with Eve when she and her boyfriend were fighting. It was always the usual drama and Eve didn't understand why April put up with it, but she didn't push and she always made it understood that if her little sister needed her or a place to stay she was more than welcome.

However, Eve was always a bit self-conscious about her curvaceous figure and April's commentary sent her into a tizzy. "He'll be here."

"Who?"

"Elijah Mann," Eve said coming out of her closet with a hand full of clothes.

"Mann? Is he white?" April asked scooping ice cream into her mouth.

"No."

"I guess it really doesn't matter," April shrugged. "It's not like he is your man-or is he your man?"

"No April, he's not my man," Eve said rolling her eyes. "He's the guy I told you about that came to town as a consultant, remember?"

"Oh yeah," April said and put the empty container on the bedside table. She then began chipping fingernail polish off her red painted nailbeds. "So why are you two going out and is he married?"

"No," Eve said watching her sister flick the ruby colored shavings on to her comforter and area rug. "No," she restated, distracted by her sister's actions. "He's not married."

"And he's in town because?" Her sister inquired again, now brushing the red flakes off her blouse onto the floor.

"He's in town on business and it doesn't matter because... are you going to pick that shit up before you leave?" Eve asked perturbed by her sister's audacity.

April ignored the question and continued her interrogation. "What kind of business?"

"Well, you remember six months ago when our company was bought out by Clearview Corporation?" Eve asked as she went and pulled the dust buster off the wall and handed it to April. "He was one of the outside consultants they hired to help the transition go smoothly. I met him then. They contracted him to come in every three to six months for the first two years to help monitor how the change is affecting the workplace. I became friends with him because being the Director of Operations I had to convince him my job is important-or rather that I'm important to the company."

"So why are you two going out?" April asked clicking the

switch of the Dust Buster off and on.

"Did you not hear me when I said I'm trying to save my job?" Eve was irritated by her sister's actions and questions. She was not going to admit that she was going out with this man because he was gorgeous and she was tired of being alone. Although she wasn't one to mess with men in a relationship, lately the only men who came for her were married. At least Elijah wasn't married. She had no intention to get involved with him, but one date wouldn't hurt.

"Girl please, your job ain't going nowhere," April dismissed. "And, how you know he's not married?"

"Didn't I just tell you… look it doesn't matter if he's married, anyway. He's a friend and that's it."

"Do you always run around worrying about what you're going to wear with all your *friends*?" April grinned. She loved to get under Eve's skin.

"Shut up," Eve said, throwing a pillow at April and hitting her in the head.

She and Elijah had been flirting off and on for a while and she didn't want to admit that the flirting comments he made did indeed get to her. She wasn't sure what he was after, but tonight she planned to find out. She also wanted to play a little and didn't see the harm in that.

Eve took out a pair of jeans and a white blouse and began to change. April lay across the bed and watched her sister dress.

"Well, how long has he been with this woman?" April pushed. She knew the type of man her sister attracted.

"I don't know. The rumor around the office is that it's been a while," Eve answered as she buckled her sandals.

"You been involved in the gossip around the office? That's not your style," April teased.

Eve threw her sandal at her sister and it hit the wall.

April rolled over, picked it up and tossed it back to her. "Do they have kids?" she continued.

"Yes."

April shook her head and rolled her eyes to the ceiling. As she got up and walked back into her room, she mumbled loud enough for Eve to hear, "You messing with a married man."

"I heard you," Eve yelled after April. "And don't you forget to get this polish off my floor."

At the same time the door to her sister's room clicked, Eve heard a car pull up. She did the last check of her appearance and then ran and opened the front door. She watched Elijah stroll up the walkway toward the door. He was dressed in a gray fitted sweater and black jeans. He smiled when he saw her standing in the doorway.

"You know you have frogs out here," Elijah said as he approached the screen door.

"Where?" Eve asked, closing the screen before he reached it. She was terrified of frogs.

"There's one right there by the door."

"Well, I'm sorry. You're not coming in and I'm not going out until that frog is gone." Eve wasn't even looking at Elijah, but looking for the frog.

"You're that scared of frogs?" He was amused by her reaction.

"What was your first clue?" She sarcastically glanced up at him and quickly returned to locating where the frog was.

"You wouldn't have done well in that whole 'let my people go' thing with Moses, huh?" he asked, laughing. "Don't worry. It just hopped into the bush."

"Are you sure?" she asked, peeping through the screen door.

"Yes." He opened the screen. "Are you ready?"

"Let me get my purse."

Eve grabbed her purse from the couch and hurried through the door. Elijah chuckled as he watched her look for the frog, and he outright hollered when the frog showed itself on the lawn and she sprinted to his rental car. By the time he made it to the car, Eve had found the humor in the situation and they both laughed.

He opened the passenger door for her and closed it as she got in. *At least he's a gentleman.* She noticed the nice comfortable feeling of leather as she nestled into the seat. When he got in, he noticed her relaxed posture and reached over and changed the satellite radio to smooth jazz. Eve found herself taking in browned butter skin and his beautiful mouth that revealed straight white teeth.

This man is fine. Her thoughts made her even more aware of her situation. It was a warm summer evening with a good-looking man and beautiful music. Lord, what in the world was she doing?

When he called, the low timbre of his voice was straight seduction, even when they discussed work. When he started calling for personal reasons, Eve knew she shouldn't have even entertained him but she was drawn in. Truthfully, it was the texts that got her. The sexual innuendos were strong and captivating. She found herself rereading them. And when she would finally delete them, another would come.

His quest seemed to come out of the blue. She was never aware of any mutual tension between them prior to a mysterious text he sent her. She was sitting in her living room at the computer answering all of her emails and her phone rang indicating a text. Looking down, she noticed his name and thought nothing of it. He was good about sending jokes and different things, so she had no apprehension reading it. It wasn't a laugh that she got.

Hey, I was on a business trip in Texas and I had a dream about you and me in a compromising position. What do you think that was about?

Eve was surprised by this and didn't know what to say. She decided to respond sarcastically:

Don't know what to think other than you shouldn't eat big meals late at night. Everyone knows that it causes bad dreams.

He sent back a smile emoji and she didn't hear from him for another two months.

Then one night she was checking her social media when a

message from Elijah popped up. That was when all was revealed. Eve found herself engaged in one of the most provocative text conversations of her adult life. At first, she tried not to take it too seriously, but they began to occur quite often. First it was texts, and soon they graduated to the phone. Although this activity increased, they fell short of full on phone sex. She made it clear to herself that she wasn't interested in actually crossing the line. She didn't get involved with men in relationships.

But their relationship moved from platonic to full on sexual tension. Anytime they found themselves in each other's presence, they exchanged secret glances and spoke in secret code. Eve was paranoid thinking somehow someone knew. To her, everything seemed so obvious, but Elijah was really cool. The flirting was becoming more intense and the desires were actualized. She stayed mindful and always on guard so as not to be made a fool. Now was the first time they were alone face-to-face. Knowing partly what he wanted, she found herself curious as to whether that was all.

Eve and Elijah went on a hunt for ice cream. Every place they went was closing soon, which gave them no time to talk, so they settled for coffee at the twenty-four-hour diner not far from his hotel.

They were sitting in an isolated booth in the back of the diner. This meeting was not late by her standards but late enough for the diner to be virtually empty. Their waitress came to take their order and Eve used this time to get her nerves together. When the waitress left, Eve got up enough nerve to catch Elijah's eyes searching for the reason she was there and what he was thinking. Elijah sat there sipping on his coffee, watching her watch him. She made mental notes about how beautiful he really was. He was tall, with smooth skin, short black hair perfectly edged with tiny waves. His eyes were sultry brown and his smile, surrounded by a black hair goatee, could knock any woman to her knees. She was so completely taken by him.

Eve held his gaze as long as she could. Then she turned her head, sighed, and took a sip of her water. She noticed that he adjusted in his seat. When she looked up, he was leaning with both arms folded on the table.

"You look like there's something you want to ask me," he stated, watching her closely.

"What gives you that impression?"

"I don't know. Maybe it's the way you were looking at me and then you sighed."

She shrugged her shoulders but didn't say anything. He settled himself back into his seat and cocked his head to the side.

"I'll give you sixty seconds to ask me anything you want to," he said abruptly.

"Wha...what do you mean?" she asked surprised.

"I'll give you sixty seconds to ask me anything," he repeated smiling. "And make it good."

"You can't just spring something like that on someone." She threw herself back in her chair. "I would want to think about it."

He placed his hands behind his head. Her attention was drawn to the power displayed in his arms. Her heart fluttered.

"Are you trying to tell me there isn't one thing you've wanted to ask me?" he asked, regarding her intently.

"I'm sure there is, but to spring one minute on me and tell me to wade through all the thoughts in my mind is unfair," she said preoccupied with those very thoughts.

His smile broadened. Looking down at his watch, he simply said, "You had sixty seconds, to be exact, but now you are down to fifty seconds."

She stared at him and held an unspoken conversation with herself. *Ask him 'Why' you idiot. But do I really want to know? Well, that is what you came here for, is it not?*

"Are you going to be totally honest with me?" she asked, trying to build her confidence.

"Yes."

"Ok. I have it," she declared. He lifted his eyebrows and nodded his head. She took a breath. "Why me?"

"Why not you?" He responded quickly, not surprised by the question.

"I call bullshit. You can't answer a question with a question," she challenged. *He's cool. He's too cool. Maybe he's been through this before. Well, if he has, he has never been through it with me.*

He moved closer to the table to be closer to her.

She leaned forward until she was inches away from him. "Now, I will repeat my question. But allow me to be more thorough." She cleared her throat and took a drink of the water sitting right next to her. "Why would you choose to take an interest in me when you seemingly have everything you need? No, wait," she said thoughtfully. "That's not what I want to know."

He shifted in his seat and continued to look amused.

"I want to know what you want from me?

His smile slipped and his eyebrows drew together in confusion. He hunched back in his seat. *Aha you got him on the run now.*

She continued. "I mean, I know you like certain parts of my body, because you have made reference to them on more than one occasion, but is that all you want? Or better yet. . ." She indicated for him to come closer. He did. "Do you even like me?"

He let out an uneasy laugh and retreated once again. "You're going to waste your opportunity on that?"

"Is it a wasted question?" she asked with a lifted eyebrow.

"Yes."

She smiled and settled back into her chair. "Nonetheless," she spoke. "It is what I want to know."

He looked at her for a moment and answered. "Yes, I like you."

"Why?"

He dropped and shook his head. "If I was an asshole I would tell you I've answered your one question," he said sarcastically.

"Well, prove that you're not and answer all of them," she retorted.

"Is there something you're getting at? Because if there is, you're going the long way around."

"No, I'm asking the question, or questions, I want to know."

"Ok. Um. . .I like you because you're sexy as hell. I've had fantasies about you, about wanting to. . ."

"You do realize that I'm more than a big ass and some tits?" She interjected being purposefully crude.

He laughed at that.

She became annoyed.

The waitress came and refilled their coffee cups.

They sat in silence both sipping the strong brew. Finally, he broke the silence. "Eve, I think you're a beautiful person. I think you're smart and funny. I really do like you as a person. I also have an insane desire to fuck you."

His bluntness, although appreciated, caught her unaware.

Lord, now I'm on the run. She took in a deep breath and exhaled it slowly and asked, "Do you always get what you want?"

"Most of the time."

"Is that all you want from me?" she asked.

He stared at her for a long time before he answered. "Yes."

Her breath caught and she closed her eyes so he wouldn't see how deeply that one word stung. Although she knew it was an honest answer, her heart still clenched together. It's a harsh flattery to know someone wants you but only to have sex with you. It's like being slapped in the face, and then having that same person, kiss it to make it feel better.

She took another breath and opened her eyes. He was sitting back against his chair with his own eyes lowered. At that moment, she really looked at him. She knew one of the reasons this attraction was so strong was because she was lonely and he had a lot of the qualities she would want in a man. This man was a rescue from her dull life. She knew it would be dangerous to think she could just be a sex partner with him and embark on the fulfillment of his and her fantasies. But goodness the man looked delicious. Maybe she could?

At that moment, he opened his eyes and caught Eve's stare. She blinked once and nodded her head.

The hotel room.
Chapter 2

They ended up back at his hotel room because he spilled coffee on his shirt. On their way back to his room, she teased that he didn't have to spill coffee on his shirt to get her to go back to the room with him. They laughed. As if he detected her apprehension in her attempt at humor, he reassured her that he was simply going to just change his shirt. The idea was for him to go up to the room and change, and then they would continue to talk downstairs by the hotel's swimming pool. He did go and change while she waited by the pool. Not long after he returned, the manager told them the pool was off limits and they would have to leave. He asked where she wanted to go, even offering to take her back home. She declined and suggested they go upstairs. She was having a good time and she anticipated no problem going back to his suite.

As he opened the door to the room, she was still under the illusion that she was in control of the situation. She went in and sat on the sofa. He followed, removing his jacket, and walked into the bedroom. When he came back, he was without his jacket and walked straight to the radio trying to find some nice, smooth music. When the Stylistics' *Didn't I Blow Your Mind This Time* came on, he turned to her and smiled.

"Earlier today, I bought some ice cream. Would you like some?" he asked, moving toward the refrigerator.

"Sure. But if you had ice cream here, why did we go in search of ice cream this evening?"

"That was for you," he tossed over his shoulder.

"Whatever." She slipped her shoes off and pulled her feet under her on the sofa. "What kind you got?"

"I have Chocolate-Chocolate chip, Mint and Chip, and Chunky Monkey." He pulled different pints from the freezer of the small refrigerator.

"I think I'll have the Mint and Chip."

Grabbing the Mint and Chip for her and the Chunky Monkey for himself, he put the other back in the freezer and walked over and handed her the spoon and ice cream. He moved to the opposite end of the sofa. They both sat listening to music and enjoying the first taste of their ice cream.

"You need to taste this, girl. This is some good stuff," he said, sucking the smooth cream from the spoon. "Here, taste this."

He scooped out the ice cream and leaned over to feed her. She, quite aware that they were sharing a spoon, reached over and covered the spoon with her own mouth. She caught his eyes as she removed the banana flavored treat from the utensil. He smiled as he watched her reaction to the flavor in her mouth. She eyed him with a smirk and almost choked when he licked the spoon behind her.

"That is tasty, but it's not as tasty as my Mint and Chip. You want some?" she offered.

"No, thank you. I'm satisfied with this." She was a bit disappointed but managed not to let on.

They sat and talked and laughed for the next few hours. He sang all the oldies that came on the radio and she tried to hang. He was too good for her. They talked about when they were younger and different experiences they had when they got older. It seemed that he was always a ladies' man and she also got a lot of attention from the opposite sex but had been really careful. They were so different, but she was intrigued and he seemed to be too. So caught up in conversation, it was only by accident he noticed the time.

"You know it's 3:00 a.m.," he said stretching and twisting his neck.

"Yeah, but I don't have to work. Unless you have to be somewhere," she said, stretching her legs out on the table.

"No, it's cool. Can you give a massage? My neck is killing me."

"I'm not a good masseuse, but I can try."

He scooted over and turned his back to her. Her hands rested on his shoulder and began to work the muscles. His arms felt as powerful as they had looked in the diner.

"You can apply more pressure. I'm not going to break," he said, still trying to work out the kinks. She began to laugh and apply more pressure. After a few moments, he moved away and laughed.

"Honey, you are right. You cannot give a massage. That's alright."

"I told you," she said a bit embarrassed. "I'm sorry."

"It's not a problem." He looked at her and played with a piece of her hair as they sat in an awkward silence.

"What am I to do with my desire to fuck you?" he asked, breaking the quietness.

She was expecting him to say that, but she felt strangely daring.

"I'm not sure what you're going to do with your desire."

He looked at her. She held his stare. There was more silence. Feeling her initial bravado fading away, she finally looked away and let out a breath.

Their conversation somehow detoured back to that of music and work. They continued to laugh and enjoy each other immensely. She felt so comfortable sharing and expressing herself with him, confiding in him things that she told only a few. He received it with no judgment of her, sharing stories of his own that revealed more than she should have known. They felt so relaxed with each other that she couldn't remember when he placed his head in her lap. Nor did she realize when they fell silent.

He lay still as she traced the waves in his hair. She allowed the backs of her fingers to fall gently across his face and trail along his side burns and goatee. She sat there not thinking about anything except the comfort she took in comforting him. He rested there in her protection—still and receiving of her tender teasing. Time moved on without notice. When she looked up and noticed the time, she was surprised.

"Look, it's 4:30 a.m. You can take me back to my house later this morning. I'm tired and I can see you are. I'll sleep here on the couch."

"That's fine," he said, "but you're not going to sleep on the couch. You can go ahead and use my bed." She tried to argue, but it was futile and she finally gave in.

She got up to walk to the bathroom. Closing the door behind her, she tried to calm her racing heart. *You are playing a dangerous game, little girl. This is a game that you can't afford to play. Stay strong and do what's right.* She decided right there in the bathroom she would not let anything happen. She wanted to kiss him, but she would not have sex with him. He was living with another woman. She could not and would not be with him.

When she came out of the bathroom, he was standing by the door. She turned to walk into the room and his hands moved to her waist. He was close to her and she kept telling herself, *I will not have sex with him.*

He led her to the king-size bed and, when she climbed on, lying across the bedspread, he turned and left her alone. She closed her eyes and fell into a shallow sleep. She tried to rest, but she remained fully aware of where she was. When she felt a slight pressure on the bed behind her, her body immediately tensed. His arms snaked around her waist and she lay still. He made no immediate attempt to move closer, but soon his hands begin to roam along her leg and thigh. Without thinking, she turned and faced him. He didn't say anything; he just looked at her. She leaned over and took his delicious lips into her mouth.

That kiss was the best kiss she had ever experienced in her life. His lips were soft and undemanding. He ran his tongue along her bottom lip and nipped at it. She closed her lips in a soft caress with his and she felt it all the way to her toes. His tongue never invaded her mouth but snuck and took a taste and moved out. This man could not have known what he was doing. If he did, he would have taken possession of her mouth, mind and the rest of her body.

She moved away and caught her breath. He pulled her back toward him and she allowed her body to be moved while her mind screamed *Idiot get up and get out. You are going to mess up. You are going to mess up.*

He continuously ran his hands along her legs, thighs and hips. He murmured erotic things in her ears and begged her to be with him. Her conscience reprimanded her. *You told him too much about you. He pumped you for information through phone calls and now he is using it all against you. You are already an idiot, but don't be more of one. Get UP!"*

Her shirt was off and she felt his hands on her body. She didn't know if he took her shirt off or if she did. It was all out of control. She didn't know if she was coming or going and at this point really didn't care. This man felt good. His touch, lips, words were all she craved. However, with the snap of her jeans, reality came flying back from its distant land and made itself known. Eve pulled away and looked at him. Tears began to well in her eyes as she began to take in her situation.

"What's wrong?" he asked in a low, husky voice. He moved to kiss her shoulders and continue to stroke along her sides.

"I can't do this," she said, trying to hold in the tears. She was so embarrassed. How could she have let herself get to this point? "I'm sorry but I can't do this." She moved off the bed and looked for her shirt.

"You're not doing this alone. We're in this together." He whispered trying to reassure her.

"I can't be with you knowing that you're with someone else. That isn't the kind of woman I am." Eve put her shirt back on.

Elijah sat up on the bed and ran his hand over his head.

She noticed that he had on shorts and a white t-shirt. She moved to the other side of the bed to find her shoes. She hid her face so he wouldn't see the tears she let escape from her eyes. She was so disappointed in herself and her lack of judgment.

So wrapped up in her thoughts, she didn't hear him get up. She jumped when she felt his arms meander around her waist and relaxed a little when he rested his head in the side of her neck. She had to admit it; she wanted this man. He rocked her slowly back and forth in order to soothe her obvious distress. As she relaxed, one of her many tears rolled down her cheek and dropped on his face. Startled by the wetness he turned her around to face him. Still embarrassed, she turned her head and put her hands up to keep him from looking at her. He removed her hands and lifted her face to him. He looked into her eyes as if he were trying to read her feelings. She closed them so he couldn't see. His hands moved to her back and tried to pull her to him, but she tensed her body and wouldn't allow him to move her. She finally moved away from him all together. *What am I doing? What in the hell am I doing?* She felt him move on the bed and without looking at him she motioned for him to stay away. He did.

What have I done?
Chapter 3

"Girl, what are you doing? You don't have to be second best to any man." Teresa ranted and raved around her living room. She was one of the two best friends, Lola Bennett and Teresa Jenkins, Eve had. Both women were surprised by her confession. "When we were in college, we agreed that we wouldn't play ourselves like this. Do you remember?" Teresa continued.

"Yes, I remember," Eve responded. "You were supposed to concentrate on economics, I was to concentrate on business and Lola was always the one concentrating on men."

"I still don't know how she managed to graduate with her degree in performing arts," Teresa cut in. She and Eve laughed.

Lola threw a look of annoyance their way. "Don't you think we should be dealing with Eve's situation and not how I got my degree?"

"You're right, Lola." Teresa turned to Eve and picked up where she had left off. "Don't be one of these foolish women that we have talked about or that you see on the Rachel Winters show. Don't get caught up."

"Well damn! Would you give her a little credit?" Lola interjected. "First of all, she ain't simple enough to end up on that damn show or Oprah Winfrey, or Jerry Springer. Secondly, they didn't have sex. Although I think if you didn't, the whole thing was a waste of time."

"She did everything but have intercourse, damn it!" Teresa screamed, "You both know what sex is. At least I know you do, Lola."

Taking in Teresa's countenance, Eve sat silently. She had no response to that. She knew she was far gone, but she knew it still wasn't too late to backpedal. What happened the other night was not supposed to happen. Their situation was really not supposed to go past the simple flirting. But it did and now what was she going to do?

Teresa watched Eve's changing expressions and felt pity for her. She knew Eve better than any other friend, and she knew Eve was under a lot of pressure. Eve had always been known as the one that used the most wisdom in her choices. In fact, back in college, Eve was the one that lived vicariously through her and Lola's relationships. Teresa knew there was no wisdom in the decisions Eve was making and she wasn't sure what Eve was really thinking. Knowing this, she decided the ranting and raving she was doing wasn't helping. She moved the papers on the couch next to Eve and gathered her friend in her arms.

"Evie baby, I'm so sorry that you're struggling with this. But you have to know that we as women can never underestimate the power of a man who knows what the hell he is doing."

"Girl, you get all the "amen's" from the amen corner over here." Lola agreed and moved to the couch where her friends sat.

Teresa looked Eve in the eyes. "So what's your plan of action?"

"I plan to stay away from this man," Eve announced, getting up from the couch. She wasn't ready to be sandwiched between her friends and receive what-you-gonna-do pats on her shoulders. She walked into the kitchen so that they wouldn't see her face. From the kitchen, she continued. "I can't fight his power. He is so smooth that, even when we're not in a conversation with innuendos, I find that they are there just the same." She came out of the kitchen with a glass of water and a bottle of aspirin.

"He scares me, excites me, confuses the hell out of me." Eve sat in the chair next to the couch and sipped some water. "And I want him and that in turn scares me more."

"I don't envy you, girlfriend," Teresa said shaking her head.

"I don't envy me neither," Eve said taking two pills from the open container.

"I envy yo' ass," Lola said leaning back against the couch. Both Eve and Teresa looked at her surprised. "I don't know why you both are looking at me like that. Eve, you have a fine ass man after you and you trying to stay away. I don't understand that shit."

"Girl, he is living with a woman," Teresa argued. "That in and of itself should scream to her to stay away."

"Fuck her!" Lola interjected referring to Elijah's girlfriend. "His ass ain't married. If he were going to marry her, he would've done it by now. But he hasn't and that makes him fair game."

"Lola, you are such a slut." Teresa responded in disgust. "It's that attitude that keeps men thinking they can do the shit they do."

"I'm not a slut. However, I'm always down for getting mine." Lola flipped her stylish locs over her shoulder and winked at Eve. "If he were married, I'd say stay away. I've been there and that ain't no joke. But girl as long as he is nuptials free, he'd be free to play with me. It ain't like you want him to put a ring on it, right?"

Teresa rolled her eyes at Lola and turned back to Eve. "Just use the sense that God gave you."

<u>Consequences, can you live with them?</u>
Chapter 4

Lola, Teresa, and Eve all met up at the club, a little jazz spot that had spoken word on Saturday nights. They agreed Eve needed a girl's night out to clear her head. The three of them loved to read and listen to poetry and Lola, being the artist of the group, would occasionally perform open mic. Although Lola wasn't reading tonight, they were determined to have a good night.

When Eve got out of her car and noticed that Lola and Teresa were dressed to the nines, she looked down at her on Black jeans and silk blouse and felt like she should have gone home and changed. On the phone, Teresa convinced her that she looked fine, but after seeing them she wasn't sure. Lola's cocoa brown skin was flawless and her makeup looked good. Her shoulder length locs bounced around her face and her mischievous smile added to her mysterious look. Being the fashion plate that she always was, Lola stepped out in a beige and black mock turtleneck, a pair of tight black leather pants that fit all the way to the ankle and finished off with a three-inch ankle boot. She carried her black leather jacket on her arm.

Teresa, the lightest complexioned of the three, was blessed with a coffee with cream flawless skin and had long, thin auburn hair. It was the color people pay for and she paid for it too, but you would never know it because she never let the new growth show. She was dressed a bit more conservative wearing a blue, long coat, single-button pantsuit with a matching heeled boot.

"Hey Eve, you ready to have fun?" Lola asked coming up to give her a hug.

"Yeah, but you all should have let me go home to change. You look too fly to hang out with me," Eve suggested as she adjusted her blouse.

"Girl, please. With your behind in them jeans, no man is going to have time to look at us," Teresa teased.

"Bite your tongue, girlfriend," Lola interjected. "I plan to get plenty of play."

"Whatever Lola wants. . . Lola gets," Eve sang snapping her fingers. Teresa joined her. "There's no exception to the rule."

Lola smiled. "And don't you heifers forget it. Now, let's go hear some poetry."

They entered the club and were shown to a little table just to the side of the stage against a wall. The room was dimly lit, but she could tell it was a classy place all the way. The small round table allowed no more than four at the most. They created small pockets of intimacy. Each table was adorned with floating candles in glass dishes and flower wreaths surrounding the dish. Eve absolutely loved the feeling of this place. They all ordered drinks and waited for the show to start.

The first poet who took the stage commanded her audience with a poem called Consequences.

"This poem represents the struggle of wanting something you can't have. I hope you all enjoy it." The poet stood before her audience with a bassist strumming a jazzy rift on his strings behind her. She spoke from somewhere deep inside her and Eve's heart began to beat the rhythm of the music and her words.

"I want affection that is not mine to have and it is tearing me up inside.

I want of something I have never tasted and the urgencies hard to hide.

I want to feel important to someone, who can't be by my side.

I want it without the guilt. I want it without the pain.

I long for affection that is not mine yet is a stirring in my soul.

I long for kisses I've never had, scared I'll want more.

I long to be the one, if only one time, with one who can't take hold.

I want it without guilt. I want it without pain.

I want the smile that is not meant for me.
I want the looks that really can't see me.
I want to be in a place I shouldn't be.
I want it without the guilt. I want it without the pain.

I long not to feel this way, the yearning with need.
I long for this not to make a difference, when it does indeed.
I long for tears not to well in my eyes, and choke me like a weed.
I want it without the guilt. I want it without the pain.

I want just one night, just one moment, when I don't deserve.
I want just one touch, one breath, when I don't have the nerve.
I want the feelings to skip up my spinal curves.
I want it without the guilt. I want it without the pain.

Will I get what I want or get what I long for?
Will my conscious allow or must I ignore?
The fact that I can't receive that affection; I can't receive the kiss.
I can't imagine the touch or what I would miss

I long for one reaction.
I long for a piece of the action.
I long for a glimpse of satisfaction.
I want it without the guilt. I want it without the pain.

I'm willing to accept the consequences!"

The audience roared in applause with approval. Eve sat there spelled bound as if the poet communicated directly to her. How could someone capture so much of what she was feeling?

"Girl, that was some deep shit right there," Lola said as she sipped her drink.

"Hell yeah," Teresa agreed. "That girl has definitely felt some stuff."

"Let me get another drink on that one," Eve said and excused herself from the table.

Teresa and Lola laughed at their friend and asked her to bring back drinks for them. Eve walked over to the bar and waited for the bartender to get her drink.

I'm not alone. I want Elijah in very much the same way. I wonder if Teresa and Lola saw the parallel with me and sista poet up there? I hope not. I don't need to be psycho analyzed by Teresa then turn around and have Lola telling me to fuck the consequences.

The bartender sat the three drinks down in front of her and she paid him. She grabbed the handle of Lola's beer and managed to carry Teresa's and her drink.

When she reached the table, Teresa got up from her seat and grabbed two of the drinks out of Eve's hand. "Oh, we weren't even thinking," she said.

"Yeah girl, I'm sorry," Lola said automatically but not really paying attention. She had her eye on a gentleman sitting at a table across the room.

"Oh no, there she goes." Teresa laughed. "She is in mack mode tonight."

"Hell yeah, because that man right there is fine," Lola said licking her lips.

"Damn Lola, he could be an asshole," Teresa commented.

"True," Eve agreed. "But the man is fine and his boys are fine too."

Lola gave her friend a high five. "Watch this ya'll," Lola said. She got a waitress' attention and sent a drink over to the man.

"Now, however he responds will tell me what's up. If he refuses, he is married or gay. If he accepts it, he is taken, but available. If he beckons me over, he is an asshole."

"Lola, that don't make sense," Teresa mumbled clearly

confused. "If he calls you over why is he an asshole?"

"It's like this, Teresa darlin'. If he calls me over, he thinks that he's all that. Now, if he is available, he will acknowledge me and before the night is over will make his way over to thank me. Or he'll tell the waitress that he won't allow me to pay for his drink, but he will pay for ours. Girl, if he does that, I might have to give him some on G.P." Lola turned around and gave Eve a high five who had been signifying the whole time.

"You are such a slut," Teresa said laughing at Lola.

The women watched the waitress walk over there and place the drink in front of the man. When he looked over at the table where they were sitting, he smiled and nodded his thanks. The waitress made her way back over to the table and informed Lola that the gentleman thanked her, but would not allow such beautiful women to pay for the drinks, so the next round was on him.

"Ah shucky ducky quack, we got potential on the horizon," Lola said pleased with her efforts.

"Nah, we just have a "ho"- rising at the table," Teresa restated.

Eve laughed and Lola rolled her eyes and called her a bitch. "Now, we just have to wait and see what he does," Lola continued. "I have a feeling about this one. He's going to come thank us and, when he does, ladies he's all mine."

"Well, you don't have to worry about me," Eve said sipping her drink.

"Me neither. Michael and I are just fine," Teresa said sitting back in her chair with a grin.

Lola rolled her eyes again.

Eve turned and looked at her smiling friend. "So Michael has been behaving himself?" she asked Teresa.

"Yes, very much so," Teresa said allowing her smile to broaden. "Girl, I love that man. I didn't think we would be together this long, but it's working."

"I thought you said he was stepping out on you?" Lola

interrupted.

"I thought he was, but I was tripping. I had been dealing with some stuff with my dad and I was hatin' all men at that time."

"That seems to be always," Lola said turning to look at the man at the other table. He was engrossed in his own conversation.

"What is that supposed to mean?" Teresa asked.

"Well, you're always having problems with your father. So your father stepped out on your mother. At least he didn't leave all together like mine. It's time you grow up and realize our parents aren't perfect."

"I will, Lola, as soon as you realize to mind your own business."

"Ah, hello?" Eve interrupted. "Are we not here to have a good time? I'm not trying to have you two fighting over some dumb shit, so just let it rest."

Teresa threw up her hand yielding to Lola, and something caught the light and Eve's attention. Eve grabbed Teresa's hand and examined the marquise-cut diamond solitaire on her left hand. She looked at her friend and saw the toothy grin. They both squealed and hugged each other. Lola, who had turned around to watch the gentleman once again, turned at the sound and let out a whoop when Eve told her the news. She jumped up and hugged Teresa. She then turned and flagged the waitress down.

"Bring our drinks now. We have to celebrate our friend's engagement," Lola said trying to make amends. After the waitress left the table, Eve and Lola got the low down on how Michael asked Teresa to marry him.

Michael and Teresa met in college and dated. Not too long after graduation, they broke up and did their own thing. They met up again at a Christmas party at Eve's job. He was escorting a friend whose husband couldn't come, and Teresa was there because Eve wanted someone to talk to. Michael was still everything Teresa wanted in a man. He was tall and attractive. He was educated and had a nice paying job. Most of all, he had no ex-wife and no children. This was a big plus for Teresa, but his player reputation followed him from college into his adulthood. Teresa knew this, but he managed to convince Teresa those days were behind him. Now, with the engagement ring, it was like proof positive that he was serious about settling down.

"Girl, the only thing that makes me nervous is if we have kids he wants me to stay home. I cannot stay home. I want to keep my career. I don't want to depend on a man for shit," Teresa said while admiring her ring.

"Well, that's something you all are going to have to really discuss because that's some serious stuff," Eve added.

"Girl, don't quit your job and lose your skills for a man. That is insane," Lola added her two cents. "Women are fully capable of working and raising a family."

"I know. That's what I told him," Teresa said. "He said we'd discuss it later."

"Well, that's something you have to get together, beforehand," Eve felt compelled to add. At that time, the waitress came back with their drinks.

"To our sister girl who is the first of us to be married, cheers!" Lola gave the toast.

Eve and Teresa looked at her with a knowing glance. Lola was married for about three months when she was in high school.

"Ok, the first of us to get married for real. Not as a stupid girl trying to get out of her mother's house."

"Cheers."

***

The night was good and the poetry was all of that. Eve enjoyed herself far more than she had anticipated. Finding out her girl was getting married was icing on the cake. And she managed to get through the evening without mentioning Elijah. She was sorry to see the night come to an end, but the club was going to close and

Lola had to work in the morning, even though it was a Saturday. Working at the cultural center meant sometimes working on Sunday. Before they left, the gentleman that Lola sent the drink to walked over and thanked her personally. Teresa and Eve moved on outside to give Lola a chance to work her magic.

"Eve, so have you decided what you're going to do about Elijah?"

Damn. Well almost all night. "Ah no, I haven't."

"Damn, your problem sounded like the first poem we heard."

"You ain't lied when you spoke that truth. They were killing me softly with them poems," Eve said unlocking the door of her car.

"Well Eve, as I said before, use good judgment."

"I will. Tell Lola I'm gone."

"Okay, bye."

Eve drove home thinking about the night's events. She thought about Lola and her ways and Teresa and her non-understanding of Lola. Most of all, she thought about that poem. Was she willing to accept the consequences of fulfilling her sexual desire? Could she differentiate between lust and an emotional need?

Damn! Why does shit have to be so hard?

When she got home, she pulled out her journal and began to write pieces of the poem down. She didn't know what she was going to do, but she knew she was going to have to figure something out.

Another meeting.
Chapter 5

Eve agreed to meet Elijah again. He was to be in town for business and she agreed to meet with him again to prove something to herself. She went to this meeting protected with the assurance that this thing they had was not what she wanted. The voice inside her head was constant in asking her if she didn't want it, why then was she meeting him? She ignored the voice and convinced herself that she knew what she was doing. And she did, right?

He sat in the same booth where they had met before. He had taken the liberty to order her coffee and it was being poured as she sat down.

"Can I get you folks some menus?" the waitress asked as Eve scooted into the booth.

He looked at her and she shook her head no. He ordered himself a hamburger and fries and the waitress left. "How have you been?" he asked leaning back in his chair and folding his hands in his lap.

"I'm. . ." she started. A slight, embarrassed smile flicked across her face, and she put her head down. "I'm still ashamed and embarrassed. And you?"

"I'm well, although I don't understand why you are ashamed and embarrassed."

"I'm sure you can figure it out."

He studied her for a moment. "Yes, I guess I can."

He moved the coffee to his lips and her eyes followed the movement secretly wishing that she were the coffee cup. *Girl, you better get it together. Remember you don't want this.*

Eve looked away and started to add sugar to her coffee. Elijah leaned forward to get her attention. His shoulders were hunched over and his elbows steadied his body against the table. His muscular upper body bulged through his leather jacket and he looked extremely inviting.

"Why won't you let your full sexuality out?" he asked, unrepentantly bold. She was dumbfounded. Her hand stopped stirring the sugar in her cup.

"What did you say to me?" she asked.

"Why do you sexually inhibit yourself? You ran from me the other night, and I just want to know why?" He seemed as if he was really trying to figure out some deep dark secret.

She felt uncomfortable. She searched his eyes for his agenda and she couldn't find one. *Don't you fall into this man's games, girl. You know this is a danger zone.*

She ignored the voice of good sense and answered his question. "It's not my desire to be caught with my nose wide open behind some man that ain't mine."

Ignoring her statement, he asked, "Do you know how many men think you're sexy?"

"You discuss me with other men?" she asked indignantly. She immediately didn't like the idea that she was the topic of discussion among other men. She began to pull on her jacket and run her fingers through her hair.

"You don't have a clue how many men want to be where I was the other evening?" he continued, amused by the fact that she was uncomfortable.

"What is it? Do I have slut written across my forehead? Is this why I would be the topic of conversation?" she went on, disgusted with the whole idea. *He talks about me with men at work. This is just wrong.*

"You don't understand." He shook his head and settled back into his chair. The waitress brought him his food at that time, and he began to prepare his hamburger.

Eve sat quietly waiting for him to continue. Growing tired of waiting, she spoke up. "Well, no I don't understand."

Looking at her, he dipped a French fry in some ketchup.

"No, you don't have a sign on your head and it's not how you dress," he said slipping the fry in his mouth. "It's who you are. The way you are. It's in your walk, your talk, your smile, your hair, your eyes, and mouth. . .It's your essence."

She sat there trying to digest what he was saying. She didn't know whether to be flattered or be insulted. On one hand, she was totally put out being the fodder for conversation, but there was a part of her that was thrilled that she was considered one of those women. *Get it together, Eve. You know why you're here, so don't get caught up.*

"So, you participated in these conversations?" she asked, not giving him a chance to answer. "Did you decide that you were to be the first one to brag about being with me? Am I a bet among the boys? Did you set me up?"

His head was bent to take a bite of his food when she attacked. His actions ceased immediately. He looked at her incredulously. He placed his food on his plate and picked up the napkin to wipe the crumbs from his mouth.

"Do you think so little of me? Do you honestly believe I'm the kind of person that would relegate you to a bet?" The expression on his face was one of disbelief and hurt. Then it changed into anger and audacity. Her heart began to tighten and guilt tried to pry it open, but she wouldn't let it. He glared at her, his own mouth thin and strained.

"I don't know what to think of you? There are definitely many layers to a person, and you have only revealed certain things to me," Eve retorted. She didn't trust herself with him, so believing she couldn't trust him made it easier. "I have been introduced to many proclivities that you have through our conversations, but yet I never know what you're really thinking. That's unusual for me. I usually can read people. Somehow though, I think you know that so you say or do something that will occupy my mind so that I don't read you. Am I giving you too much power? Probably."

Elijah allowed an ironic smile to cross his lips.

Eve kept talking. "I do believe you manipulate situations and people. You have been gifted with discernment and you use that to your advantage. You've definitely used it on me. This was made known to me when you admitted that you usually get what you want. In your manipulations, I would never suggest malice or harm, but human nature. Wanting what you want, when you want it. To a thinking person, it's intriguing and sexy as hell. That's how you got my attention. But don't get it twisted; I'm not sure entirely what to think of you."

Elijah sat back in his seat.

When she saw him sweat, she smiled. *Ha, Eve look! You got him on the run.* She leaned forward on the table and cocked her head to one side. "It's amazing to me how when I met you I didn't look at you as someone I might possibly be intimate with, and yet here I have it hanging over my head. But I will admit one thing that bothers me is your cavalier attitude about it. You dismiss my musing as something that doesn't matter or superfluous. Anytime I mention your woman, you shrug and think nothing of it. When it comes to you, the insecurity monsters that I try to suppress are now sitting on my walls looking at me. And in order for me to deal with them, I need communication beyond my big bouncing black ass. So yes, I think you might be capable of 'regulating me to a bet,' because you haven't shown me anything different."

Elijah sat there with shock registered on his face. He didn't know whether to be impressed with the way she expressed herself or offended that she didn't trust him. After a moment he spoke.

"Let me tell you something. I have watched you for a long time. You wouldn't believe how long. When I come into town I watch your interaction at work, in social gatherings, and everywhere we happen to meet. I have seen in you the things that I mentioned long before I have been privy to the discussion."

He leaned forward again and gripped her hands in his.

"I have wanted you a long time. What happened the other evening was a part of my fantasy. It was very difficult for me to stop, but I respected you enough to forego what I wanted to do. The reality of that situation was I could have had you then. We both know that. I know you wanted it just as much as I did. I remember your response to me. I remember the look in your eyes. I remember the sounds you made when I touched you. I can feel that right now. I can feel the tension in your arms."

She tried to pull her hands from his. He held them tighter and an easy smile slid across his face.

"Girl, there are two things that are essential for you to know. The first is I would never do anything that would purposely hurt you or embarrass you. You do not have to worry about the men at work, or anywhere for that matter, knowing what occurs between us. Secondly, we are inevitable whether you believe it or not. I'm a patient man and I will wait on you. And we will be good."

He stared intently in her eyes, and she noticed the blatant lust that was reflected in his. She hadn't even noticed that the grip held on her hands had now turned into a caress. He had turned her palms up and rubbed their center with the pads of his thumbs. The sensation moved through her body all the way to her core. She felt herself give up resistance. She pulled her hands away and did everything she could to bring it back. It was gone. She knew it and he knew it too. She excused herself at that moment and went to the bathroom.

Going into the bathroom, she let out the breath she hadn't realized she'd been holding. *Damn, am I that much of a punk? I give an impassioned speech about how I don't trust him and he says a few words proving everything I said didn't mean a damn thing. This man is beautiful. He is funny, he is intelligent, he is sexy, and if he was single we'd already be in position number 76.*

She rested her body against a stall door and lowered her head into her chest. She wanted this man. She wanted him despite all her misgivings. She wanted him despite the "I nevers" she spoke in her life about messing with another woman's man. She wanted *him*. She didn't know what to do and she refused to pray about it. She couldn't pray about it because she knew the answer would be to leave him alone. She didn't think she could do that. She knew she didn't want to. She began to sort out all of the random thoughts in her head and only one thing was really clear. Being with him was inevitable and she was willing to deal with the consequences.

Coming out of the bathroom, she returned to the table as he finished the last of his hamburger. She sat down and reached over in his plate and lifted a fry. He smiled at her and watched her place the fry between her lips. She knew he was watching and she bit slowly into the tip of the fry and let her tongue roll it in her mouth.

"Were you feeling kind of moist?" he asked suggestively. It was like the conversation they had before she went to the restroom never happened.

"For the last hour." She chewed slowly and worked a seductive smile across her face. He lifted his eyebrows in recognition that her attitude had changed and her smiled broadened as she ate the rest of his fries.

After the brief look and conversation, they sat and continued to laugh and talk about everything except sex, her sexuality and his desire. She was so settled in her decision that even the subject of his kids or their mother didn't rattle her. Periodically, through their discussion, she would indicate her intentions without being obvious. If he understood, he did very little to acknowledge it. He continued to talk and act goofy. They laughed into the wee morning hours.

She glanced down at her watch and noted the time was 2:30 a.m. She knew if she was going to go through with this she couldn't go home. If she was going to do it, it was tonight.

"It's time we leave this place," Elijah said nodding at the server. "I think we have sat through a shift change."

They both laughed.

She grabbed her purse and moved out of her seat. He stood and threw money on the table and grabbed her elbow. He walked her out of the restaurant into the night air. She looked up and the stars were shining brightly. He was standing directly behind her. She could feel his body pressed against her back and sensed his breath against her neck.

"Are you coming to my room?" He whispered in her ear.

She closed her eyes and took a breath. She stepped away from him and turned around to face him.

He simply looked at her.

She smiled and grabbed his hand. "Yes."

Let's gets it on.
Chapter 6

Déjà vu. Wasn't I just here? Her thoughts pounded in her head as she watched him open the door of his hotel suite. She held her breath. *There ain't no turning back now. Ok. What now? Do I make a move or do I just go in and sit down?*

He moved to the side and allowed her to enter first. As she walked past him, he grabbed her waist and followed in behind, keeping close to her body. She wasn't but a few feet inside the door when the light from the hallway disappeared and she found herself turned around and pressed against the door.

He leaned forward and began with the softest kiss on her lips. He then moved to nibble on her bottom lip, occasionally swiping it with his tongue to ease the stinging nips. His hot breath on her face had a hint of mint that mingled with the cologne from his body.

Hmmm, this man smells so good. She ran her hands over his shoulders and moved up to grip his low shaven head. This act alone deepened their kiss to a full onslaught of fierce passion. His hands traveled around the fullness of her hips and began to gather the skirt to her waist. Her legs were exposed, and he left her mouth, bent down, and ran his hands along her bare thighs and his lips across her ample breast.

"Please, if you don't want this, tell me now because I can't stop tonight." He whispered, pulling back a little and allowing her skirt to fall back down. He looked at her with such intensity it was as if he was telepathically willing her to continue.

"Ah stop?" she asked, confused by what he was saying.

His gaze dropped from her face, withdrew from her and he took a step back. He placed his hands on his hips and dropped his head. His chest was heaving as he labored to catch his breath. Exasperated, he turned around and walked into the other room.

She realized what she had done when she heard the faint click of the restroom door and the distinct sound of running water. *Damn, I didn't mean for him to stop. Do I go in after him or do I take this as a detour not to get myself into this? Damn, I came off like a little girl playing grown up.* She didn't want him to have that impression of her.

Good sense was telling her to leave and don't worry about the impression it may make, but lust, dressed up in her momma's home training, said that it would rude. So she sat on the sofa with her head leaning back and closed her eyes. Her eyes popped open when she heard the restroom door unlock. When he walked out, he found her sitting there looking down at her hands.

"I'm sorry," she said barely audible.

"For what?" he asked sharply.

"I. . .I wanted to but. . .I came here to but. . ." she flustered. "I'm so sorry."

Sighing deeply, he moved to sit next to her on the couch. "It's alright. I'm a patient man."

"I'm not a tease."

"You sure?" he said looking down in his lap at the evidence of the tease. She followed his eyes. He grabbed her hand and placed it on his manhood.

"This is what you do to me, even when you walk into a room. You can't help but tease me."

She tried to remove her hand, but his stronger one kept hers there. She could feel him moving and admittedly she was feeling the heat. She barely noticed that he was caressing the nape of her neck. Responding to his manipulations, she began to massage him.

"Girl, just relax. I won't hurt you." He whispered in her ear. Her mind was swimming with thoughts.

Fuck the consequence! Go for it!

"Baby, just let go. I will make it so good." His hand moved over her breasts and squeezed them. Her nipples hardened through her blouse. "Let it go." He chanted.

She removed her hand from him, and he moved away from her looking into her eyes. She didn't say a word. She held his gaze and began to lift her blouse over her head.

She felt his hands on her so quickly that she wasn't sure if they had ever been off. He helped her lift it over her head and tossed it to the floor. He stood up and pulled her from the sofa. His hands moved quickly to the waist of her skirt and slipped it down over her hips. She felt a flash of self-consciousness. *Oh God, why did I chose this day not to match my underwear. Black lace bra is attractive, but it doesn't quite match my stark white cotton panties. Well, at least they are a high-cut brief.*

He didn't even seem to notice. His breath caught in his throat as he looked at her body. He took in her plentiful breasts barely contained in lace. Her flat stomach showcased a small waist, which in turn highlighted her rounded Black-woman hips. He looked at her and smiled.

"Damn girl," he said taking the tension out of the moment.

She laughed and walked into his arms.

He squeezed her in a bear hug and let his hands slide down her back and rest on her bottom. "This is what I want more than anything," he said with a slight squeeze.

"Oh really?" She boldly stepped outside herself. "Well, tonight, it's all yours." *Hell, if I'm going to do this, I'm going in all the way.*

"For me?" he asked in a falsetto childlike voice of surprise.

She smiled and nodded her head.

He pulled her to him and began kissing her once again. His adept hands moved quickly. In a matter of minutes, her bra was lying on the floor by her skirt. His mouth was all over her breasts and her hands were pulling at his shirt. Coming out of his shirt, she found that his body was solid. He didn't have a six-pack stomach like a well-oiled body builder, but there was an obvious strength. He had fine hairs in the center of his caramel chest and a sexy trail of tresses making a path into his pants.

She pushed away and began unbuckling his pants. He watched her undress him, and it was made obvious that he enjoyed every moment. Her heart skipped a beat when his pants dropped around his ankles. She didn't know if it was the boxer brief that caused it or what was no longer hidden inside them. *Oh God, this man is beautiful all over. Damn!*

"I'm glad you like what you see," he said with an amused look on his face.

Her eyebrows drew together, wondering if she had praised him out loud.

Laughing at her, he reached over and tweaked her nipple and moved his hand to the curve of her breast. She heard him murmur something about a perfect fit. Continuing to manipulate her breast, he grew extremely quiet. He moved in close to her again and began placing fine kisses all over her face.

"I'm tired of playing games," he said licking her lips. "This is the last time I'll offer to walk away." He leaned down and let the roughness of his beard run across her already sensitive nipple. "It will take everything that I have in me, but I will."

Eve wasn't a hairy woman, but he traced a line of small hairs laid across her stomach leading to her womanhood with his tongue. He followed that path all the way down to the top of her underwear. She jumped from the instant sensation he sent through her body.

"Girl, you have to tell me right now, because once I taste you, it will be too late."

She took only few seconds to think then she slid her panties off. Elijah lay between Eve's legs and began to kiss and lick the inner part of her thighs.

Eve heard whimpers in the distance and realized they were coming from her. She started to gyrate. He continued around her honey pot and sucked on each lip. Eve's moans grew louder. He continued to slowly tease her by licking her from the top of her clit all the way to her anus.

"You are like sweet caramel." He whispered. "I don't think I can get enough." Elijah tasted her, taking care that time to avoid her most sensitive spot.

Eve started to squirm and moving her legs. Elijah's powerful arms grabbed hold of her ankles and spread her wider, moving in with his tongue to lick across her pearl. Her body jerked as he sucked it into his mouth. Not too hard, just enough so that Eve began grabbing at his back. He let go of her legs and maneuvered his shoulders to keep her wide open and grabbed her arms. He increased the activity faster and harder. Moving both of her wrists to one hand to allow his other hand to grab at her breasts and his thumb to flick her nipples, setting her on edge. He tasted her like a fine wine savoring every drop and sending her into another world. She was so close to her climax that she couldn't keep a coherent thought in her head.

"Come honey. Come on." Elijah encouraged her. "Release it, Eve. Get yours, girl."

Eve began to ride on the orgasm wave. She came so fast and long that her body shuttered for a matter of minutes, and Elijah somehow continued licking her clean, tasting all of her sweetness, not leaving a drop.

Eve lay quietly trembling and trying desperately to gain her composure. Elijah continued to nip at her shoulder and breasts. His dick was so hard that he thought he would burst, but he wanted to wait until she was ready to feel him in her warm glove.

When her tremors ceased, Elijah lay beside her on the bed and began rubbing between her legs. Her juices were still present. His fingers glided easily in and out of her.

He slid his index finger into her palm side up and curled his finger up so that it curled around her pubic bone. He started rubbing in that area. Eve shifted at the discomfort, but she didn't have the strength to make him stop. He moved his fingers as if he was searching for something. Eve was about to stop him when an extreme wave of pleasure hit. Her pussy muscles tightened and a sharp breath left her body.

"Gotcha," Elijah said in her ear. "That's your g-spot, Evie. How many men have even hit it on accident? Can you tell me how many?" When Eve tried to talk, Elijah stole the words from her mouth with the pressure of his fingers. "I don't want you to talk, Eve. I want you to squirt."

Elijah began to massage her spot in circular motions and suck on her areolas. Eve's body began to thrash on the bed. She jerked so hard that she inadvertently caused pain. As she began to reach her peak, Elijah talked her through it.

"Let it go, Eve. You've never felt anything like this. Let it go. This is how it's supposed to be. Squirt for me. Squirt honey from your honey comb."

Eve's body began to build a sensation like she had to pee, but she couldn't stop it no matter how she tried. Soon, she found herself squirting a clear liquid from between her legs and saturating Elijah's hand and arm.

Elijah moved away from her. He reached for a towel, wiped his hand clean and watched the expression on her face go from pure ecstasy to utter panic and surprise. When Eve caught his eyes, he smiled at her that cocky male smile. And he had every right to that smile with the things he had just done to her body. She was so satiated that she didn't think she could move.

"You ready for the main course?" Elijah asked running the back of his hand along her stomach.

"What the hell was that if it wasn't the main course?"

"That was the appetizer," he said with a wicked smile. He leaned over and invaded her mouth with his tongue.

She began to get into the kiss and move her arms around his neck.

Elijah reached over for a silver packet on the table next to the couch. She hadn't noticed it before. He broke their kiss and tore it open with his teeth. She took it from his hands. She rolled the sheepskin sheath over his manhood and led him to the gateway of her heaven.

"Oh shit!" He groaned into her neck. "This is sweet heaven." He began to pump her moist center and with every grind he seemed to give her strength, as she became an active participant. "Yeah Evie, give it to me. That's what this is all about, me pumping this pussy."

His words caused her heart to beat a little faster. She found the energy to rise up from the bed sending him on his back. With Elijah still deep inside her, she began to explore him with her mouth. She tasted his lips, his ears, neck, chest, and licked on his nipples. She felt him shutter and looked down to notice his eyes closed. She felt his iron hard rod in her stomach and felt her own body responding again to him. Slowly moving her hips, Eve closed her eyes. She suddenly found herself flipped over onto her back.

He began to drive his rod deep into her honey pot, and he knew that he had found heaven. He moved methodically and filled every inch of her. Eve didn't know it was even possible to be so full. She felt every fleshy inch of him and reveled in it. When he began to move more intensely, Eve felt her own crest begin to break. Reaching his climax, Elijah growled into Eve's neck and raked his teeth across her shoulder. That one action sent her over the edge.

Elijah shifted his weight to where he partially covered her and continued to kiss her. Eve began to recover and it became clear what had transpired. Her body stiffened and she was getting ready to move from underneath him. He sensed it and moved his mouth to her breast taking her nipple into his mouth.

Eve gasped. The stimulation was almost sensory overload.

Elijah's hand began to explore the length of her body. Eve could feel him getting hard again and her pussy acted like a homing device. With one shift, Elijah was back in heaven and he toured heaven all night long.

Ten things I hate about him.
Chapter 7

Eve sat on her couch after work feeling like the burden of loneliness was going to be the death of her. It had been some time since she gave into Elijah, and they hadn't communicated with each other much after that. She wanted to touch herself at the thought of what he did to her that night, but that wouldn't make her feel any better. Every thought she had about him was accompanied by guilt. She felt guilty about being with him, guilty about wanting it to happen, guilty about wanting it again. Sighing, she slung herself back on the couch and recalled how she told Teresa and Lola about what she had done. The morning after her rendezvous, Eve called Teresa who called Lola. They went to Eve's place for breakfast. Teresa was disappointed and Lola was excited.

"Well, what did he do?" Lola asked munching on a piece of toast.

"Girl, you should probably ask what he didn't do." Eve responded with the excitement of being able to share her experience.

"Well, what didn't he do?" Teresa asked much more reserved and pensive than Lola.

"I don't think there was anything we didn't do." Eve giggled.

"That's what I'm talking about," Lola interjected giving Eve a high five.

"Y'all, I have never been twisted up like that before. I mean, Elijah found my spot. Girl, I was sure I didn't have one, but that man found it."

"Girl, it ain't nothing like a man finding your spot," said Lola.

"I didn't know it was physically possible to be able to come three times in an hour or so. I swear it seemed like every time I collected myself he was getting me wound up again."

"Damn Eve," Lola grabbed a bowl of grapes. She popped one

into her mouth. "Girl, start from the beginning."

Teresa sat quietly while Eve and Lola did an instant replay on Eve's night with Elijah. Finally, she spoke.

"Well, Eve, did you get it out of your system?"

"What?" Eve asked knowing what Teresa was referring to.

"You know that man has a woman. I'm asking did you get him out of your system?

"To be honest with you. I don't know," Eve admitted. She sat down as if Teresa had thrown cold water on her.

"What don't you know? Either you got enough or you're going back." Teresa's visceral sound caused Eve to frown.

"Damn Teresa." Lola interjected. "Can you get out of your right now and be a girlfriend? Yo' ass about to give me heartburn."

"I heard everything Eve described and, if this was a man she was dating, I would have brought the champagne for mimosas, but that ain't the case."

"Well, I haven't spoken to him since that night, so it is probably out of both our systems." Eve conceded. *I hope that's just a lie I got to tell Teresa because I want more.*

"I hope so for your sake," Teresa added twisting her ring on her finger.

Eve noticed that action and decided to change the subject. "Have you started planning the wedding?"

That was just what Teresa needed to get off the subject of Eve and Elijah. They talked wedding, work, and friends. Eve found herself thinking about how her two friends reacted; Teresa's disillusionment and Lola's elation. Eventually, the conversation made its way back to Eve and Elijah.

"So Eve, you never told us did you taste it?" Lola asked picking up a banana.

"I don't want to know that," Teresa interjected.

"Then go into the other room," Lola said peeling the fruit. "I want to know did it taste like caramel or Dulce de Leche?"

Eve laughed and shook her head at Lola. "Lola, you are too much. I'm done telling you anything."

"Now, that's the most sensible thing I heard you say all morning. Look, I got to go and meet my man at the mall." Teresa picked up her purse and walked over to Eve. "Honey girl, you know I love you. I just want what's best for you. Please think about what you're doing."

"I love you too, sister friend," Eve said hugging Teresa.

"Well, I guess I'll go to the museum since it seems like all the fun has stopped," Lola pouted as she grabbed her purse. She walked over to Eve and gave her a quick hug. "Call me when you ready to dish again." Lola walked past Teresa and tried to pull her out the door.

"Eve, I read an article that said if you're trying to get over someone you should write a list of why you shouldn't like him," Teresa suggested.

"What in the hell were you reading, Seventeen?"

Teresa smiled and walked out the door. Lola, being a smart ass, chimed up and said, "Why don't you write a list of Ten Things That He Did That Made Me Holler." After that comment, Teresa was pulling Lola out the door.

At that time, Eve never really considered writing a list, but that night, in the midst of her angst, she thought about Teresa's advice to make a list and decided to do it. She got up from the couch and found her journal. Settling back in the corner of her couch, she began to write.

"The ten things I hate about him"

1. I hate that he is with someone.

2. I hate that he has done things to me that I didn't know could be done.

3. I hate that he has a woman that might as well be his wife.

4. I hate that he has kids with this woman.

5. I hate that he is fine and sexy as hell.

6. I hate that I want him.

7. I hate that when I'm lonely that I long for that experience again.

8. I hate that I didn't say no.

9. I hate that I said no, but I didn't mean it.

10. I hate that I made a decision that got me making a list like
*   this.*

Reading over her journal entry, she tossed it on the other side of the couch. That exercise didn't help at all. She looked at the book and considered writing the list that Lola suggested. Laughing at herself she got up and began straightening up her living room. She was dumping the trash when the phone rang.

"Hello."

"Hello yourself." The low timbre and smooth sound of his voice tickled her ears as if he licked them. Her breath caught. She didn't say anything. "Are you still there?"

"I'm still here."

"What, might I ask, are you doing?" he asked quite seductively. At least, that's what she thought.

"I'm cleaning."

"I was hoping you would meet me for dinner. I'll be in town this weekend."

Her mind was once again flooded with opposing thoughts.

You've been wanting him. Here is another opportunity.

What about your list? Don't you care about what was on that list?

Damn girl, you've already had him, go for it. You might as well enjoy this man like you did last time.

"Hello? Are you there?"

"Ah, yes." She stammered. "I'm here. Sure, I will meet you for dinner."

"Friday night okay?"

"Friday is fine."

<u>All girls; all the time.</u>
Chapter 8

Eve was trying to get ready for her "All Girls All The Time" party. She started having these parties once a month when she saw her favorite talk show host, Rachel Winters, host one on television. On the third Thursday of each month, she and all of her girlfriends had a get together. Usually, it was a book club kind of thing, but this month they hadn't decided on a book yet, so they just decided to Netflix the old school classic, *What's Love Got to Do with It*, and bash Ike Turner. Since everyone contributed money for the snacks, Eve assigned Teresa and Lola to bring wine and cheese and she would take the rest and make sure to have the crackers and other snacks ready.

By 7:30 everyone was there and the movie was on. The comments of Ike's mistreatment of Tina were in full swing when Moniek, one of the ladies that Eve knew from the gym, asked about the fine ass man she saw Eve with at the diner. All attention was drawn away from the movie to her.

"Girl, he ain't nobody but a colleague." Lola piped in. "He works as a consultant on the merger for the company she works for."

"Oh, is she talking about Elijah Mann?" one of her co-workers asked. "That man sho' is fine."

"Before you all get extra happy," Teresa said, jumping up and grabbing the chips off the table. "He's living with a woman and has kids by her." Everyone in the room looked at her and Lola wondering why they answered for Eve. Reading their mind, Teresa answered, "I asked her too and she gave me the download. So damn, quit looking at me." She shoved a potato chip in her mouth.

"I don't care if he's married to Halle Berry. He is fine as wine on a cool summer day." Moniek chimed in. "Sexy, sexy." She sang as the other women laughed.

"Well," interjected Teresa, "I heard that he was a scoundrel."

"Look who's talking." One of the women muttered under her breath. "She's getting ready to marry one."

"Excuse me?" Teresa pinned the lady with a glare. The woman said nothing and took a sip of her drink.

"If it's who I think it is, I heard that too." One of the women on the couch reiterated, bringing the subject back to Elijah.

"He tried to talk to me the last time he was here." Another co-worker of Eve's said sitting in the recliner and sipping her wine. "He thought I would want to go to dinner with him. He is so tired."

"Girl, please." Lola laughed. "Everyone in here knows that if a man says excuse me to you on the way to greeting his wife you will swear that he was trying to get with you." The whole room exploded into laughter.

"That don't keep him from being fine," Moniek insisted.

"True that. But still, the man might as well be married. Hell, I have seen pictures of his kids." The woman in the recliner continued.

"What's wrong with that?" Lola asked.

"Well, hell! When your woman's big face is in the picture strung across you, you can't think that makes me want you more." There was a burst of "amens" on that statement in the room.

"Don't matter," Moniek insisted again. "The man is still damn fine."

"Damn girl. Is that all that matters to you?" The girl sitting next to Lola retorted in disgust. "So what, he fine. So are half the men where I work. But I ain't trying to screw a married man."

"As a matter of fact, that is all that matters to me right now." Moniek spat back. "I want to do things with him, and I don't care about his half wife. If she were worth her salt in gold, she would have had him locked up in the marriage vow. But she didn't; therefore, he is fair play, unless he's taken by our hostess?"

Everyone in the room turned around and looked at Eve. Eve had been silent through this whole conversation up until now. She shook her head and waved everyone off like they were crazy. His admirer, taking her cue, went on.

"I want to be used, abused and excused by something that scrumptious." She reared back with laughter and was joined by the rest of the women.

Lola and Teresa looked at Eve. She smiled at them and began gathering the plates and cup to take them in the kitchen. As the ladies continued to laugh and talk, she looked at Teresa and wondered to herself. *What does she mean she heard he was a scoundrel? Is she talking about what we did? Or does she know he does this a lot? What if I'm not the only one? Am I really stupid enough to believe I'm the only one? Oh my God!*

"Hey girl." She turned at the sound of the voice and saw her co-worker there behind her.

"Hey yourself. Did you need some more to drink?"

"No, I just wanted to know if you had anything going on with that guy ole girl saw you with?"

"No," she said indignantly. "Didn't you hear? He is practically married."

"Well, hell," she said before taking a swallow of her drink. "I heard he was really married and he was keeping it under wraps."

"Where did you hear that?" she asked, trying not to react too strongly.

"A few months ago when he was in town, I heard him walk into our boss man's office. The big boss man congratulated him on his nuptials and he didn't deny it, at all."

"When was this?" Eve said, trying to act as if it was good gossip rather than affecting her personally.

"This had to be about two to three months ago," her co-worker said. Distracted by another conversation in the room, she excused herself from Eve and walked over to join the other women. Eve sat there trying to take in what she had just heard. That fool was married. She was with a married man.

For the rest of the night, she didn't sit still at all. She acted like the perfect hostess and watched the clock until it came time for the women to go, so she could get in a good cry.

A married man.
Chapter 9

After the party Teresa and Lola both stayed behind to help her clean up. They didn't stay long, but Lola tried desperately to convince her that it wasn't her fault that he was a liar and a scoundrel. Teresa didn't say too much. After they left, and after the cry, she was still confused. She didn't know what she wanted to do. She didn't know why she hadn't canceled their meeting. She didn't want to be seen with a married man and, more than that, she didn't want to talk to a liar. What was she going to actually say? What really could she say? It was bad enough that she had been with him, but she even more wrong because he was in the ultimate committed relationship.

Friday night, Elijah arrived at her door with black leather pants and a blue pullover sweater with a neckline that opened just below the shoulder line revealing a gold chain and the sleeves were long enough to cover half of his hand. He had grown a low beard and his hair was still neatly cut low on his head. He was absolutely divine.

"Hello Momma." He leaned over and kissed her forehead. "You look beautiful."

She had taken great steps to look her best. She wore her hot pink wrap dress and matching strappy heels. She wanted to be unaffected by his touch, but her heart jumped and raced to the bottom of her feet. It paralyzed her for a second, and she just stood looking at him.

"Are you ready to go?" he asked, slipping his hand to the small of her back and gently pulling her forward.

Her feet shifted under her from the pressure and she stumbled forward. "Damn, you don't have to push me," she said, more irritated at her response to him than that actually push.

"Damn Momma, I'm sorry!" He let his hand drop to his side.

"Where did you pick up this Momma shit, anyway?" she asked as she strolled to the car.

"It was just something I picked up. Why?"

"Because I don't like that shit."

Ignoring her apparent attitude shift, he opened her door for her and walked around to the driver's seat. As he got in, he looked at her and noticed that she refused to look at him. Not really knowing what to say, he just drove to one of the nicer restaurants in town.

Throughout the ride, she had thoughts of nothing else than his marriage and his deceiving her. When they arrived at the restaurant, she was fuming. He walked around to open her door, but before he had the chance she hopped out of the car, slammed the door and headed towards the restaurant's entrance. He looked annoyed as he followed her lead. Just as she reached the door, he was right behind her. He reached around her to open the door. As he opened the door, his other arm snaked around her waist. She tried to pull away, but his grip tightened.

"Don't make a scene." He whispered in her ear. "I don't know what your problem is, but I would like to find out. You pissing me off is not going to allow me to do that."

"What the hell is that supposed to mean?" She whispered back to him.

"It means calm the hell down and let's get a table."

"Is this just for two?" The hostess interrupted holding two menus. Elijah smiled at her and nodded yes. Having not removed his hands from her waist, they followed the hostess to the table.

"I can walk," she said, irritated.

"Yes, you can. I have seen it for myself." He responded sarcastically.

"Well, then let me go."

"Here is your table. The specials tonight are the smoked salmon, the halibut steak, and our fillet mignon. Your server will be with you in a moment." The hostess left and they both sat down.

"So are you going to tell me why you're acting the way you are?" he asked as he looked at the menu.

His manhandling and nonchalant attitude did nothing to calm her. She meticulously moved her water glass and menu to the side. She looked at him in his face and caught his eyes. She leaned forward on the table in a posture that to the outside world suggested an intimate moment was going to take place. He smiled and moved in closer to hear what she was going to say.

"Let me apologize for my behavior," she said in a whisper. "You know, I just find being lied to annoying." His smiled slipped off his face and his eyebrows drew together. She smiled. "Oh yes." She continued. "When someone deceives me in order to become close to me or even intimate with me I have a problem with that."

"What are you talking about?" he asked through his teeth.

"I'm talking about. . .well, let me explain something to you about women. Some women love to be treated like fine China unless it has to do with the truth. Then, we want to be treated like Tupperware. You see, fine China is to be adored, admired, touched carefully, be considered beautiful. Tupperware is dependable, reliable and cherished for its durability. Men must learn to know when the woman needs to be treated like China and when she needs to be treated like Tupperware.

"What the hell are you talking about?" he asked, completely confused.

"Ask your wife if she is fine China or Tupperware."

He looked as if she had just slapped him. "My wife?"

"Oh, yeah her. That one you told me you weren't married to. Yeah, ask her if she's fine China or Tupperware."

"What does she have to do with us?"

"Excuse me? What do you mean what does she have to do with us?"

He leaned back against his chair and allowed that easy smile to spread across his face again. "If I recall, when we were together, you weren't thinking too much about her."

"If I recall, I didn't know yo' ass was married!" she retorted. She glanced around her and noticed other people looking at them. She didn't want to make a scene so she lowered her voice. "You are that woman's husband."

He looked at her. "And that is a damn song by Shirley Murdock," he said nonchalantly, looking back to his menu.

She let out a huff and cut her eyes at him. At that moment, the waiter came to take their order. She hadn't even looked at the menu so he ordered for the both of them. When the waiter left, he returned to the conversation at hand.

"What's the difference? I was living with her. You knew that. I have children with her, you knew that too. What, pray tell, is the difference? A piece of paper?"

"Your level of commitment is the difference." She justified.

"Sweetheart, do you hear how asinine that argument is? My commitment level isn't different. You would like it to be, but it's not. I love my "wife," and that hasn't changed. I have no intentions of leaving her, at all. I felt that way before I met you, when I was screwing you, and I have that same commitment now." He leaned forward again and caught her chin in his fingertips. "Your problem is that a piece of paper makes a difference to you because you feel guilty. But that commitment is not yours, it's mine."

His words stung. She knew he didn't want anything other than sex from her, but damn, to have it laid out in front of her was something else. Her face must have reflected her pain, because he became sincere and sympathetic.

His fingers left her chin and traced her lips. "There is no reason for you to feel guilty. We enjoyed each other. There should be no guilt in that. I have done nothing but think about how we could enjoy each other again. That is inevitable. You can't taste anything that sweet and not want some more. You have to change your mindset."

She felt stupid. Despite her pain and irrational self-righteousness, part of what he was saying was right. She was more upset with herself. She felt humiliated and embarrassed and wanted to go home. He had shown where his commitment was and it wasn't in a relationship with her.

Why am I mad about an actual marriage certificate when before I knew about it he was still doing the same thing? He was still living with the mother of his children, sleeping with her, having a family with her. What was the difference? Nothing was different except the knowledge of a paper certifying his family as his own. What about the principle? What principle? That is the point. What principles am I standing on that can make a difference anyway?

Trying to get a hold of her senses she pulled away from his touch and dropped her head. He sat silently looking at her. He couldn't read what she was thinking, so he had not a clue what to say. He waited.

The waiter returned with their order and they ate in silence.

And he waited.

She finally lifted her head and met his eyes. "You're right," she said, defeated.

"Excuse me?" He wasn't sure what exactly she was talking about.

"You're right. It really doesn't matter at all." She continued to speak as she traced her plate with her fork. "I have wanted you ever since I knew you had a thing for me. Hell, I want you now. I know this is wrong and so I fight it. When we had sex, it was the best and worst thing I have ever done in my life. What made it the best? It was *damn good.* What made it the worst? I will regret the fact that I was with another woman's husband for the rest of my life, especially now since I know you are her *husband.*"

He sat looking at her for a moment.

"There you go with quoting songs again. What is your point?"

"My point is. . .hell, I don't know." Eve sighed." Well, that is not entirely true. I do know. I have a decision to make."

He sat waiting.

"I have to decide whether I want to continue to deal with the consequences or cut my losses."

"What have you lost?" he asked, truly confused. "If anyone loses, it will be me, but I don't think either one of us has to worry. We are both intelligent and discreet."

She didn't quite know why what he was saying to her surprised her, but it did.

"What do you mean what have I lost? I have lost my self-respect. My sense of right and wrong has been blurred beyond measure. My friends don't even seem to know who I'm at this moment and, most of all, I'm not sure if I know my damn self." She took a breath and went on. "Do you know I sit and think strange thoughts about how my life will be affected by my decisions? The other day, I sat in my car and thought if I ever got married and my husband cheated on me I would be forced to forgive him, because I've been the other woman."

He smirked at her.

"Yeah, I know that shit sounds ridiculous to you. What would you do if you walked around the corner over there and found your wife talking cozily to another man?"

"That shit wouldn't happen," he declared and was offended she said such a thing.

"Are you sure?" she asked with a raised eyebrow. He had broken his cool and that was unfamiliar to her, outside of the bedroom anyway. "Would she say the same about you?"

"Don't project your fears onto me," he said, resuming his cool demeanor.

Eve could still tell that he was disturbed.

"You are an adult woman, in every sense of the word. You can make the decision on your own, but I want to tell you something.

What we have is unescapable. You can run and you can hide, but sooner or later you are going to have to meet it head on again."

He got up from his chair and pulled out his wallet to pay their bill. He came around and pulled out her chair. She got up and grabbed her wrap and purse from the back of the chair. Walking toward the door, he murmured in her ear, "Since I know the inevitable will not happen tonight, let me take you home. I have to be up early tomorrow."

She wrapped her wrap around her shoulders and followed him out into the night air.

This just ain't right!
Chapter 10

Eve got up to go to the gym at 5:30 a.m. When she returned to her house, she put her cell on speaker to listen to her voicemail as she got her clothes ready for work. The first two calls were her mother's usual wake up calls. The third was Lola calling and canceling their plans for the upcoming Friday. It seemed that the man from church had called her after she got home from their shopping spree on Sunday and invited her to a dinner party. The fourth call was Teresa telling her that she was planning on traveling to see her parents this weekend, and the last call was from Elijah.

"Hey, what's up? I will be in town this weekend and I have made reservations for dinner and what not." Eve smiled at the statement *what not*. She knew what not meant *Why not?* "Anyway, I'll give you a call sometime later this week."

She tried to make herself uncomfortable with this whole thing, but she was at the point of no return. She had changed her mindset. Deciding not to dwell on it, she rushed through her shower and headed to work.

Eve went to work and plugged away at the mundane everyday tasks. Every morning she walked in and got her coffee. Her assistant laid papers down in front of her to prioritize and put due dates on and by midmorning she was in the swing of things.

She worked through lunchtime and didn't emerge from her office until about two. She walked toward the breakroom where her candy fix relief would be waiting for her in the vending machine. Walking in the room, she acknowledged the folks sitting and headed straight for the machine.

"Girl, you and your candy," a co-worker commented and laughed.

"I can't live without them," Eve replied laughing. As she counted out the change in her hand, she listened to their ongoing conversation.

"Girl, I heard that Mr. Mann has a regular honey pot that he sees any time he's here."

"Girl, please. How does he do it? Every time I work late and he's here in town, he walks out of this office the same time I do and you know I do extra time, not getting out of here until about ten or eleven o'clock."

"Well, he must meet her after eleven. It's not like they're trying to be seen. His ass is married."

Eve, realizing this was a conversation she'd rather not hear, got her candy bar and walked out the door after bidding her co-workers a farewell. She got halfway down the hall when she realized she didn't get her soda. She headed back towards the breakroom and overheard her name.

"Well, I did hear that something was up with him and Eve," one of her co-workers whispered.

"Eve who? Eve, Eve? The Eve that just left? Miss, innocent-probably-don't-know-a-dick-poking-her-in-the-face, Newborn? That Eve? Girl, please! That woman ain't been laid in so long that you know her stuff done closed up."

"If it was ever opened up." The initiator added on.

Both women laughed.

Eve standing outside the door decided that at that moment she would give up soda. She turned around and walked back to her office.

At the end of the day, Eve was exhausted. Ever since she heard her coworkers talking, she couldn't seem to concentrate on anything. *Am I really that big of a prude? What should it really matter anyway? I ain't screwing they husbands. I think it's good that they don't' think I get any. Hell, that is a great cover, but I wonder who is spreading rumors about me and Elijah?* Lost in her own thoughts she didn't hear her assistant walk in.

"Miss Newborn? I'm leaving now. Is there anything you would like me to do before I go?" Eve looked at her watch and the minute hand struck 5:00 p.m.

"No, Patricia, have a good evening. I have some things I'm still working on. I'll have a list of different things that need to be done before noon tomorrow on your desk when I leave this evening. I'm going to be coming in late tomorrow morning and I'll need those things finished by the time I come in."

"Not a problem Miss Newborn. Should I prepare to come in early?"

"Patricia, call me Eve. And no don't come in early. It won't be that much."

"Ok Miss New . . ."

Eve gave her chastising look. She had been trying to break Patricia out of the habit of being so formal. They had worked long hours together on projects and had been subjected to each other's early morning breath. Eve felt they were past titles and had reached friendship.

Patricia smiled. "I mean Eve. Have a good evening."

"You too," Eve said, watching her assistant walk out the door to go home to her adoring husband who was waiting for her. Eve thought to herself *what do I have waiting for me at home? Not a damn thing but a frozen pizza. And maybe not that if my sister is there.* Taking a deep breath, Eve worked a couple of more hours before she called it quits.

Planting herself on her couch as soon as she walked into the door, Eve was glad her sister wasn't there. She wanted to have the place to herself. Grabbing the remote control, she flipped on the TV and began perusing through her mail. Hearing the familiar sounds of the opening song for the *Rachel Winters Show,* she put her mail down, snuggled on the couch and turned the volume up.

Damn that Rachel wears some bad shoes. That heifer is so bad she out dresses Oprah every day of the week—although I did like the way Oprah dressed before she lost that weight.

"Before we get started today, I would like to warn the audience that this show is not about confrontation. Today's show is about women in our society who do exist and who claim their life works for them. Though this is not my usual format, I found the arguments these women make are fascinating, even though I don't agree with them. These women may enrage you, but more than that, I hope they draw attention to your own relationships, so their lifestyle isn't made possible. We will be right back."

Lord what is this show about? Eve got up from her sofa and walked into the kitchen. She prepared her soda and grabbed her fruit bowl form the refrigerator. When she heard Rachel's voice once again, she hurried back to the couch.

"Today on our show we are going to talk about women who say that the married man in their lives is just what they need. They recognized that being a career-minded woman makes it virtually impossible to be a mom and wife. So they have decided they would establish intimate relationships with married men."

Damn! You sure this is Rachel Winters? Eve thought to herself as she settled back into the indention her generous behind had made earlier in the sofa. Rachel Winters usually stayed above the typical drama talk show format. She reached for the remote control and pressed the information button so the channel and show would appear on her screen. *Yes, it's Rachel Winters.*

"Well, I'm classified as a workaholic and it's very difficult for me to maintain a relationship because of my work," one of the women on the show explained. "In the type of business I do, ninety-nine percent of the males I meet are all married. About six years ago, I met a business associate that I was to work on a project with. We spent long hours together and our attraction grew. Eventually, the attraction grew to the point where we didn't care what anybody thought; we wanted to be together."

"Well, what about his wife?" Eve yelled at the television. Right after that, Rachel Winters asked the same question. Applause arose from the audience who obviously agreed with Rachel and Eve's question.

"I have to be honest with you, Rachel. She was not my concern; she was his. You see, I knew I could walk away from this, because I didn't have the commitment. He was the one who was going to have to face the music."

At that time, Eve's telephone rang. So engrossed in the show, she picked it up and barely got out a hello.

"Girl, what are you doing?" It was Teresa.

"Girl, I got on Rachel Winters Show. You will never guess what they are talking about."

"Yes I would. I'm a loyal fan and it's a re-run."

"Girl, you could have warned me. Or maybe you knew I would watch it today and you could try to make a point with it." Eve muted the TV on the commercials.

"If I need to make a point," Teresa retorted. "I'll just make it. I'm not going to use a nationally syndicated talk show to make a point with my girlfriend."

"What side of the bed did you wake up on?"

"The side with no one in." Teresa snapped.

"Oh honey, you need a little lovin'," Eve said recognizing the source of Teresa's irritation.

"I don't need a little; I need a damn boat full."

"Now, you're beginning to sound like Lola."

"Bitch, bite your tongue on that one," Teresa said too quickly. Although Lola and Teresa were friends, they were so opposite that it was an insult to suggest that they were alike in any fashion.

"Where is Michael?"

"Michael is out of town on business for the next two weeks."

"Dang Teresa, you work in a building full of men. What's the problem? You can scratch the itch if you want to," Eve said before she thought about what she was saying. Every time Michael went out of town, Eve would say something stupid like that, knowing Teresa would not take her seriously. Now, her heart sank at the possible response.

"First of all, I'm not going out on Michael. Second, the problem is that they are all white, married, fat, bald men." Eve was relieved Teresa answered the way she usually would when she was teasing.

Teresa worked in the city planning office in the economic development department. Everyone asked her why she wanted to go into a white male dominated field, she just answered, "'Cause I can."

They both laughed.

"Well what happened. . ." Eve voice trailed off when the TV caught her attention.

"What happened with what?" Teresa asked.

Eve didn't answer.

"Eve!" Teresa yelled realizing her friend was watching TV.

"What?" she answered half listening.

"Damn girl, hit the DVR. Turn that shit off and talk to me."

"Well, you've seen this already, right?" Eve said pressing record and then muting the television.

"Yeah," Teresa whined. "But I need to bitch right now and you ain't listening."

"Okay fine." Eve turned the television off. "I'm listening now. What's up? What happened to Chris? Didn't you have him as a backup when Michael was acting up?"

"I'm engaged now so there are no more backups. Anyway, I had to cut him loose a long time ago."

"Why?" Eve asked slipping another grape into her mouth.

"He called out the name Pamela in the middle of having sex." Eve almost choked on the fruit.

"What? Who the hell is Pamela?"

"Girl, Pamela Anderson."

"The white girl with big breasts from that old show, *Baywatch*?"

"The one and only."

"Why would he call out her name when he was with you? You ain't white with blonde hair. Although you're definitely *not* an active member of the itty-bitty-titty committee." Eve giggled.

"Damn straight and yo' ass is jealous of these ripe melons," Teresa boasted. They laughed then. "Anyway, I guess he was fantasizing about her when he called out her name. He was trippin' when I told him to get off me. He said I shouldn't trip because he was just fantasizing. I was like damn is your momma thirteen years older than you?"

"No you didn't, girl," Eve said laughing

"Yes, I did, and that mofo acted like he didn't have any home training. I was like damn all these beautiful sista' celebrities and you go to a 1980's white one? Miss me with that."

"Girl, Yeah." Eve agreed. Right then, Eve's phone beeped indicating another caller. She looked and didn't recognize the number.

"And so you are going to be in need of lovin' until Michael gets back," Eve asked, sending the call to voicemail.

"Nah. Michael bought me a little toy for when he is gone."

"Really? Ha, it sounds like you need to get busy." Eve's phone beeped again. "Hold on Teresa; there's a call on the other line."

"I'll call you later." Teresa interjected before Eve could click over. "I have to finish up some stuff."

"Alright sweetie, make sure you have fresh batteries." They both laughed. Eve clicked over to the other line.

"Hello."

"Damn girl, what took you so long to answer the phone?" It was Lola.

"I didn't recognize the number, and I was just talking to Teresa."

"I'm calling from my work phone. What y'all talking about?"

"She just tired of being horny."

"Damn. I hate that too, but I don't let it last as long as Teresa. I will go hunt down some dick."

"I know."

"Anyway," Lola went on, "have you heard from you know who?"

"Girl, no." Eve lied. Some of this stuff she just had to keep it to herself. "But, I heard he was coming into the office later this week. I'm nervous about seeing him."

"Girl, you already done fucked him. What's the problem?"

"Lola, it's not about sex. It's about getting caught up. I could fall in love with him and where would that leave me?"

"Eve, first of all, you are not going to fall in love with him. You are going to fall in love with the sex. However, if you can't handle it, then don't do it."

Eve sat quietly for a moment. "But Lola, I want it *bad!*"

"I don't know what to tell you. Hold on for a minute," Lola put Eve on hold. Eve absent-mindedly reached for the remote control and turned on the television. The Rachel Winters show credits were going up the screen. "Okay, I'm back."

"Did you see the Rachel Winters Show today?" Eve asked Lola.

"Are you talking about the one where women are talking about how married men fit their lifestyle? Yeah, I saw that. I was cracking up when one woman stood up and said she agreed with the women on stage. She said there was a married man that definitely fit into her lifestyle; her husband. Girl, everyone on the show started hooting and hollering."

Eve sat there, not saying anything. Lola noticed her silence.

"What's up Evie?"

Eve was hesitant at first. Then she spoke. "I can see how the women on the show could justify their relationships. They're not trying to break up the marriage, they are just. . ."

Lola cut her off in mid-sentence. "Don't pay attention to that shit! If you're going to do this thing, be woman enough to make your own decisions and not excuses."

"I know Lola. I know."

Change my mindset.
Chapter 11

When Eve went to work on Friday morning, she saw him talking to her boss. He looked up at her and smiled. She smiled back and walked in her office. Five minutes later, her secretary came in and announced her boss, Gerald McClintoch, had called a meeting of all department managers. Eve walked into the boardroom and Elijah was seated around the round table with the other managers.

The only seat open for her was the seat directly across from him. *Did he do that shit on purpose?* She made it her number one priority not to stare at him, but, as the meeting began, her eyes subconsciously traveled in his direction. Realizing what she was doing, she momentarily closed her eyes.

Get a grip! I cannot ogle this man in this meeting. You're going to have to pay the same amount of attention to everyone else if you don't want to look so obvious. This is insane!

When Elijah spoke, her eyes were riveted to him. Giving him her seemingly undivided attention allowed her to take in the sight of him. She noticed every move. She noticed when his bottom lip dropped slightly revealing white teeth. She noticed his hands as the expressed his thoughts and implied others. She noticed his clothes, the fit of his pants, the clinging of his shirt to his well-defined arms, his perfectly coiffed hair, and shiny black shoes. She took all of this in, in a matter of minutes. When he finished, she pretended to be as interested in everyone else. She wasn't. Her mind was wandering. *Is he wondering about me? Of course not stupid, he just got through going over his assessment of the takeover thus far.*

Sitting back in her chair, she felt her skirt give way revealing her leg. After shifting to adjust the split, she found that it kept opening. She noticed him taking in her legs with a side glance. The way she was sitting he had a direct view of her leg and anything else she wanted to show him. She was in a quandary. Should she leave it alone? Or maybe she should try to undo him as he did her? Or should she be a more modest person because of the other men in the room? Allowing herself to get caught in this predicament led her to become self-conscious about everything. She wondered if her lipstick was still on, and was it on her teeth. *Oh how stupid am I? He is not even available to me, although he has made himself available to me. Good sense should tell me to worry about this board meeting and the task at hand and not about this man.*

She adjusted her skirt to cover her leg, and she noticed a slight curl of a smile on his lip. She, again, focused on the speaker trying to forget Elijah was there. She finally managed to get her head out of the clouds and became a productive participant in the meeting.

A small lull in the conversations allowed her attention to slip and she noticed him pull out a mint and slip it into his mouth. She followed that mint into his mouth and it was as if he noticed her watching. His mouth remained open at tad longer than necessary, allowing her to watch his tongue sensuously wrapped around the mint. His mouth closed and his tongue snaked across his lips and her concentration had abandoned her like a reckless train derailment. She physically moved in her seat and hoped no one noticed.

Taking in a deep breath, she exhaled loudly enough for the person sitting next to her to glance over. She smiled sheepishly and began to rub the back of her neck. It was at that time they dismissed for a ten-minute break. Thankful to be out of that room, she went straight to her office and closed the door.

Walking to her desk, she pulled a mirror from the drawer and examined her face. She was flushed. Her skin was clammy and beads of perspiration trekked across her nose. It was not that hot. This is her workplace and she shouldn't be looking and lusting, like a teenage cheerleader in heat for the quarterback of the football team. She was smarter than this. *Snap out of it, girlfriend!*

Gathering her papers she would need for the meeting, she opened the door. Elijah was standing right there. She smelled the cologne on his body and the faint mint of his breath. A smile slipped across his face with ease and his eyes narrowed. Human instinct says that if you are too close to fire you should back away, so she did. He took advantage of her movement and stepped into her office and closed the door. She looked at the door and at her watch.

"Gerry is on a long distance call. He sent word for everyone to take an early lunch and we'll resume at one o'clock."

She glanced at her watch again. It read 11:30 am. Looking back, she noticed him leaning against her office door watching her. She could feel the sweat pop up on her nose and she became extremely self-conscious. Not thinking, she removed her blazer and reveal the camisole tee underneath. It wasn't inappropriate in any way, but she regretted that move as soon as she had done it. She knew the tee fit snugly and outlined her shape. She didn't want to seem silly and put her jacket back on, but she didn't want to just stand there either.

"Well, shall we go for lunch?" he asked, still leaning against the door.

"I think I'm going to stay and catch up on some things." She moved around him and sat down at her desk. She kept her head down and stared at the papers on the desk. Eve felt so stupid. She was a grown woman acting like a twelve-year-old who just discovered the opposite sex and the fact that a boy liked her at the same time.

He moved away from the door and walked around her desk. So lost in her own thoughts, she wasn't aware of him until she felt strong, firm fingers run through her hair.

"What are you doing?" She stammered as she jerked out of the reach of his hands.

"Relax. We're the only people in this office. Everyone who was at the meeting is gone already." He moved towards her again and began massaging her neck. "As a matter of fact, I told them I was coming to ask you if you wanted to join us at the Chinese restaurant up the street."

"Well, I don't," she said letting her eyes fall close and enjoying the exquisite ministering of his hands along her scalp and neck.

"I can see that," he said.

She heard the humor in his voice, but his touch rendered her useless. Totally relaxing her body, his hands moved further down her back and inside her shirt. Still nothing was said. His hands were strong. He massaged the muscles along her neck and back allowing his hands to unhook the snaps of her bra. She tensed at the loosening, and his hands continued to massage the tightened muscles.

Her breasts were full enough for the bra to cling, but the black straps began to slip down her shoulders. As the straps slid down, she felt his hands move up her back and his fingers lightly clasped around her neck. His fingers danced along her throat and moved her hair away to expose her ears.

Hello, sleepy head. This man is taking your clothes off in your office.

I know, but he has magic hands. They feel so good and I need this massage.

Rationalization was such an ugly thing. "Hey now," she said, welcoming good sense into this situation. She pulled away and adjusted her clothing. He grinned at her while she watched his chest heave, trying to catch his breath.

"This is the workplace and this is inappropriate behavior," she said, slipping her straps onto her shoulders and adjusting her breasts in her bra.

"Yes, it is and yes to the second statement as well." He sighed deeply and leaned against her desk. "I want to apologize. I know that was unprofessional behavior. I would never want to make the workplace uncomfortable for either one of us."

She nodded and continued to dress.

He stared off in deep thought for a moment.

She watched him in her peripheral vision.

"So what do we do about it?" he asked, suddenly causing her to jump a little.

"What do you mean?" she asked and tried to look confused as to the meaning of his question.

"Oh, we're playing dumb, huh?" he asked, uncrossed his arms and moved toward the door. "How professional is that?"

"Are you insinuating that I'm a professional?" she asked, emphasizing the double meaning.

He glanced back at her with a slight curl on his upper lip. "Touché." When he reached the door, he turned completely around and looked at her.

She ran her fingers through her hair and her eyes caught his.

He said nothing.

She calmly reached down and opened the drawer that held her purse. She opened it and removed her compact. Looking in the tiny mirror, she adjusted her hair and put on a fresh coat of lipstick. Looking up a minute later, she realized he was still standing at the door watching her and saying nothing. She grabbed her bag, shoved the compact in and rose from the chair. Walking to the door, he moved to the side and opened it for her. She paused in the doorway and looked boldly in his eyes.

"You pay for the hotel. Never will we meet at my home, nor will I ever call yours. This is strictly between us. If I hear the slightest bit of gossip, it ends, and if I feel at any point uncomfortable with this, it will end with no other discussion. And, you will always wear a condom."

He smiled and moved to the side allowing her to walk through. She wasn't sure but she could have sworn she heard him say "inevitable."

Inevitability is a mindset
Chapter 12

That evening, Eve went to Elijah's hotel suite and knocked on the door. Waiting for him to answer, she looked up and down the hallway. He had a different hotel than where he stayed before. She had no idea if someone there would recognize her or not. She smoothed her red sundress across its buttons and adjusted the straps on her sandaled heel. She was expending nervous energy. *Dang is he going to open the door?*

When Elijah had called her and invited her to dinner, she immediately became unsure of herself, but she suppressed all of that. She decided to come. She wanted to see what exactly she'd gotten herself into. She could always get out if she didn't want it.

When Elijah answered the door, she smiled. He stood before her in a pair of slacks and white shirt buttoned halfway. She noticed that he had no shoes on and his even feet were nice looking.

He smiled at her, moved out of the way and allowed her to walk in. "Would you like a drink?"

"No, thank you," she answered, noticing the glass in his hand filled with a brown liquid.

"You sure? I hate to drink alone."

"Yes. No, thank you. Are you going to get dressed?"

"No." He walked over to the coffee table to refill his drink.

"I thought you said that we were going to dinner."

"I decided we could order room service. What would you like? The menu is over there on the table."

Eve sat in the chair next the love seat. She picked up the menu and looked it over. She decided on the chicken salad, although she was so nervous she didn't know if she could eat.

She gave him her order and he picked up the phone to order for both of them. She surveyed the suite and it was nicely decorated with a beige and cream theme. When Elijah was finished with the call, she pretended to study the art on the walls as she watched Elijah take a seat on the sofa and watch her. He sat at an angle with his right leg lifted on the couch and his right arm resting at the back.

"It will be here in about forty–five minutes," he said and sipped his drink.

"That will be fine." Eve smiled at him and returned her attention back to the artwork on the wall. Eve became aware of the silence in the room and began to fidget. Willing herself to look over at him, Elijah sat swirling the ice around in his drink, staring at her. "What?" she asked self-consciously.

He didn't say anything.

Eve frowned at him and began touching her face feeling for something that may be out of place. "What?" she asked again. "Do I have something on me?"

His demeanor was making her paranoid.

"No," he said, drinking from the tumbler he held in his hand. "No. I was just thinking." He sat back in his chair with his legs crossed sipping his drink. His voice was soft and seemingly reflective.

"Thinking about what?"

"Eve, do you trust me?"

She hesitated and looked at Elijah curiously. "Yes. I guess so."

"Take off your clothes."

"Excuse me?"

"Take off your clothes."

"Why?"

"I'd like you to."

"I'm not sure I want to take my clothes off."

Elijah set his glass down, leaned back in his chair, placed his hands on the back of his head, and looked her in her eyes. "Eve, what did you come here for?"

Eve smiled and looked away embarrassed.

He knew what she came for. She had come to have her mind blown.

"Take off your clothes," he challenged.

Eve sat for a minute longer.

Girl, you wanted to play. Don't chicken out, now. You could go home, but I think it's a little too late to be running scared. Gurl, look at that man. You already know what those soft lips can do. Eve shivered. *You know what his touch feels like. Gurl, he is not going to hurt you. Just do it!*

Eve rose from her seat and allowed a smile to spread across her face. She began to slowly unbutton her dress. She unfastened the last button and allowed the dress to fall away revealing her red lace bra and panty set. She moved her shoulders allowing the straps to fall down her arms and the dress fall to the floor. She heard his breath catch and she smiled broadly.

"Run your hands over your breasts," he instructed.

Eve, feeling self-conscious, shifted her feet but somehow managed to keep looking straight into his eyes. She knew he was testing her and she was determined to pass with flying colors. He lifted one eyebrow at her and waited.

Eve moved her hands across her breasts slowly. She cupped them together as she had seen women do in porno and presented her ample cleavage to him. She allowed her fingers to hook inside her bra tracing the lacey edges encasing her caramel hills.

"Flick your nipples with your thumbs. Make them hard."

She began to get turned on as she ran her thumbs across her sensitive peaks. She gasped at the sensation and her body began to warm and tingle. She moved her thumbs back and forth quickly so her distended nipples would push out the lacy fabric that covered them. She could feel her liquid lust floating through her body.

"Now, I want you to follow directions as I give them to you. Remove your hands from your body and rest them at your side."

Oh shit. What the hell is he going to want me to do?

Eve did it.

"Now, get a chair and come and sit in front of me."

Eve pursed her lips and looked at him.

He merely nodded toward the chair and waited.

She walked slowly to get the chair. She knew he was watching her. She also knew her body was hot and she looked good. When she picked up the chair, she leaned over further than necessary to give Elijah a glimpse of her ass. When she turned, she could tell by the smile that he enjoyed the show. She walked the chair back over to him and sat it in front of him.

"Have a seat, Eve."

She moved and sat in front of Elijah and waited for her next instructions.

"Now, lovely lady, I want you to put your hand in your panties and touch yourself."

I know he did not just ask me to get myself off? I came here for him to get me off.

"Is there something wrong, Eve?" he asked as he sat back in his chair and sipped his drink.

Hell yeah, there is something wrong. I have never did shit like this before. I'm used to just getting busy – not this stuff.

She shook her head no.

"Good. Now, take your left hand and put it in your panties. I want you to use your index finger to stimulate your clit and your middle finger to work in your sweet place."

Eve smiled at his reference to her "sweet place." She held his eyes and allowed her left hand to move slowly down her stomach and the tip of her fingers disappeared under the elastic waistband. She stopped and peered further into his eyes. They were unreadable.

Elijah waited.

Eve was uncomfortably titillated sitting before him semi-nude with her hand covering her heaven. Eve closed her eyes and allowed her fingers to hit her small erection. She gasped as her self-imposed restraint began to crumble away. She began to enthusiastically give herself pleasure.

"Make sure you make it juicy." Eve heard Elijah's confident voice develop into a deep huskier version of itself. "Use your right hand to keep your nips tweaked."

Eve's left hand moved rhythmically between her legs and her right hand ran over her breasts. Each time her fingers brushed her nipples, her essence saturated her hand. Her female sex smell began to permeate the room. Her legs began to quiver as she continued to stroke.

"Do you like that, Eve?" Elijah asked moving toward her and allowing his own hand to began to roam over her body. He lifted the bra up allowing the firm breast to bounce out into his hands. With her own hand covering his, he tweaked her nipples.

She shivered.

He then traced a path down her stomach to the elastic where her other hand was submerged. He tugged at the band. "Lift your hips."

Eve barely heard him in her world of pleasure. She lifted her bottom and he slipped her underwear from her. Her honey pot was open to him with her distinct smell and flavor. He grabbed her hands and held them away. Eve instinctively moved to close her legs, but Elijah had positioned himself between her legs so that she was wide open to him. Eve's eyes popped open and her body writhed.

"Wha. . .What's wrong?" Eve asked gasping for her breath.

"Nothing at all."

Elijah held her hands up over her head with one hand and traced her mouth with the other. Eve opened her mouth and allowed Elijah fingers to sneak in. She wrapped her lips around his fingers and sucked them.

He pulled them away and began to trace the lines of her neck.

Eve meowed and allowed her head to drop to the side exposing her neck. Elijah continued to move his hand down across her chest, flicking each nipple and causing a pinch of painful pleasure. Racing down her stomach, he stopped and circled her belly button. The little hairs on her stomach stood up. His finger finally made it to her pleasure button. Her ragged breath expelled and his sweet torture began.

"I...I...I...don't...know...if...I...can...take...anymore." Eve panted between each word as Elijah used his finger to stroke her to her ultimate pleasure. "Elijah, I'm there. I'm there. I am..." Eve let her body succumb to an overwhelming release that lifted her from the chair trembling, allowing the quake to run its course. Her body finally collapsed and slumped in the chair.

She opened her eyes to look at Elijah, who still was holding her hands over her head and was still dallying between her legs. He looked at her with a smug smile and brought his hand to his mouth licking his fingers slowly. Eve was so turned on by what she saw that her body involuntarily shivered again.

"Go ahead and clean up in the restroom. You can put my robe on." Elijah let go of her hands and they dropped lifelessly to her sides.

It took every ounce of her strength to get up and move into the restroom. When she came out, she was wrapped in an oversized robe with the hotel insignia. She padded barefoot across the floor to the bar to pour herself a drink.

Elijah was sitting in the very same chair, sipping on another drink. "I see you need a drink?" she heard him say from behind her.

"I guess I do." Eve didn't say much more. She had never done anything like that before and she was so turned on that she was a bit ashamed. And to watch him lick her essence from his fingers sent her senses to the roof. *Damn, I never know what I'm going to get with this man.*

There was a knock on the door and Eve jumped a few feet.

Elijah smiled and eased himself out of the chair to answer it. Eve sat on the couch trying to catch her breath and get some clarity on what happened moments before. When she looked up, Elijah was pushing a tray into the room.

"Dinner is served."

<u>Dancing in the dark.</u>
Chapter 13

"You did what?" Teresa screamed at her. "What do you mean you agreed to do this? You told him yes?"

"Back off, Teresa," Lola interjected. "He ain't the only one getting his groove on. Our girl has finally stepped out on the wild side." Lola jumped up and circled the couch.

"I say she go for it." Lola started singing, "Don't stop, get it, get it." She backed her behind on Eve and bumped up against her. Eve laughed.

"Lola, sit yo' ass down. You know this shit is serious," Teresa berated. "As a matter of fact, wasn't it you that told her don't fuck with a married man?"

"Yes, I did, but it wasn't my choice to make. I'm not the one that made this agreement. Eve did. Now that she has, I just want to support my girl in the decision that she made."

"Even if it's the wrong one?" Teresa retorted.

"Yes," Lola said unapologetically.

"It ain't too late to call off the deal." Teresa looked pleadingly at Eve who sat in silence.

"But does she want to," Lola said sitting down by her best friend.

Eve decided not to let them know that she already technically did the do. "Hell, I don't know. Yesterday when I agreed to this I was confident and sure. I would have gone to the hotel room right from the office, if our boss didn't come out of his office and ask us to go to lunch with him. Parts of me want to whip it on him." *Be careful what you say Evie. Your girls ain't dumb.*

"That's my girl," Lola said popping her fingers.

"Shut *up!*" Teresa hit her with a pillow.

"But the other part of me knows I need to walk away." *Dang you laying it on a little thick.*

"Which part is stronger?" Teresa asked earnestly.

"To be honest, I know I'm probably going to go through with it." *You've already been through it.*

Teresa sighed and removed herself from the couch and gathered her coat.

"Where are you going?" Lola asked standing up.

"I'm going home."

"You can't leave. Our girl needs us."

"I cannot and will not sit and support her in this mess." Teresa looked at her friend sitting on the couch. "When he hurts you beyond what you can bear, call me and I will be right over here. Until then I don't want anything to do with this. I don't want to know any of this. I don't want to hear about it. I would rather stay out of it."

"What the hell are you talking about?" Lola yelled. "You mean to tell me that you're willing to walk out on a friend when she apparently needs you the most. What the hell kind of friend are you? You are a sorry piece of..."

"Shut up, Lola." Lola stopped upon hearing the hurt in Eve's voice. "Don't say another word that might further alienate the two of you." She turned to Teresa.

"Teresa, don't go." She pleaded with her friend. "I need you and Lola."

"Girlfriend, I know you need a friend, but I can't sit in approval of this. You put me in a position where I have to make the hardest decision and distance myself away from my best friend," Teresa looked up at Lola who was pissed off. "My best friends," she restated, "until this is over. Girl, bye."

Lola interrupted again. "Stop trying to sound like a fuckin' martyr. I know where this shit it coming from," Lola continued on. "This shit is from your daddy, right Teresa?"

"You know what Lola, just leave it alone," Teresa said grabbing her purse and digging in it for her keys. "This is not about me. It's about our friend and her choices."

"Oh, you damn skippy it's about you. You trippin' about finding out about your daddy's extramarital activity."

Teresa looked at Lola and sent her a look to warn her off, but Lola was too far-gone. Eve stood back in shock that Lola would attack that low.

"This about you and your inability to accept that your daddy was a fuckin' man like the rest of the sons of bitches out there that skipped out a couple of times. Well, hell, welcome to the party, Miss Teresa. So glad you could join us here in the real world," Lola's sarcasm oozed out of her mouth like a foul tasting pudding.

Teresa's eyes glossed over with tears. The things that Lola spoke of were some of the most difficult things Teresa had to work through in her life. Her father's infidelity ruined her relationship with him for a long time. It took a while before she realized that his infidelity was none of her business. That was an issue between he and his wife, her mother. Her mother didn't leave, so she had no right to make judgments on those things. Lola knew the struggle that Teresa went through and for her to mention it was cruel.

"Lola you're wrong and way out of line." Eve interjected into Lola's tirade.

"I'm out of line?" Lola asked Eve incredulously. "No, she is out of line. You are her best friend, getting ready to charter unfamiliar territory, and she is abandoning ship."

"I know Lola, but that's her choice. I wish she wouldn't, but she has a right to tell me when she can't handle something. And since I'm trying to be a friend I'm going to respect her wishes." Eve turned to Teresa. "I won't call with this, but I will call."

"Thank you for understanding, Eve," Teresa said and gave her friend a hug. Lola looked at the two shaking her head. When Teresa released Eve from their embrace, she walked to the front door and opened it. Teresa turned around and looked at Lola. Lola met her look with a challenging look of her own. Teresa raised her right hand as if she were going to wave and then turned it around and flipped her off.

"Bitch," Lola muttered after Teresa left.

"Let it go, Lola," Eve said, standing in the middle of the room. She didn't know what to do with herself.

"Well, since this get together was a bust, I will let it go and I will go." Lola grabbed her purse. "I will never understand why you always cater to her, but I'm gonna let you do you and I'm going to do me. I'll holla." With that, Lola walked out the door.

We will pray about it.
Chapter 14

It had been a few weeks since Eve had any real communication with Teresa. Meanwhile, Eve was with Elijah almost every night he came into town. She was home by herself tonight, so she decided to call Teresa.

"Hey T. What are you doing?"

"Hey. I just got in and put a frozen lasagna in the oven. What's going on?"

"I just called to see how you are."

"Girl, I'm busy planning this wedding. Last night, I met some of Michael's frat brothers and they were off the chain."

"I know you expected that. Whenever fraternity men get together, they tend to be a bit much."

"I know." Teresa laughed. "I hear a grown man bark one more time I will howl at the moon."

"Then prepare to howl at your wedding reception," Eve said in a fit of giggles.

"Oh my God!" Teresa screamed. "These guys are in the wedding too, so if they bark during the ceremony, I will kill someone." Eve and Teresa both roared with laughter. "I will say this about them though," Teresa added. "Them brotha's are fine as hell. And each one is single."

"Well, Lola will be happy about that," Eve said. "She asked me the other day if I knew who the men were in the wedding."

"That doesn't surprise me at all. I made sure both of you are with single guys."

"Well, thank you," Eve said. There was a long pause and Eve knew Teresa wanted to ask about Elijah. Eve waited, letting her decide if she would ask. She didn't.

"How come you haven't been to church lately?" Teresa asked,

instead.

I know this chick did not ask me about church. "I've been real busy working overtime." *Yeah like I can tell you I've been spending Sunday mornings in bed with Elijah.*

"Oh, I will let the pastor know. He had been asking about you."

"Really?" Eve asked, confused as to why he would ask about her. "Why?"

"He said he wanted you to meet his nephew."

"Wow." Eve laughed. "Even my pastor is trying to set me up."

They both laughed and talked for a few more minutes until Teresa had to pull the lasagna out of the oven. When they hung up, Eve thought about how she had been avoiding the whole church scene and felt guilty. She promised herself she would get there Sunday and she was going to convince Lola to go with her.

***

Sunday morning, Eve and Lola walked into First Missionary Baptist Church and Teresa was sitting right there saving their seats, as if she knew they were going to be there that Sunday. Lola, loving to make an entrance, walked inside the church with her cream colored tailored suit that fit every single part of her curvaceous figure. Although some would deem the skirt too short for church, Lola was just one of those women who could pull it off. Her legs where beautifully encased in Barely Brown pantyhose and her three-inch cream pumps. She topped it off with a wide brim red hat that partially covered her eyes. She always had to work a splash of color into the mix. Eve, on the other hand, choose a simple blue suit with a long skirt and equally long jacket. Her feet were adorned by matching heeled boots with zippers up the back and a pointed toe. Her own hair was in a simple bun at the nape of her neck.

Teresa turned and saw them come in. She moved her purse and motioned for Eve to sit next to her. Eve smiled and moved to sit down allowing Lola to sit on the end. Lola rolled her eyes at Teresa and sat down beside Eve. Teresa smiled and squeezed Eve's hand.

Everyone knew Lola only came to church to scope out a man or to listen to the choir. Lola had been blessed with a beautiful voice and loved to sing especially gospel, but when she found out that to be in the choir you must attend a bible class she decided she was too busy. Now on Sunday she came to hear them sing. Lola would sometimes tiptoe out of service if the choir was finished and there wasn't a new man to meet. Eve had gotten in the habit of holding her hand in service trying to make her stay. Sometimes it worked and sometimes it didn't. The choir began singing Lola's favorite song and she was on her feet in an instant singing louder than anyone in the choir.

Eve was smiling at Lola and almost didn't notice the hand on her arm. She turned and looked at Teresa and Teresa glanced toward the door. In walked Elijah and a very beautiful woman on his arm. Behind them were two boys, and in her arms she held a sleeping bundle wrapped in pink. Eve's heart dropped.

Is that her? Oh My God if that's her. It's his family! Damn Eve, that is what you are messing with, that picture right there. What are they doing here? They don't live in this city. Out of all the churches in this area, why did they have to walk in here?

Eve allowed her eyes to follow him and the woman until they were seated; only tearing her eyes away when he placed his arm along the back of the pew and she nestled closer into his side.

Teresa squeezed her arm again. Eve didn't turn to see what she already knew was in her eyes. She didn't need "I told you so" right then. Eve just sat and tried to concentrate on the choir singing, but her mind would drift back to his lips, his chest, and his kiss. She immediately bowed her head to pray. *Oh Lord, this is not the place to be thinking these thoughts like this. Satan get thee behind me. Lord, if you can just get me through this service, I will be alright.*

Pastor Gregor was up to preach.

Lola grabbed Eve's bible, and Teresa turned to the scripture in her own. Lola leaned over and asked. "Eve, what did he say the scripture was?"

Eve shrugged her shoulders and Lola looked over at Teresa. Teresa waited for her to ask; she wasn't going to volunteer the information. Lola turned her back completely to Teresa and asked the good-looking gentleman behind them. He didn't know either. Finally, Teresa leaned over and whispered it to Eve, but loud enough for Lola to hear. "Romans 7:14–through the end."

Eve thanked her while Lola grabbed the book out of Eve's hand and opened it to the scripture. As Pastor Gregor read, the words spoke to both of them, but Eve was convinced she was the only one that could hear it.

"We know the law is spiritual, but I'm unspiritual, sold as a slave in sin." The congregation participated in its traditional call and response with "Amen's and Ah Hun's."

Pastor Gregor went on.

"I do not understand what I do. For what I want to do I do not do, but what I hate I do...For I have the desire to do what is good, but cannot carry it out. For what I do is the good I want to do; no, the evil I do not want to do – this I keep on doing..."

Eve's mind stuck on that point. *What I want to do I do not do, but what I hate I do? Is that applicable to me and my situation? Can I blame it on the sin in me? Maybe I need to blame it on the sin in him?*

"Oh, what a wretched man I am!" The pastor read vociferously.

It was at this time Eve turned and saw Elijah looking at her. He nodded in acknowledgement and turned his attention back to the pastor. Eve didn't know what to think. She just turned around and prayed for church to be over soon. *Oh, what a wretched woman I am.*

Pastor Gregor preached on the scripture for forty-five minutes—forty-five agonizing minutes. Eve tried to ignore what he was saying, but she knew this was her chastisement. She kept getting bits and pieces of his sermon.

"We are nothing but filthy rags. That is why we need Jesus. He is the only one that can deliver us...But you have to want to be delivered...You have to repent not just confess, but repent..."

When the benediction was given, Eve didn't notice Lola grabbing her purse and heading for the exit until she was nearly out the door.

"Lola, where are you going?" Eve yelled after her puzzled. They had planned to go for brunch after church.

"Girl, I will meet you at the restaurant. I have something I need to take care of." With that, she ran through the door. Eve watched Lola head for the gentleman that sat directly behind her.

"Well, what do you have planned this afternoon?" Eve heard a voice say and turned seeing Teresa standing with her purse in hand.

"Lola and I have reservations for brunch. I made a reservation for three just in case you wanted to come." Eve looked at her with a questioning smile.

Teresa smiled and shook her head no. "How did you know I would be at church today?"

"Girl, please. I know you. You were here to see if I would show up," Eve said laughing.

"That ain't true," Teresa said laughing along with Eve. "Anyway, I don't think that Lola would appreciate me coming with you."

"Girl, please. Lola was just fronting. She ain't still mad. She is over herself and you. Anyway, I think I might get stood up." She indicated for Teresa to look out of the door. Teresa turned and saw their friend talking to the man she had asked for the scripture.

"She is so predictable," Teresa said laughing. "Well, I might go. There is something I want to share with you, anyway."

"Well then, come on girl, let's go." Eve grabbed Teresa's arm and pulled her towards the door.

"Were you going to leave without saying hello?" The soft, deep tremble of his voice penetrated her flesh to the core of her bones.

Eve slowly turned and faced Elijah and his companion with a forced smile on her face. Thoughts flew through her head. *I'm not ready to meet this woman. What am I supposed to say, "Hi, I know what your husband looks like in the silk boxers you bought him last Christmas. And by the way, he doesn't like it when you blow into his ear, but he does like you to lick down his spine." Oh Lawd, I'm trippin'. Calm down girl, you are in the house of the Lord.*

"Oh. Hello Elijah." Her eyes stayed on his face. She couldn't bring herself to look at the woman. Out of her peripheral vision, she noticed Teresa giving the woman the once over. "I saw you come in, but I thought you had left already."

"No, I was waiting to introduce the two of you." He grabbed this beautiful woman next to him and Eve was forced to look at her. "Eve, this is my sister, Jenifer. Jenifer this is Eve, the young lady I was telling you about. The one I work with when I come to town."

"It's a pleasure to finally get to meet you." The woman was smiling and reached her hand out to Eve. Eve didn't remember taking her hand, but apparently she did because she felt a slight squeeze and release. *His sister. His sister. Not his wife, his sister.* Eve felt her grin get wider.

"You never told me your sister lived in this area."

"I didn't think about it, truthfully." His sister playfully jabbed him in the stomach. He bent over from the slight pressure and laughed. "It's not like that, sis. It's just I usually stay in a hotel room and, when I see Eve, we don't have a lot of time to just talk. We have a lot we need to accomplish in a short period of time." Elijahs' last words hung awkwardly in the air.

Eve managed an agreement through a mouth curled into a half grin.

Teresa cleared her throat.

"Oh, I'm sorry. Teresa, this is Elijah Mann and his sister

Jenifer."

"It's a pleasure to meet you both," Teresa said smiling and shaking each of their hands. "I don't mean to be rude," Teresa interrupted, "but if we don't go, we'll be late meeting Lola. You know how she hates to wait."

Eve took the clue, turned and smiled broadly. "She's right. It was nice meeting you, Jennifer. And Elijah, I shall speak with you later." With a light wave, Eve and Teresa walked out of the sanctuary doors to the waiting car on the curb.

Eve and Teresa rode to the restaurant conversing just as old friends should. Their conversation, since the time they left the church, never included Elijah or his sister, and both seemed comfortable with that. After arriving at the restaurant, Teresa excused herself to the ladies' room.

While Eve waited to be seated, she noticed a man sitting at a table by himself and he was totally engrossed in the menu. This man was absolutely gorgeous. His chocolate brown skin was a delicious compliment to his black wavy hair and dark brooding eyebrows. His goatee was cut close enough to be a shadow and his lips were as ripe as pomegranate.

Feeling her eyes on him, he looked up.

Eve smiled and averted her eyes. In her peripheral vision, she saw him flash a set of perfect white teeth. *Oh, God that man is fine!*

"How many in your party?" the hostess asked.

"There are three."

"Just a second, they are clearing a table now." With that, the hostess went to check on the table and Lola walked in.

"Hey girl, we haven't got a table yet?" Lola asked.

"No, I was waiting on you."

Right then, the hostess returned and seated them. "Follow me," she said and laid down three menus on our table.

"Where have you been?" I asked, after we placed our drink orders and the waitress walked away.

"Girl, you remember that fine specimen that sat behind us at church? Well, let's just say I'll be in church more often." Lola giggled and Eve smiled.

"So what does he do?" Eve asked glancing at the menu in front her.

"He's a partner at Martin, Dulles and Lansky Law Firm. He's the Lansky part."

"So what's up? When will you two hook up?"

"Oh my girl, you know me too well."

"So I guess you scored big time." Lola flinched at the sound of the voice behind her. Teresa moved around to take the seat next to Eve.

"So what's she doing here?" Lola asked, glancing at Teresa and then turning and looking at Eve.

"I asked her to come. Just chill out. You know you ain't even mad anymore."

"No, I'm not, but I can't see how she would want to be here considering she can't have nothing to do with you anymore."

"Lola please!" Eve said rolling her eyes. "You know I told you I understood from jump. I'm cool with Teresa here. So get over yourself."

"Whatever," Lola said flipping her hand in the air in front of her face as if she were swatting an annoying fly.

The ladies ordered and ate their lunch talking about everything except what Eve's situation was with Elijah. Occasionally, Lola would say something in reference to Teresa's decision to stay out of the Eve/Elijah situation. Eve even had to kick Lola under the table. Although Teresa knew what was going on, she never let on.

When Eve excused herself to the bathroom, she was hesitant to go. She didn't want to come back and find the restaurant tore up because her friends couldn't be civil. On her way to the restroom, the man she saw earlier was paying his bill. He glanced up and caught her eye. She smiled and walked on into the ladies' room. A few minutes later, when she came out, the gentleman was still waiting.

"Hello, my name is Nathan Garrison. I noticed you when you walked in and I would have come to the table to introduce myself, but I didn't think it would be appropriate."

"Hi, I'm Eve." She offered her hand and he shook it.

"Eve, so as not to detain you any further, may I ask for your number? I would really like to talk to you and possibly take you to lunch."

"Okay, you know that was corny right?"

Nathan smiled.

"I think that may not be a good idea."

"I hope this is not too pushy, but may I ask why?"

Eve looked at him and thought of Elijah. *Hello Eve... Elijah is married.* Eve glanced at Nathan's finger and there was no ring. "Well, Nathan, are you married?"

"If I were, I would not be asking for your number," he said as if he may have been offended.

"Well, a young single woman has to ask the right questions."

"Touché."

Eve smiled. She decided she did want to get to know this man and there was no reason for her not too. "Mr. Nathan Garrison, so as not to detain *you*, here is my card." She reached in her purse and pulled out her business card. She handed it to him with the backside up. "That kind sir is my personal cell. I hope to hear from you soon." She smiled and walked back toward the table. She could sense his eyes running all along her backside.

She made it back to the table and there was an awkward silence. As soon as she sat down, the waiter approached with a dessert menu. Eve and Teresa passed, Lola didn't.

"Ah yes, I would like a double fudge chocolate brownie sundae. I want pecans instead of peanuts and lots of whipped cream."

"Girl, I don't know how you do it. I even think that way and five pounds jump on my booty." Eve laughed.

"The better to rump-shake with," Lola said getting up from her chair shaking her backside in the air. They all laughed, especially when Lola got through shaking her thang and was applauded by the gentleman sitting at the bar.

"Girl, you are so crazy." Teresa laughed. Then growing serious, she reached for her friends' hands and whispered, "I miss you two."

Eve squeezed her hand gently and Lola forced a smile.

"Eve, I wanted to come to explain a few more things to you. I'm going to tell you some things that I'm not proud of. I never told you and Lola because it...well anyway. I was involved with a married man."

"Ah hell!" Lola threw her arms up in the air and shook her head. "Now that shit is rich."

"Shut up, Lola," Eve managed. She still was shocked by her friend's confession. "Teresa when was this? What happened?"

"I will tell you what happened," Lola interrupted. "She got booty bumped by a married guy. He made all the promises and she fell hook, line and sinker. And I just bet the weekend he was supposed to leave his wife he never showed up. She hasn't seen him since."

"Lola, where the hell do you get this shit?" Teresa said disgusted. "If your mind is that fertile, you need to write a damn book." She turned to Eve.

"Unlike you, I didn't know he was married until about six months into dating him. He and his wife had a bi-coastal marriage. I found out at one of the big BBQ fests that he always had. I went into the kitchen and overheard his best friend asking his sister when he was going to get a divorce."

"Oh that shit is unreal. Girl please, they got better drama on *Days of Our Lives*." Lola laughed and spooned some of the ice cream off the sundae.

"Look Eve," Teresa said ignoring Lola. "We were kickin' it like everything was chill. I was feeling him and he was playing me. Even after I heard the conversation in the kitchen I didn't say anything. I stayed in denial. He treated me like gold. The sex was off the hook," Teresa paused and let out a deep breath. "And his ass was married."

"So what you saying is Eve is getting dissed because you mad at a man for playing you and you mad at your pops for playing your moms?" Lola asked looking at Teresa and taking a drink of her water.

"It's not that easy, Lola. I'm not dissing Eve. I just told her I can't be a part of what she is *choosing* to do. I was played. My momma was played. But Eve is the one playing a woman she doesn't even know. I can't get with that. To me, that is cruel." Teresa looked at Eve. "Eve, you know I love you with all my heart, girl. I'm just asking you not to include me in your tales of Elijah."

"I already understood that, Teresa." Eve leaned over and hugged her friend. "But I need you to understand that our circumstances are different. And I'm a different woman."

Teresa released her hand and reached for her water glass and took a drink.

Eve continued, "Yes, I feel bad about this woman who he's married to, but I don't want him for anything more than what I have him for." *Yeah right, heifer you know you lyin'.* "We have the bomb sex and we laugh and talk. That's all I need right now."

"Oh please, Eve." Lola interjected. "I was with you on the first part of your statement until you started lying."

"What are you talking about, Lola?"

"Girl, you know that your nose is spread wide open. I know you and if this man was available to you emotionally you would be in there."

"Well, hell, Lola. Do you support Eve in what she is doing or are you against her?" Teresa asked sarcastically.

"I do not support being with married men," Lola restated to Eve, ignoring Teresa's sarcasm. "If I gave you that impression, I'm sorry, that's not where I stand. However, I do support my friends." Redirecting her attention to Teresa, Lola went on. "That is the difference between me and you, Teresa. Even when my friends are making some fucked up decisions, I got they back."

Teresa was about to protest the insinuation but held her tongue. It would do no good. She knew how Lola was. She knew once Lola had you pegged, there was no changing her mind. The only person she seemed so forgiving of was Eve.

Although they were all friends, Eve had special relationships with both Teresa and Lola. There were some things Teresa had shared with Eve that she knew Lola wouldn't understand and Lola had confided secrets in Eve that Teresa could never be privy to. Eve never judged Lola the way that others did and for that reason she was the only person that benefited from Lola's loyalty.

"You know what? I'm through with this conversation," Eve announced. "What are we going to do with the rest of our Sunday?"

Lola and Teresa smiled at each other, calling a truce for the sake of Eve.

"Are you both thinking what I'm thinking?" Eve grinned.

"Shopping!" They all said simultaneously and laughed.

A conference call.
Chapter 15

When Eve got to work Monday morning, her boss informed her that he needed her to attend a conference that another supervisor was scheduled to.

"When? I need to add it to my calendar."

"You'll be leaving today."

"Why such short notice?"

"Mike was supposed to go, but his wife went into labor this morning. I you need to go home and pack a bag within the next hour. You and the other conference participant will be riding together."

"Who's the other partici…?"

Eve didn't get a chance to ask her questions. Gerry was headed down the hall on his cell. Rather than wasting time, she called her sister and asked her to go by the house and pack a bag for her and bring it to the job.

Eve called Patricia in to her office and gave her instructions on things that needed to be taken care of over the next couple of days. When Patricia left the office, Eve leaned back into her chair and closed her eyes. *Maybe this trip will be a good thing. My life has been a bit out of sorts and maybe I will get some perspective on some things.*

Eve jumped at the sound of the buzz on the phone and Patricia's voice.

"Miss Newborn?"

"Yes?"

"Your sister is here with your bag."

"Okay. Tell her to come on in."

April bounced in wearing her signature jeans and t-shirt. Her midnight black hair was pulled back into a ponytail giving a far younger look than her twenty-five years.

"Here you go, sis. I got everything in there. I even put your favorite lounge socks in."

"Thank you, April," Eve said getting up to hug her sister. "Gerry just came in this morning to tell me about this and you know how I feel about last minute anything."

"Yeah, I know. But you need more spontaneity in your life."

"You have enough for the both of us," Eve replied, circling back around her desk to sit in her chair.

April sat on the chair closest to Eve's desk and began rummaging through her candy jar. "So who is going with you?"

"I have no idea. I just know we're driving in a company car and I don't have to pay for anything."

"You are living the life. I wish I could get an expense account and take off on trips."

"You could if you kept a job longer than six months."

"Don't start, Eve," April said and popped a mint in her mouth. "You know better than anyone that I'm a free spirit."

"Yeah I know, but..." The phone buzzed.

"Yes Patricia."

"Mr. Mann is waiting to see you."

"Damn." Eve muttered under her breath. "Okay send him in." Eve got up from her desk. April sat there watching her sister curiously as she opened the door. Elijah stood there in a black three-piece button suit. He wore a mint green shirt with a tie of the same color. He looked damn good. April let out a sigh and Eve shot a look at her sister.

"Hey Eve, I'm sorry if you are busy. I just wanted to see what time you wanted to leave."

"Leave what?" Eve asked unsure of what he was saying.

"Leave for the conference. We're supposed to be riding together, or didn't they tell you that?" He smiled at her.

Damn, Damn, Damn! I was trying to get away to get some perspective on him, but now he is all up in my face. I wonder if April thought to put some protection in my bag? Knowing Elijah like I do, he probably has some.

"Oh. I didn't know who I was riding with. Why are you going? As a consultant would that be something you would do?"

"It's something I want to do." He looked closely at her. "I wanted to see what kinds of conferences the employees are being sent to and to see if they are something worth continuing."

To anyone else, Eve guessed his reasoning sounded reasonable, but she didn't think that was it at all. She began to think he had something to do with Gerry's suggestion that she go, but she knew she couldn't guess that Mike's wife would go into labor.

"Ah, can I get an intro?" April stood up and faced Eve and Elijah. Eve had forgotten she was even there. Before she could properly introduce Elijah, he was already shaking April's hand.

"I'm Elijah Mann."

"Hi. I'm April Newborn, Eve's sister. It's nice to meet you."

"No, the pleasure is mine," he said with charm oozing out of his pores.

"Well, April, thank you for bringing my clothes. We are going to get ready to leave. Tell Mom I will call her when I get settled. Oh yeah, and call Lola and Teresa for me please. They were coming by tonight."

"No problem, dear sister. Be safe." April gave Eve a quick kiss and repeated, "Be safe." Turning to Elijah, she smiled. "Nice meeting you."

Elijah nodded and winked. April bounced out of the office closing the door behind her. Eve returned to her desk, grabbed her purse from the drawer, and her jacket from her chair.

"Let's get out of here." Elijah smiled and picked up the bag April left in the middle of the floor.

***

As they rode up the highway, Eve leaned her head back and

closed her eyes. She didn't realize how tired she was. She was just drifting off to sleep when Elijah started talking to her.

"Talk to me. I don't want you to go to sleep on me."

Turning her head to face him, she spoke. "What do you want to talk about?"

"Tell me about your relationship with you sister."

"Not a lot to tell. I'm older than she is, but we get along great."

"Are there any more of you?"

"No. Just me and her."

"Is she married?"

"No. She is involved on a bi-weekly basis with this guy. One week they are in love, the next she's living with me."

"Does that bother you?"

"Yes, but she is a grown woman. I can't tell her what to do."

"That's true." Elijah let the conversation fall and they lapsed into a moment of silence.

"Elijah, how long have you been a consultant?"

"About ten years."

"What made you go into it?"

"The company I was working for had no upward mobility and I heard that Elite Consultants was looking for more employees. When I started, I was low man on the totem pole, basically being an errand boy, but then I began to get my own mergers. Now I'm at the top of my game."

"Ah." Eve clucked her tongue. "No modesty there."

"I know what I'm doing. And when I know what I'm doing, I do it well." Eve let that dance in her head for a moment.

"I suppose you do. So how did you meet your wife?" *Did I just ask that? Dumbass I don't want to talk about this man's wife.*

"I met her when I was a consultant on a merger. She was an office supervisor."

"Did you work with her directly?"

"No, I didn't. I started dating her after my job was finished."

"Was it love at first sight?"

Elijah smiled. "I wouldn't say love at first sight, but I was taken with her. She is a beautiful person inside and out."

"Oh." *Okay Eve, you can shut up now.*

Eve quickly let that conversation drop and they went on to discuss other things. She always enjoyed talking to him. He was a very intelligent man with a great sense of humor. They often found themselves in a match of wits increasing the sexual tension they had between them. This road trip was no different. Eventually, their conversation became riddled with double meaning. When they arrived at the hotel, she realized she liked Elijah as a person and she was hot and bothered.

They checked into the hotel and got rooms next door to each other. Upon entering the room, they found that their rooms shared a common door which allowed them to move between the rooms. Eve didn't know if Elijah arranged it that way, but it was very convenient for them.

Eve was putting her clothes away when Elijah walked in behind her. He grabbed her breasts from behind and began to kiss her neck. Eve leaned back into him and relished the feel of his hands on her nipples. She began to grind her ass into his crotch and she felt him harden with every push. She felt him pulling her shirt and lifting it over her head with her bra somehow following suit. Her breasts bounced freely and were caught in his palms once again. He began to knead them and her peaks became like pebbles.

"I need to fuck you." He growled in her ear and ground his pelvis against her behind. "I have wanted you since I came into your office today. If your sister hadn't been there, I would have taken you to your desk, bent you over and caught you from behind."

Eve became wetter with everything he confessed. She reached down between her legs and began rubbing herself. "And I would have let you," she whispered.

Elijah's hand was on left her breast and he lifted her skirt to her waist with the other. Eve wore thigh highs that day and Elijah felt like he was going to burst. He pulled her underwear down and reached around between her legs. Eve moved her hand and let Elijah take over her manipulation. They were both on fire. Elijah managed to move Eve over to the table and then bent her over it. He was in her so fast that she couldn't breathe. It wasn't long before they both had a release.

After a few moments, Elijah backed away from Eve and sat on the bed. Eve sprawled across the table, slowly peeled herself up and walked to the restroom. After she cleaned herself she came back to find Elijah laid across the bed.

"Damn, what you do to me girl?"

"I didn't start this," Eve said while going to sit on the side of the bed. "If I recall, I was putting my clothes away and you came in from behind."

Elijah laughed at her choice of words and Eve playfully punched him.

"Get up, Elijah. We got to get some rest. Our first meeting is at 8:00 in the morning. I want to go to sleep."

"You're not going to dinner tonight?"

"I will order in."

"You want me to stay?"

"No. You go on. I need to rest and I won't if you stay."

"Okay," he said getting up from the bed. He began walking toward their adjoining door. "Are you going to eat at the table?" he asked smiling.

"Get out, Elijah," Eve said ignoring him. He knew she wasn't going to eat anything on that table.

***

The conference was all the next day. Both Eve and Elijah picked up some valuable information for the company. After their last session, they went to an early dinner and came back to the room and had mind-blowing sex.

Afterwards, Eve had her arms snaked around his waist and snuggled her body against his. He absentmindedly played in her hair as the basketball playoffs were going on. She reveled in his smell and his body. She let her fingers dance in the soft patches of hair on his chest and her hands smoothed down the flatness of his stomach. *This man is delicious. I don't think it is possible to get enough.*

"Don't start nothing you can't finish," Elijah said stroking her back but still watching the game.

"I always finish what I start." She replied boldly letting her fingers slide down the hairy road leading to the place just beyond the waistband of his boxers. They had been together a while now. Each time, she was more comfortable to explore her sexuality a bit more.

"Eve." He warned.

"Yes?" she asked as she continued her journey.

"You are going to wake the sleeping giant and he will want to play."

"Really? I'm always amazed at the games that the sleeping giant can play." Her hands circled his manhood and she could feel the giant awakening.

Elijah moved so fast that Eve was not prepared. In three seconds, she had let go of him, was under his body, and his mouth was attacking hers. Getting her bearing, she pulled the sheet away from her body, exposing her nakedness to his eager and waiting mouth. She snatched his boxers down and released the no-longer-sleeping giant. He grabbed one of her nipples with his teeth and gently pulled.

Eve groaned and grabbed his head pulling him closer. She felt his hardness on her stomach and the ache between her legs began to pulse with her heartbeat. Elijah let go of one breast and attacked the other. Eve reached down between them and grabbed his hot steel and guided it to her center. His hands reached behind her legs and drew them up so her knees were just about at her shoulders and her body completely open to him. He had learned that she enjoyed this position and she was waiting with great anticipation when his cell rang.

"Don't answer it. Please don't answer it." Eve whispered with ragged breath.

Elijah let his head fall and his hands released her legs. He sat for a moment trying to call back his labored breath. "I have to answer it."

"No, you don't," she said pulling him toward her. "Just let your voicemail get it."

He waited and the ringing stopped. He moved to enter her again and his phone rang again. This time, it had a special ring that signified it was an emergency. He sighed heavily and began to move away from her. "I can't," he said finally. "It could be my wife."

At those words Eve's hands dropped to her sides.

He rolled away from her and grabbed his phone. Before he could even get his greeting out, she bolted for the bathroom. She couldn't bear to listen.

Why are you trippin'? You know what he came with. He came to your bed with a wife and children, so don't pretend otherwise. The thought of him out there whispering sweet nothings to her makes me so...so...Oh my God! I'm jealous.

Eve heard Elijah raise his voice. "Look Janelle, what am I supposed to do? I cannot come to the game, because I will be here working. Tell him I will be at the next one."

Eve turned on the water at the sink to drown out his voice. She thanked God for squeaky pipes. She washed her face and looked at herself in the mirror.

Lord, I don't want to be getting excited over a fight that he is having with his wife. I don't want to be so naïve to think that means something for me. Girl, just take it as it comes. There is nothing more than a friendship and bomb sex.

Eve dried her face and hands and opened the bathroom door.

Elijah had hung up the phone and allowed his attention to drift back to the game, although his hands nursed the giant with gentle strokes.

"Would you like me to do that?" Eve asked playfully standing in the doorway of the bathroom.

Elijah grabbed the remote control and turned the television off. He got up slowly and removed his boxers completely. Stark naked, he walked to her and stood directly in front of her. "I'm sorry about that, baby. Can I make it up to you?"

She looked up into his face and dropped to her knees. She grabbed his mighty giant with her right hand and fit her lips to the tip of it. She had never done this before, and she wasn't sure what possessed her to do it now. She began to move and emulate what she had seen on pornographic movies. She felt his hand touch the back of her head guiding her forward; then his hand tightened in her hair. She wasn't sure what really happened, but her gag reflex responded to the invasion and her stomach began to churn. Her body began to jerk with heaves and it seemed to her that Elijah wouldn't let go. Trying to pull away, her jaw tightened, her teeth ran across his sensitive shaft and he let out a yelp. Eve never felt the shove he gave her, only her butt hitting the floor.

"Damn Eve, what are you trying to do?" Elijah yelled and held onto his manhood. "You trying to take my shit off?"

Eve tried to speak, but she was humiliated. She sat wide-eyed and watched him nurse himself. After a moment, the situation grew funny. She tried her best to hold in the laughter, but she couldn't do it. Eve began to laugh until tears ran down her face.

"What the hell are you laughing at?" Elijah asked, thinking nothing was funny.

"Baby, I'm not laughing at you. I'm laughing at me. Here I thought I was about to turn you on and turn you out and it ends up that I... fucked up big time."

"Ya think?" Elijah replied sarcastically.

Eve giggled and moved toward him.

"I'm sorry, Elijah. I meant for it to be a good thing."

"I'm sure you did, Eve, but if you don't know how to do the shit you could have asked me how or chose not to do it."

Sobering, Eve stood up with her hands on her hips.

"Are you saying you didn't enjoy your dick in my mouth?" Eve asked with an attitude. *Damn, I sound like Lola.*

"Sweetheart, I'm going to always enjoy my dick in your mouth." Elijah joked trying to diffuse the situation.

Eve, never being one afraid to make a mountain out of a molehill, decided that she wanted to fight. In that second, she realized she was being purposely antagonistic because she couldn't fight about his wife calling. She knew where she stood in his life. Yet, she was jealous and she had to let it out somehow, so she would fight over this. Elijah, oblivious to the inner turmoil, continued.

"Fuck you, Elijah."

"That's what I want you to do, Evie." Elijah smiled and reached out massaging her neck. Not wanting him to know that he was getting to her, she moved away. "Look Eve, you almost castrated me and then got mad when I was upset? That is crazy. And on top of that it becomes amusing? Was I supposed to just grin and bear it?"

"No, asshole. You could have just handled it better."

"Better than what?" he asked, moving to sit on the bed, "I didn't bite your head off."

Eve couldn't help but smile at his pun. "No, but you did shove me on my ass," Eve said as she plopped down on the bed beside Elijah.

They both fell silent.

Eve watched a little while and then got up and walked into the bathroom. A few seconds later, Eve felt two arms slip around her waist.

"Look, we have one more night together. Let's not go through these changes." Elijah nipped at her ear and settled her bottom against his manhood. She felt his tongue sneak around to her ears and his arms tighten.

Eve folded her arms tightly trying to resist. *Girl stop trippin'. If you were going to resist, you would have been out of here as soon as your behind hit the floor.*

"Damn...you are so sexy." He whispered in her ear.

Eve turned in his arms and smiled.

This man is too delicious to be trippin' off the dumb stuff.

Yeah, but he still ain't yours.

Well, that may be true, but he is mine for tonight.

Yeah, that is why I'm about to rock his world.

"Well, Mr. Mann, this sexy lady is about to turn you out," she said, slipping her hand between their bodies.

"I'm looking forward to that, Ms. Newborn."

Eve began kissing Elijah and decided she was going to mentally access her sex files. She had waited too long and read too many books not to have some surprises for a brotha. After so many sessions with Elijah, she felt the need to do some homework and she did. Eve broke out her well-researched work and showed him she was a straight-A student.

"We're going try this again," Eve declared, moving to the side of the bed on her knees. Elijah swung around and sat facing her.

Eve began to kiss his chest with soft butterfly kisses. She noticed that his nipples were very sensitive and she began massaging them with her fingers. She heard him groan. Her mouth worked every inch of his chest steadily heading downward. She felt him rubbing her shoulders and running his fingers through her hair. She listened as his breathing became more ragged.

Working her way between his legs, she allowed her tongue to explore his essence, tasting him and enjoying the chorus of groans he sang. Taking him fully into her mouth was almost his undoing. His body rose from the bed and his hands clinched on her head. Then Eve remembered something she once heard Lola say. She smiled to herself and began to hum. She was delighted when Elijah took up her song and sang it with all of his heart. *Got him,* she thought as they spent their last night together fucking so good and so sweet that Eve dared to think they were making love.

<u>Remember me?</u>
Chapter 15

Eve arrived home exhausted. Even though she loved being with him, she was happy to see Elijah go. As a lover, she couldn't get enough of him, but as someone she had to work with, he was ruthless. He wanted everything the way he wanted it, and there was no way she could keep up this pace permanently. He only had about six months left of his contract. But she wondered, after that, would he be gone as her lover too?

As she sat down on the couch and removed her shoes, her phone rang. "Hello."

"Ah yes, I'm trying to locate Eve Newborn." Thinking it was a telemarketing call, she hesitated in revealing that it was her.

"And this is regarding?"

"Well, I met her in a restaurant a few weeks ago and I was giving her a call. This is Nathan Garrison calling."

Oh damn, this is that fine ass man from the restaurant. That man was scrumptious. "This is Eve," she said, quickly.

"Well, it's nice to finally catch up with you. I thought you had given me the wrong number. Every time I have tried to call over the past few days there was no answer."

"I'm sorry. I have had a pretty hectic schedule in the past week and I don't return calls to numbers I don't recognize. Truthfully, the only reason I picked up was because my phone was in my hand." Eve stretched out her body along her couch and gazed at her aching feet.

"Well. I'm hoping that you would go ahead and lock my number in your phone and that you are not too busy for lunch this weekend. I have been thinking about our chance meeting ever since that Sunday."

Well, if you were thinking about our chance meeting," Eve thought to herself, *what the hell took you so long to call?*

"I didn't call right away," Nathan answered, suspecting what she was thinking, "Because I, too, have had a hectic schedule."

"Oh," Eve said. "Well, what do you do for a living?"

"Right now, I'm the manager of security in the I-Tech building. I have a background in police work, but I left due to an injury. Now, I deal with I-Tech's security and I go to school online studying for my MBA."

"What do you plan to do with your degree?"

"I'm planning to build my own security business that caters only to corporations like I-Tech. "

"Well, the little guys need security too," Eve said teasingly.

Nathan chuckled with a warm burning timbre. *His voice is sexier than Elijah's.*

"Well, there are plenty of little guys to take care of that. After working for I–Tech, I'm almost guaranteed they will be my first client. I spoke with the CEO and she likes what I'm doing."

"She? E.L Parkhaven is a she?"

"Yes and *she* is no joke."

"I know." Eve responded. "They were bidding against the company that eventually took over my employer. From what I understand, she was ruthless in negotiations. Rumor has it, her hard nose business demeanor is what stifled negotiations."

"Well, you know how it is when women get in a position like CEO. Some feel they have to be a man in negotiations."

"Well. Damn. She did a good job because most don't know she is a woman."

"If you saw her, you would know that she is all woman."

"Oh," Eve said, not really knowing how to take that comment.

"Why are we talking about the woman I work for? She is really of no concern to us, unless you are trying to pump me for information so the company that you work for can plan a hostile takeover." He joked.

"Now that you mention it...," Eve replied teasingly. They both laughed. *I love a man with a sense of humor. Elijah has one.*

They continued talking and getting to know each other. Glancing at the clock, Eve mentioned that an hour had passed.

"Oh damn. I lost track of time and I'm supposed to meet my boys at the gym."

"Well, I hope that you have a good work out," Eve said trying to imagine him in some sweatshirt and a muscle man shirt. *Oh damn, he works out too! If I remember correctly, this man is something scrumptious.*

"Ms. Newborn, I plan to. Can I take you to lunch this week?" Nathan asked again.

Eve sighed deeply and asked herself if she really want to start something with this man. "I have to look at my schedule, but I don't anticipate it being a problem. Can I call you tomorrow and let you know when I will be available?"

"I'll be waiting. Please lock my number in."

"I will. Goodnight, Nathan Garrison. Thank you for calling."

"Trust me, Miss Newborn, the pleasure was all mine."

***

Eve called Teresa and Lola and asked them over for dinner. Teresa's man was out of town on business and Lola's date cancelled because of work. Lola hated to be stood up, so Eve knew she would be in a pissy mood. Lola arrived about five minutes after Teresa.

"Okay y'all, what kind of pizza do you want?"

"Damn Eve," Lola said, flopping onto the couch. "You invite us to dinner and you ain't cooking? I thought since I wasn't going to get screwed tonight at least I could have a home cooked meal."

"Lola, I made your favorite cookies to help you get over your spell."

"Really?" Lola hopped up with a smile. She ran into the kitchen.

"They are in the cookie jar," Eve hollered to her. Then she

turned around to Teresa. "She is such a cookie monster."

Teresa laughed.

Eve ordered the pizza.

Lola came back in the room with a Ziploc bag full of cookies and three wine coolers. She handed one to Teresa and the other to Eve before she took her place on the couch.

"So how was your day Teresa?" Eve asked, taking the top of the bottle and taking a sip.

"Girl, it was something else. All them old white men get on my damn nerves. Here we are sitting in a meeting on revitalizing the downtown area, and I asked what they were planning to put down there. You know I'm concerned with the Black folks living down there. Well, they busted out with let's put a baseball stadium in that area."

"What the hell?" Lola interrupted with cookie in her mouth. "We don't even have a baseball team."

"I know," Teresa said. "That was my whole point. Somehow the mayor has it in his head that if we build it they will come."

"Did you tell him that this ain't *Field of Dreams*?" Lola asked.

Teresa and Eve laughed.

"I wanted to, believe me, I wanted to."

"Why don't you tell them to build an art center? It may be made up of different museums and performing arts theatres. This town already has a ballet company, albeit small, but it will grow. The people have an appreciation for art. Remember they came out for that artist.

"Wasn't that that the man who took pictures of naked homosexuals." Eve laughed. "What was his name?"

"That was...damn I can't remember. I think it was Oglethorpe or something like that."

"Well anyway, I don't know what we are going to do about it. I just know that my ass is tired and hungry." Teresa plopped another cookie into her mouth.

"If they need a director for the art center, keep me in mind because I'm tired of the Cultural Centre," Lola piped in. "If I'm forced to teach one more tap dance class to those no-dancing white senior citizens, I think my ass might just break my own legs, so I can't dance."

"Now that is extreme. Why did the director leave?" Eve asked grabbing the cookies from Teresa's lap.

"The fool was embezzling money. He was a damn idiot. I think they said that he took himself off the payroll and then wrote himself personal checks under reimbursement. Who the hell is reimbursed fifty-five hundred dollars a month?"

"Did he actually think that no one would catch that?" Teresa asked.

"I guess so."

The doorbell rang. They all jumped up and ran to the door. When they opened the door, Lola grabbed the pizza box out of the delivery person's hands and she and Teresa opened and starting eating as they walked back to the couch. Eve paid for the pizza and gave a generous tip.

They sat, ate pizza and talked about Teresa's upcoming nuptials. Teresa was planning a simple wedding and Lola and Eve tried to talk her out of making them wear green. They laughed and talked as Lola clowned around. Eve pulled up a movie on Netflix, but they ended up talking through it. After the movie, Lola entertained them with the story of her date with the man she had met at church. He ended up being a nice guy, but way too nice for Lola. He wanted to take things slowly and Lola was trying to jump him the same night. When he said no, she was shocked, but Eve could tell that Lola had gained some respect for him. She wasn't sure if Lola would date him again, but she wished she would. Lola needed someone that would slow her hot behind down.

Teresa picked up the comedy by telling them how one of the men she worked with came on to her in the copy room. He had written a letter and left it on the copy machine for her. Apparently, he forgot that there were other people in the office that used the machine because she was the last one to know. She walked around all day getting strange looks from her coworkers. It wasn't until Teresa's personal secretary went to make copies and came back and told her. Teresa was so mortified that she packed her bag and left before check out time. She was relieved when she got the message to come to Eve's for dinner.

"Girl, you are a mess for leaving early. What made this man do some stupid shit like putting an offer on the copy machine?" Lola asked. She was slouched on the couch working on her third wine cooler.

"Girl, I don't know. The only thing I think of is the fact that the only time I see this man is when we meet in the copy room. I think we have seen each other every day for the last week around the same time. I guess he thought that was an everyday thing that I do. I don't know." Teresa turned to Eve. "How was your day?"

"Ya'll know I just got back from the conference." *Don't tell them you went with Elijah.* "Well, when I got home my phone rang. I answered it without looking at who it was because I assumed it was one of you. You guys remember when we went to lunch the other Sunday and Teresa and I saw that fine man sitting at the table by himself?"

Teresa nodded.

"I didn't tell you he met me at the door of the restroom. We exchanged numbers and he called today."

Lola leapt to her feet. "Girl, you have been holding out," she yelled. "Who, what, when, where, why? Give me the details heifer."

"He was so damn fine, girl. How come you didn't tell us when you got back from the restroom?" Teresa asked equally as excited as Lola just not as dramatic.

"I didn't think he would call and it wasn't important."

"Excuse me?" Lola interrupted, plopping down in front of Eve.

"What do you mean it wasn't important? All fine men who you give your phone number to are important enough to tell your friends."

"Yeah." Teresa agreed. "Hell, what if he was some kind of stalker? You know I'm still friends with Daryl and he is still a police officer. He *can* run a check on him."

"I'm sure Daryl would." Lola injected, "and he would probably check him out for himself." They all laughed.

"It don't make no sense for someone that look like Daryl to be gay," Eve added.

"To be gay means to be happy. He ain't happy," Teresa laughed. "His ass is a homosexual." They all fell into a fit of giggles.

"Don't let us get away from what we are talking about," Lola said scooting away from Eve and stretching her legs out in front of her. She reached over for her warm wine cooler and took a sip. "So who, what, when, where, and why?"

Eve took a deep breath. She began telling her friends about Nathan from the time she met him until he called. As she filled in the five Ws for Lola and filled in the details for Teresa, the night grew late.

"Well, what do you think about him?" Teresa asked finishing up the last slice of pizza.

"I think he is beautiful, he is smart and from what I can remember he smells damn good. Oh and the man has some beautiful lips. They were full and red. I remember thinking I wouldn't mind sucking on those juicy lips."

"All of that?" Lola slurred. The five wine coolers she consumed were taking their toll.

"And then some," Eve replied and looked at the clock. She looked at Lola's heavy eyelids and shook her shoulder to get her attention. "Lola you are slurring. Why don't you head for the guest room? I think one of your gowns is still in there from the last time you stayed over."

"Good looking out, girlfriend," Lola said as she got up and

headed toward the guest room.

"Are you okay?" Eve asked Teresa. "Don't forget I have another room."

"No, I'm cool. Where is your sister anyway? Did she move out?"

"You know she is only here off and on..."

Teresa got to her feet and grabbed all the plates, glasses and boxes taking them into the kitchen. When she came back, she grabbed her purse and jacket. "Eve can I ask you a question, but I don't want you to be offended."

Eve frowned. "Go ahead."

"Is Nathan married?" Eve looked surprised and then she laughed.

"No, he is not. Teresa, you don't have to worry that I have sworn off single men forever. Elijah is a river I fell into and I'm just enjoying the water."

"Well, since Nathan is a possibility, can't you let Elijah go?"

"Teresa, don't worry about it, okay? I will handle this all in due time."

Teresa looked like she was going to say more, but she decided not to say anything. She picked up her purse and walked toward the door. As she walked to her car, Eve stood in the doorway until she drove down the street.

Eve walked through her house putting things away and turning off lights. She walked by the room where Lola was and the door was ajar. She pushed it further open and found Lola fast asleep. She smiled and closed the door all the way. She made her way to her bedroom. As she dressed for bed, she wondered about Nathan. Was he as good as he seemed? She went to sleep thinking about this man and Elijah wasn't a thought that night.

One more man.
Chapter 16

Eve was sitting behind her desk pouring over paperwork when her assistant Patricia buzzed her intercom.

"Yes, Patricia?" she asked, preoccupied with the order forms stacked on her desk.

"You have a call on line one. It is a Mr. Garrison." Eve's head snapped to attention, and she stared at the blinking light on her phone. *I could have sworn I said that I would call him.*

"Uh, thank you. I'll take it." Eve took a deep breath and picked up the phone. "Hello Mr. Garrison. What can I do for you today?"

"Well, Ms. Newborn, you can first forgive me for not waiting for you to call me. Second, you can check your calendar and see if that lunch is going to be possible this week. And lastly, you can make me a happy man by saying that the lunch can take place today, so I don't have to wait another day to see you."

Well damn! This man is something else.

"I don't know if I'm going to do all of those things, but I'm positive that I can get at least two out of three."

"Two out of three aren't bad odds."

Eve smiled. She liked him. She wasn't sure if he was arrogant or just confident. Either way, it was attractive as hell. His voice on the phone sounded like rich chocolate with an alto fullness. *I wonder if he can sing? Oh my God, if this man can sing. I wonder if Elijah can sing...*

"Mr. Garrison, I do forgive you for not waiting for me to call and, if you can hold for a minute, I will check my calendar."

"That's fine."

Eve put him on hold and opened the calendar on her desk. She buzzed Patricia and asked her to bring her schedule into her office. A few moments later, she appeared with a large calendar in her hand.

"Patricia, I want you to clear my calendar for the rest of the day. I need you to make copies of the report due to Mr. Mann and Mr. McClintoch."

"Are sure about clearing your calendar completely?" she asked with uncertainty.

"Yes, why?" Eve asked with her hand resting on the phone.

"Because you have an appointment with Mr. Mann to go over his evaluation from last week and the report on the transitional team in your department."

"Shit!" Eve said exasperated. She signaled to Patricia to wait as she picked up the phone.

"Mr. Garrison. If we can make it a late lunch, today is possible."

"That will be fine. Why don't we make it an early dinner? Let say about five thirty at the same restaurant where we met?"

"That will be fine. I shall see you then." After saying her goodbye, Eve hung up the phone.

"Okay Patricia, where and what time is the meeting with Mr. Mann?"

"It was a lunch meeting, so it was scheduled around noon. You told me to make the meeting at his hotel restaurant. He was leaving today to go back to the main office and the hotel was closer to the airport."

"Okay, that's fine. Can you please take care of everything else? After my meeting, I won't be back in the office."

"Alright, anything else?" Patricia asked before she left.

"No, I don't think so. Thanks."

***

Eve knocked on the door of Elijah's suite and waited impatiently. He always took too long answering the door. A few minutes passed, and the door swung open. There he stood in a pair of blue jeans and a black silk button shirt with the top two buttons undone. He reached through the door and grabbed her wrist pulling her inside.

"How did you get the penthouse suite this time?" she asked as he took the folder out of her hand and began unbuttoning her suit jacket and peach silk blouse.

"I was supposed to have it a long time ago, but there was a mix up last time." He nuzzled on her neck.

Eve, always so taken with him, allowed him to do anything he wanted to do. He began to kiss her neck making his way up to whisper all kinds of naughty things in her ear. He let his tongue slip into her ear and she immediately felt the moistness between her legs. His hands began pushing her skirt over her hips and letting it fall to the floor. When the skirt hit the floor, she stepped out of it and stood in front of him wearing a matching peach bra and panty set. She learned from their first experience to not be caught again without matching underwear.

He led her to the room where the bed was and removed her bra and began to suckle her nipples. Growing excited, she began to run her nails along his back. His hand moved between her legs and began to press against her womanhood. Eve's back arched toward his hand and she could feel his smile along her stomach. She looked down at him as he kissed her navel. He grabbed her underwear with his teeth and pulled them down making eye contact with her. She wanted to close her eyes, but she couldn't. Within minutes, he was inside her and they were both taking a familiar journey to ecstasy island.

About an hour later, Eve sat on the couch in his hotel robe eating a hamburger that was ordered from room service. Elijah sat in his boxer shorts, drinking coffee, going over the report that Eve brought with her.

"Who wrote out these evaluations?" Elijah asked stealing a French fry off of Eve's plate.

"I did, why?" Eve moved to see which evaluation he was

looking at.

"Just wondering. Did you type it as well?"

"No I asked Patricia to type it. What's wrong?" Eve asked moving to stand behind him. He handed her the paper and got up from the table to pick up his coffee mug.

"Nothing. I just like the format that she put it in."

"Oh," Eve said putting the file down with the rest of them. "She is very good at what she does. I thank God that she is my assistant."

"Is she still at the office? I have some things that I would like done in that format. Maybe she could do them for me?" he asked.

"What time is it? I'm sure that if she is there she will do it," Eve said throwing herself across the couch again.

"It's five minutes after five."

"What?" Eve screamed. She scrambled up and reached for her watch on the table. "Shit! I got a meeting in twenty-five minutes."

"With whom do you have a meeting?" Elijah asked watching her run into the room to retrieve her clothes from the floor.

"Oh, it's just a potential supplier. He wanted to meet with me to see if we could make a deal," Eve said so smoothly that she almost thought she was telling the truth.

"Well, is it someone that Clearview already has a contact with? If that's the case, you need to direct this man to the Clearview person."

"No, this company is not affiliated with Clearview or Oxford Corp." Eve finished buttoning her blouse and she slipped on her shoes. "I just met him recently and I thought he may have something to offer."

"Well, what does his company offer?" Elijah asked with increasing interest.

Eve's mind was whirling. *I don't know why I just don't tell him the truth. It's not like I'm cheating on him or that I have any claim. This is so awkward.*

"He's in security. I have heard rumors about Clearview and Oxford having trouble combining the security department. In those evaluation papers, you can tell there's something going on. This man is the head of security for E.L. Parkhaven's I-Tech building." Eve turned her back to him, faking an attempt to find her car keys, and let out a deep breath. *Just stay as close to the truth as possible.*

"I've been to the I-Tech building. It's a smaller company, but the security there is tight and smooth. That's also the company that was going against Clearview for the merger with Oxford isn't it?

"Yes."

"Is he thinking about leaving I-Tech?"

"I don't know. That's part of what this meeting is about." Eve hoped she was convincing.

"I see. I hope this is something you can bring to the table on Monday morning."

"Yeah maybe," Eve said pulling the keys out of her purse. She turned around and smiled. "I have to go. I'm going to be late as it is." She glanced down at her watch and it read five-fifteen. "I got to roll." She blew him a kiss and headed for the door.

"Damn, is that all I get?" He walked toward the door.

"Elijah, I gotta go," she said as he grabbed her purse on her arm.

"I just want to send you off with a proper goodbye." He grabbed her face and ran his tongue across her lips. Eve's eyes fluttered close in anticipation. His lips didn't come right away. She felt his breath on her face. She could smell the coffee with a bit of Irish cream. She didn't realize he had added that bit on the order. "Are you going to come back here after your meeting?" Elijah asked running his luscious lips across her face and mouth.

"I ... I don'.... I'm not sure." She tried to catch her breath. His nearness caused her to tingle all over. "Don't you leave tonight?"

"Yes," he said grabbing hold of one of the wild strands of her hair. "But it's the red eye. So I will be here until 11:30 this evening."

"O.K.," Eve said moving away from him and opening the door. She walked through the doorway and turned around to see him standing there. "I'll talk to you soon."

He smiled and waved at her.

She turned and ran toward the opening elevator.

She sat outside the restaurant putting her hair in a bun at the nape of her neck. She reached up and moved the rearview mirror so she could put her lipstick on and make sure she tucked fly-away hairs into the fastener. She glanced at her watch and it was five forty-five. *Damn I'm late!* She checked her face and hair one more time and opened the car door.

When she entered the restaurant, no one was present to greet her. She looked around to see if she could spot Nathan.

"Excuse me, ma'am. How many in your party?" Eve turned to look at the host smiling at her.

"Ah. I'm meeting someone..."

"Oh yes. A gentleman?" he asked.

Eve smiled and nodded.

"Right this way." He placed the menus back and led the way.

"Oh, wait a minute. I need to freshen up. Could you let him know I'm here and I will be right out?"

The host smiled and directed her to the ladies' room. Eve went in and looked herself in the mirror. She looked a bit frazzled around the edges but not too bad. She gathered some paper towels and wet them.

This is some ghetto fabulous shenanigans, Evie Girl. You're running from one man's bed to see if you want to get to another. And look at you. You in the bathroom cleaning up like a whore who just left her last john. She winced at her on thoughts. *It ain't that kind of party. One time is alright. Just don't make it a habit.*

Eve came out of the ladies' room and met the host again. She followed him to the rear of the restaurant where the lights were dimmed and candles were lit on every table. She saw Nathan sitting there in a taupe jacket and beige turtleneck. He looked up and smiled. Her breath caught in her throat. The man was much finer than she remembered. His smooth chocolate brown skin shimmered like the sun gliding on silk. His facial hair around his mouth barely revealed a small dimple and framed his beautiful smile. Eve wondered why she hadn't noticed the dimple before. His smile was so beautiful. Elijah's smile was beautiful too, but it wasn't as sincere. And it was shared with another woman. She scanned from Nathan's mouth to his eyes. They were deep coffee brown, dark roast, and were accented by long sweeping eyelashes.

"Well, well, Miss Lady, I thought maybe you forgot I was waiting. I was beginning to think I was left out to dry."

"I'm so sorry." Eve gushed. "I was in a meeting, and when I looked up at the clock, it seemed to have skipped a few hours. I apologize again."

"It is not a problem. I understand that business runs that way. Anyway, my pastor always says that mistakes and misunderstandings are a part of life, so why must I be sorry for them."

"That's an interesting way of thinking, I guess," Eve said picking up the menu. "What church do you go to?"

"I attend First Missionary Baptist, when I go. I'm usually working on Sunday, so I try to catch bible study on Wednesday's."

"Oh my. That's the church I attend, when I attend. But I'm a Sunday morning member."

Nathan nodded and sipped on his drink. "Maybe we can attend one Sunday morning when I'm not working?"

Eve smiled. "That would be nice."

The waiter came and took their order. Nathan ordered a steak, medium well, and a stuffed baked potato with cheese broccoli. Eve ordered a Chinese chicken salad with extra special dressing on the side.

"Is that all you're going to eat? You're not one of those women who can't eat in front of a man, are you?"

"No sweetheart. I have yet to meet a man that can make me lose my appetite. I nibbled on snacks in my meeting and I'm not very hungry. So what is going on at work?"

"Well, after the attempted merge with your company, I just found out that E.L. Parkhaven has decided to try to buy out a smaller multimedia firm. They deal with the local cable systems, but from what I understand they were getting heavily involved with Ivy Cable before Ivy merged with DUO. I think Ivy had promised them they would be a satellite firm, but DUO didn't want it. This company invested a lot of money in Ivy Cable's interest, but when the merger happened, their deal was null and void. Money began to drain like rain through a drainpipe and E.L. jumped in to try to save the day."

"Damn. So how does all of this affect you?"

"I have been assured that my job is not going to change much. I have to find a way to present our security system as the superior system so I won't have to reorganize but otherwise was told that the only change is that I will be the head of security over two buildings instead of one. The other security head will fall under my authority."

"Oh, so now you are a big deal?"

"Oh, don't sleep, sweetheart." Nathan winked at her and smiled. "I was a big deal before all this went down."

Eve sat back in her seat and laughed.

They laughed and talked about their jobs, friends and family. He was the oldest of three and was the only boy. His middle sister was a stay at home mom and his youngest was in Hollywood waiting on tables and her big break. His father retired from the railroad and his mom was a retired hairdresser. They now lived in Florida.

Eve felt comfortable with him and she found herself talking more about herself than she typically did with any other man on their first date. His relaxed, easy-going nature drew Eve to him. Her life had been so uptight for the last couple of months that she took advantage of this time to let her hair down. Looking down at her watch, she noticed it was nine o'clock.

Noticing that Eve looked at her watched, Nathan checked his. "Am I keeping you from something?" he asked.

"Oh no. I'm just enjoying your company and I was surprised by how much time has gone by. I'm really enjoying our conversation."

"So am I." Nathan concurred, touching her hand on the table. His hand was large, warm and rough. This man most definitely worked with his hands and that made Eve's stomach jump. It was then Nathan decided he would get a bit more personal.

"Eve tell me about your past boyfriends."

Eve wasn't expecting that. She choked a little on her water. "What do you want to know?" she asked, wiping her mouth.

"Anything you tell me."

"Well, in high school I was popular, but not necessarily with the boys. I got along with everyone, but no guys saw me as someone they would go out with. When I was in college, I think I became a bit more comfortable in my own skin, and I noticed guys noticing me. I dated a few, but nothing major was going on. Then, I met a guy named Rodney. He was everything I wasn't. He was an ex-drug dealer that had dreams of playing baseball with the local leagues and no motivation to pursue it. When I met him, he was working at one of the elementary schools as a janitor. He was such a gentleman to be so rough around the edges.

Anyway, I got involved with him and eventually he was the first person that I had sex with. I think that was the link between us that kept us together for so long. I can remember Lola and Teresa trying to get me to drop him, but I wouldn't listen."

Nathan interrupted. "Lola and Teresa are your two best friends I saw you with the other day, right?"

"Yes. We have been friends for a good little while. We were all roommates in college."

"Okay. So what finally ended your relationship with Rodney?"

"Well, it was a lot of things. Before I went to college, there was a guy that I started seeing. So at the time I was seeing both of them. Rodney knew about the other guy, but the other guy didn't know about him."

"Oh, you're a playa," Nathan said jokingly.

"Not in the least. A playa doesn't feel guilty. Ultimately, I couldn't stand doing this and I knew I had to make a choice."

"Who did you choose?"

"After I got to the point that I had to choose, the choice was made for me. Rodney was there and I got to see him and the other guy was messing around on me anyway. I have dated off and on but nothing too serious after that. So what about you?"

"Well, I was one of those men who was an equal opportunity dater. I dated anyone and everyone. I didn't date them at the same time, but they would only last about a month and then I would move on. There was this one girl who I dated. I was living in Florida at the time and she was a beautiful woman. We had so many things in common, I thought that she was the one. We were together all the time from the first time I saw her."

"Sounds like it really was something," Eve commented.

"It was."

"What was her name?"

"Erica," he answered sadly.

"What happened?"

"Well, she was ready to be married and I wasn't. She said she shouldn't have to wait and I told her not to," he said with such finality.

"Damn."

"Yeah." Nathan took a drink of his water. "Ever since then, I've had different relationships, but nothing major."

Eve looked again at her watch and it read 10:45. She noticed that almost all of the other tables in the restaurant were empty. She looked at Nathan and smiled. "I think we might want to get out of here. It looks as if we may have shut the place down."

Nathan laughed. "I will have to tell the manager I was caught up in conversation with a beautiful female. He will surely understand that."

"What if the manager is a woman?" Eve teased.

"Then, you will have to tell her that you were caught up in the conversation with a man who was captivated by your beauty."

"Oh my," Eve said shaking her head. She felt a slight blush come over her. *Damn Girl! Black folks don't blush.* "Well, would you think I was too forward if I invited you to my house for coffee and more conversation?" Eve offered as she gathered her things to leave.

Nathan smiled and took a deep breath. "If you were to offer, I wouldn't think you were too forward. But I'd pass on that offer. I don't want to put this thing we got going in jeopardy." Nathan picked up her hand and kissed it. "I want you to know that I want that invite, but I know me so well that if I'm sitting on your couch drinking coffee, conversation is going to be the last thing on my mind."

Eve titled her head to the side and twisted her lips. She thought about what he said. Finally, she allowed a sly grin to cross her face. She nodded. "I can tell you Mr. Nathan Garrison, I'm very impressed and intrigued."

"Are you intrigued enough to have another dinner with me this week?"

"Oh yes." Eve interjected. "Absolutely!"

"Let set it for the typical date night. Is Friday good for you?" Nathan asked handing his credit card to the waiter.

"I cannot foresee that being a problem."

"That's good. I figure we can go have drinks, then have dinner, and maybe a little dancing."

"That sounds like a plan to me. I love to dance," Eve said opening her purse and pulling out her keys.

The waiter brought back the ticket and card. Nathan signed the ticket, handed it back and then got up from his chair. He went around the table and pulled Eve's chair out and helped her into her jacket. Escorting her to her car, they continued to talk and laugh.

"Where is your car?" he asked as they stepped off the curb into the parking lot.

"It's back there on the right." She pointed to a little silver Jetta.

"Why did you park so far back? That's not safe."

"I wasn't really thinking about that. I was only thinking of how late I was."

When they reached the car, he suddenly bent down and looked under the car. Eve stopped and observed his bizarre behavior. He placed his hand out toward Eve. She looked at it as if he was a foreign object.

"Give me your keys," he said looking through the windows of her car. She reached in her bag and searched for her keys. Nathan turned around and let out a sigh while he watched her search her purse for the elusive keys.

"I thought you had them out already?"

"I did, but I dropped them back in when I got up to put my coat on."

After a moment, the familiar jingle was pulled from her bag and handed to Nathan. Muttering a thank you, he moved her to the side and opened the driver side door. Eve, although somewhat surprised by his action, took the time to notice his strong arms as they reached over the back seat and his backside in all its glory on display. *Oh damn! I'm happy this man did not take my offer to go home.*

Her attention was snapped back to reality when the engine of her car started. Nathan got out of the car and moved to the side so that she could get in. He placed her in the car and closed the door. She rolled down the window.

"Mr. Garrison, what was that all about?"

"Eve, you should know better. Since you're by yourself, you should have parked under a light and closer to the building. It isn't safe. Do you even check under your car or in your backseat before you get in your car?"

"No," she admitted.

"These things are important. When I was on the police force, you would be surprised how not checking simple things like that can put you in danger."

"Stop now before you make me paranoid." Eve joked trying to lighten the conversation.

"Paranoia is a good thing when it comes to your safety. I need to email you those safety tips. Do I have your email address?" he asked checking his jacket pocket for a pen.

"Yes. It's on my card."

"Good, I will email it to you tomorrow." Nathan's demeanor changed from security expert to the man she just had dinner with. "I thank you, fair lady, for having this impromptu dinner with me. I'm looking forward to Friday night."

Eve smiled. "So am I, kind sir, so am I."

Nathan leaned in the window and kissed her on her cheek. He pulled away, smiled, and then walked toward a forest green SUV. She sat and watched him until he got in his truck and then she drove out of the restaurant parking lot.

On her way home, she went over her day in her head. Work had been no different than usual, until Nathan had called. She was surprised to hear from him but was really happy that he called. Her time with Elijah was as it was. The man knew what he was doing in the boardroom as well as the bedroom. Even though the sex was unbelievable, the highlight of her day was dinner with Nathan. He surprised her by being witty, and well spoken. She had sensed that about him on the phone but sitting across from him had given her a whole new vibe. That man was all of that.

As she pulled into her driveway and waited for the garage door to go up, she noticed a green SUV parked in the middle of the street behind her. It scared her at first, until the light on the inside of the truck came on and she realized it was Nathan. He held up a cell phone and then started dialing. Her cell started to ring. She pulled into the garage and then reached to grab her phone.

"I'm sorry if I scared you," he said quickly. "I know you haven't developed your sense of paranoia yet, and I was willing to let you use mine until you do."

Eve laughed. "If you wanted to know where I lived you should have just taken me up on my offer."

"Well, now I don't have to worry about you meeting me on Friday. I can just come and pick you up."

"That is true. Hey, you want to come and check over my house before you go?" She teased.

He fell silently pensive. Finally, he spoke. "You don't have an alarm and you live by yourself?" He sounded angry.

"Nathan, I was just teasing. Yes, of course I have an alarm. And I'm not always by myself. My sister sometimes comes and stays with me."

"Oh. Well, would you like me to come and take a look around?"

Eve was tempted, but she didn't want to get into anything tonight. He was right when he said the pretense of coffee or even safety could interfere and really mess things up. "No, I got this one, but on Friday you can check out my security system when you pick me up."

"Okay Momma. Talk to you later." Nathan hung up.

She closed the garage door and as the door closed she could see him pull away from her house. Eve got out of the car and walked inside. Pressing her code for the alarm she wondered to herself, *where the hell do these men get this Momma shit?*

<u>That is a real friend.</u>
Chapter 17

Eve left work early to go home and change. Teresa was picking her up and they were going to meet Lola at the mall to try to find Eve something to wear for her date with Nathan. On the way to the mall, Lola called asking what was taking them so long because she was ready to go; shopping and men were right up her alley. When they drove up, Teresa and Eve laughed. They knew they were in for some real shopping. Miss Lola, who always wore boots or heels, was standing in front of the door in her jeans and tennis shoes. Whenever she wore them, they were in for a shopping adventure.

"Hey y'all." Lola greeted them as they walked toward her. "I have already scoped out the place and I know just where to get you a sexy little thing for Nathan."

"Did you check out the shoes?" Teresa asked. "I want to see the shoes. The wedding is closer than we think."

"Now, you know I checked out the shoes." Lola countered. "Am I not a woman? Shoes are as important as bread and water."

"Well, alrighty then. Woman shall not live by bread alone," Eve added.

"Damn skippy," Lola affirmed. "Let's go."

Eve opened the door to the mall. They hit every single store on the first floor, and at least one of them walked out with something in their hands. Coming out of one of the larger department stores, Lola was approached by a younger man.

"Excuse me, Miss. My name is Eugene and I thought it necessary to tell you that you are the most beautiful girl I have ever seen."

"Thank you, sweetheart."

"No problem. I was wondering would it be possible to get your phone number. I would really like to converse with you."

Lola, Eve, and Teresa all looked at Eugene. Dressed in a trendy style outfit and his haircut low with a designer part, he appeared to be no more than twenty-years old. Lola finally spoke.

"Babe, how old are you?"

"Why? Age ain't nothing but a number." He commented smiling and running his hands over his baby face.

"How old?"

"I will be twenty-one next week."

Eve and Teresa turned their heads and giggled.

Lola looked at Eugene shaking her head. "I'm thirty-two years old, I have a job, my own home, my own car, and investments. I'm not interested in being any boy's sugar momma."

"Oh it's like that?" The young man asked defensively.

"Yes, sweetheart, it is."

"Well, Miss lady just so that you know. I have investment in an internet company which is doing well, I'm in the process of building my own home, and I'm rollin' in the newest model of Mercedes. I don't need a sugar momma."

Lola looked surprised. She was impressed if all of this was true; however, the twelve-year age gap was enough for her to pass.

"I'm impressed Eugene. Forgive me for assuming anything else. I will however tell you that age is not simply a number but a note of experience. Get back to me in another ten years." Lola turned to her friends. "Let's go ladies." They all began walking away.

"You don't know what you're missing," Eugene yelled out.

Lola chose to ignore it and kept walking.

"Wow Lola. You handled that much better than I expected. I remember times when you made some guys feel really low after stepping to you. I just knew you were going to go off on the boy," Teresa acknowledged.

"I have grown older and wiser." Lola responded with a shrug. "And he wasn't disrespectful. The last time a young buck stepped to me, he was holding himself and talking major trash. I let him have it major Lola style. Then a nigga' got violent on a sista' and security had to come and remove his ass. I decided that I got to be smarter than that. It was a blessing he wasn't waiting for me outside. "

"I hear you Lola." Eve interjected. "April was telling me that when she was in school, she heard of some girls going from baby to bitch in five seconds flat because they wouldn't talk to these young guys."

"You see that's what I'm talking about," Lola reiterated. "I don't know how these young girls put up with this stuff. However, I took a clue from them and just started being nice."

"Wow. Lola nice? That *is* a concept," Teresa commented.

"Shut up, Bitch." Lola grabbed Eve by the arm and walked ahead.

Lola walked into the next shoe store they saw, which happened to be her favorite. When they entered, the salesperson greeted Lola by name. Eve and Teresa found the first seats they could. They knew they would be in there for a while.

"So how are things with Nathan?" Teresa asked.

"There's nothing to tell. We have a date on Friday and that's why we're here shopping."

"Don't be a smart ass. Has he called?"

"Yes. It has only been a couple of days since I had dinner with him and he has called both evenings."

"Well?" Teresa urged.

"Well what? He called. We talked. We are going out on Friday."

"What have you guys talked about? I mean..."

Eve nudged Teresa on the arm and motioned her to look behind her. Teresa turned and spotted Lola talking to a woman with a baby. The baby was beautiful and Lola was making silly faces and having a good time. When the baby grabbed Lola's locs,

Teresa braced herself for Lola to go off. Instead, Lola eased her hair out of the baby's hand and kissed it.

"Will wonders ever cease?" Eve muttered out loud. "It always takes me aback when I see this side of Lola."

"I know." Teresa agreed. "But I found out a long time ago that there is so much more to Lola than anyone knows or thinks." Right then, Lola walked up.

"Okay, bitches, let's eat. I think I'm going to get a teriyaki bowl," Eve announced.

"Hook me up, Evie," Lola said handing her the money.

"Me too." Teresa honed in.

"Damn ya'll. A sista' only got two arms," Eve whined.

"That's what they have trays for, love." Lola reminded her sweetly. "We are going to find a good place to sit to people watch."

Eve went over to the counter and placed their order. The guy behind the counter was cute and was obviously interested. When she got her order, he touched her hand and winked. She smiled and hurried back to the table.

"It must be an epidemic."

"What?" Teresa asked reaching for her bowl.

"That young guy at the counter was flirting with me. Good Lord, is he even sixteen?"

Lola looked over at the counter and noticed the guy staring at Eve.

"He's probably eighteen." She turned back around and took her bowl off of the tray. "Just think of it as a compliment. Women in their thirties are not often hit on by these younger men, unless of course you're me."

"Well damn, I hope I get a turn," Teresa said and stuffed a spoonful of rice in her mouth.

"Well, you can go get the sodas and see if he hits on you," Eve offered.

"No thank you. I'd rather eat."

"I'll go get them," Lola announced. Before anyone could give her money, she was off.

"You know Eve, Lola continues to surprise me," Teresa said thoughtfully.

"Why?" Eve said watching Lola walk to the counter.

"She's a real bitch, but I know she has a good heart. I remember in college when I was struggling in Economics. She tutored me every night."

"She did?" Eve asked surprised. "I didn't know that."

"That's what I'm saying. She has always treated me shitty and I put up with her because I knew where she came from and because of my friendship with you. But there were times when you weren't around that she showed me that she could be a friend." Teresa looked over to see Lola headed to another counter. "Eve, did I ever tell you that I got pregnant in college?"

"What?" Eve dropped her spoon.

"Yes, I got pregnant and I didn't want it. Lola was the one who tried to convince me to keep it. When I made it clear to her that I wasn't going to keep it, she took me to the clinic, stayed with me through the whole procedure, and then took care of me."

"Is that the time in our junior year when I was gone for a few weeks when my grandfather died?" Eve asked as she recovered from the shock of her friend's revelation. "I remember coming home and thinking you two were closer than ever."

"Yes. And not too long after that she was being the queen bitch again. As I watched her with that young man and the baby, I thought to myself you never know what you are going to get with this woman."

"I understand. I think I have seen that side all along. That's the reason why we're still friends. I trust her to have my back at all times."

"I guess I can say the same thing." There were a few seconds of silence between the two friends.

"I always thought she told you about my pregnancy," Teresa said looking into her plate.

"No, she didn't."

Eve and Teresa watched Lola walk up with three different juices. "Teresa, here is your Cran-Grape, Eve your O.J., and my passion fruit."

"Did you get anymore admirers?" Eve asked, opening her juice.

"Yes. This time, they were older and I did give them my office number."

"You go Lola." Teresa laughed. "You are on it today. When I grow up, I want to be just like you."

"Well then, sista' girl, pay attention and watch me work."

"So Eve, what do you say about Nathan?" Lola asked digging into her food.

"Like I told T, there is nothing to be said. We're going out on Friday."

"What about Elijah? Has he been calling?" Lola asked.

Eve looked over at Teresa and saw her physically stiffen. She looked at Lola and subtly shook her head to cut the conversation as she answered. "Yeah, I speak to him at work," Eve answered.

"Well, have you seen him for play?" Lola continued to press her.

Eve's eyebrows gathered as she frowned at Lola. "We can talk about it later."

"Oh girl, please. Don't mind T. She knows she wants to know. Don't you, Teresa?" Lola instigated.

"I think I need something else to drink." Teresa got up and walked toward the counter.

"Damn Lo. Why do you have to be so antagonistic to her? She asked that we not discuss Elijah around her. We're having a good time. Don't fuck it up with some bullshit."

"Whatever Eve." Lola snapped. "I will shut up for now, but she needs to grow up."

Moments later, Teresa came back to the table with a bottle water and sat down. As she sat, her cell phone rang. "Hello."

"This girl better not be on the phone all night," Lola whined. "We don't need the distraction."

Eve hit Lola on the arm and shook her head when Teresa grabbed her arm. Both Eve and Lola looked at Teresa with concern.

"Okay yes. I will be right there." Teresa hung up the phone.

"What happened?" Eve asked.

"Michael was in a car accident. I got to get to the hospital."

Teresa, Eve, and Lola were on their feet.

"Look," Lola said. "I'll take Teresa to the hospital, because I'm parked closer to where we are. Eve can you handle these bags? Get them to T's car and meet us there."

"That's fine. Just go," Eve said.

Teresa and Lola took off running.

"Hey throw me your keys," Eve yelled. Teresa reached into her pocket, grabbed her keys and hurled them at Eve. She caught them with one hand. "What hospital?" Eve yelled after them.

"General County," Teresa yelled, turning out of the food court and running toward the exit.

Eve managed to get all their bags in some type of order and looked around for a cart.

"Ma'am do you need a cart? I can get one for you."

Eve turned around and it was the young man that flirted with her earlier. She smiled. "That would be nice of you. Can you hurry? I'm in a big hurry."

"Sure." The young man ran out of the food court to the middle of the mall. Within thirty seconds, he was back.

"Thank you so much."

"Not a problem. Maybe when you come back we can have lunch?"

"Yes maybe." Eve answered not really paying attention. She took the cart and rushed out of the food court and mall. When she got to the car, she threw everything in the trunk and got in. On the way to the hospital, her cell phone rang.

"Hello."

"Hey little lady, what is going on?" It was Nathan.

"Hey Nathan. I'm headed to the hospital. My friend Teresa's fiancé was in a car accident."

"Hmmm. How bad was it?" Nathan asked genuinely concerned.

"I don't know. We were at the mall when she got the call. Lola took her to the hospital. I gathered our things and now I'm headed that way."

"Okay. Let me get off the phone so you won't be distracted. By the way what hospital?"

"He's at General County."

"Alright, talk to you."

Eve hurried over to General County hospital and parked in a fifteen-minute parking space. She hopped out of the car and ran into the emergency room looking for Teresa and Lola. They were sitting in the waiting room and Lola had her hands awkwardly placed trying to comfort Teresa.

Lola is not one to show affection. This must be killing her. Eve laughed to herself.

Lola saw Eve before Teresa and signaled with her eyes that she needed help. Eve moved over to sit next to them and reached to hug Teresa. That was when she noticed the tear rolling down her face.

"They say he's awake, but they are running some tests," Lola informed Eve and moved away from Teresa. "Nothing seems to be damaged, but he took a big blow to the head. They will know more after the tests."

They sat in silence until Eve looked up when Nathan walked in. "Nathan," Eve acknowledged in surprise. "What are you doing here?"

Lola looked over at Nathan and Teresa looked up in surprise.

Eve got up and walked toward him.

"I just came in case you needed something." He unbuttoned his jacket.

"Thank you. But you didn't have to come."

"I know," Nathan said sincerely. He grabbed her hand and gave it a squeeze. "I wanted to." He turned to Lola and stuck out his hand. "By the way, I'm Nathan Garrison."

Lola took it. "Lola Bennett."

Turning his attention to Teresa with his hands outstretched, she wiped the tears from her face and then wiped her hands on her jeans before taking Nathan's. "Teresa Charles."

"I hate that we had to meet under these circumstances," Nathan offered.

"Me too," Teresa answered, wiping her eyes.

There was an awkward silence. Nathan finally broke it. "Have you all eaten?"

They all nodded yes.

"Well, I will go get us some coffee," he said.

"Can you make mine a soda?" Eve asked. She needed one.

"Sure."

"I will go with you, Nathan," Lola insisted. "You can't carry it all by yourself."

"Thanks."

Lola and Nathan walked out.

Teresa looked at Eve. "You think Lola will make her move?" Teresa asked smiling.

Eve smiled back. "She ain't that bad. Plus, we never have been attracted to the same type of man."

"Well, he is fine," Teresa added.

"Yes, he is," Eve agreed.

The doctor came in. "Ms. Charles?"

Teresa stood.

"Your fiancé is asking for you. You can talk to him if you

want."

Teresa moved quickly following the doctor, and Eve said a silent prayer of thanks. When Nathan and Lola returned, Eve told them the good news and they were equally relieved.

"I'm going to see if I can find Teresa," Lola announced and left Eve alone with Nathan.

"Nathan, I appreciate you coming. You didn't have to do that. You barely know me."

"But I want to know you, and I felt that you needed to know I'm serious about that."

If I wasn't convinced, I'm convinced now. This brother is definitely interested. "Wow. I don't know what to say?" Eve admitted.

"Nothing needs to be said."

Teresa and Lola came back together. "Hey Evie, Michael has to stay overnight, so I'm going to take Teresa home. Where did you park?" Lola asked.

"I parked in fifteen-minute parking right in front of the Emergency Room."

"Good Lord, I hope you don't get a ticket on my car," Teresa said lightly. By her expression, Eve knew Michael was okay.

"Girl, your man was in a car accident and you're worried about a ticket?" Eve asked.

"Michael will kill me if I get another ticket on that car," Teresa answered truthfully.

"Well, Michael and you must both be fine if that's what you're worried about. Let's go," said Eve.

"Okay," Lola agreed. "How are we going to do this? I'm parked farther away than you."

"Tell you what," Nathan interrupted. "I will take Ms. Bennett to her car so she can pull to the front of the emergency. And we will both wait for you down there."

"Sounds good to me," Lola said grabbing her purse.

"No, I have Teresa's car," Eve remembered.

Evie, I will pick up my car from you in the morning. I'm still a bit too shaky to drive," Teresa answered.

"Well then, I will meet you outside and escort you to the car," Nathan offered.

"That will be fine."

"I will go with Nathan to my car, and Teresa I will meet you out front," Lola said gathering her stuff.

"Okay, I'm still confused about what we are supposed to do," Eve said, "but y'all go and I will figure it out."

Lola and Nathan laughed and headed down to the parking lot. Eve and Teresa went in and talked to Michael and the doctor. Teresa made plans to pick him at 8:00 a.m. As they walked toward the elevator, Teresa began talking. "Eve do you remember when we agreed that there was more to Lola than anyone thinks?"

"Yes."

"Today is a perfect example of what I was talking about. You know that our relationship was a bit strained because of your choice to be with Elijah. But despite that, she was still Johnny on the Spot for me. I will never understand her and will probably continue to disagree with her on almost everything, but tonight I thank God for her."

"Friends aren't necessarily always the ones who are nice to you; they're the ones that are there for you," Eve said as the elevator opened. They both stepped in.

"That's true, but they do need to be nice once in a while," Teresa said.

They laughed as the doors closed.

Pleasant thoughts.
Chapter 18

Eve had been so busy at work that she didn't have the chance to talk to Nathan since the accident. They played phone tag leaving messages or sending texts. She did, however, manage to print out the safety tips that he emailed her. She also forwarded them to all the ladies in her address book.

When she got home, she came in taking off all her clothes and settled into a warm bubble bath where she could relax and not think about the day. She thought about Nathan and looked at her cell. She realized Nathan had left a voicemail and she hadn't even heard her phone ring. She sent him a quick text and then leaned back to soak. A few minutes later, a text ring came in.

"We still on for Friday?"

She texted back, "For sure."

"Good. I will see you then."

She smiled to herself and found she was excited that she had something to look forward to. When she got out of the tub, she threw on her robe and listened to the messages on her house phone. Her mother and telemarketers were the only ones who called her house phone.

Her mother had left a message. She had been out of town and just got back at the beginning of the week. She had called Eve four times and sounded increasingly worried. When Eve called her back, her mother was relieved and angry.

"It's about time you called me back, young lady. I have been calling you every day this week. I was growing worried. I even called your office. When your assistant told me you were in a meeting, at least I knew you weren't dead."

"Hello Mother," Eve placated. "How was your trip?"

"My trip was fine. How is your sister? I haven't spoken to her either." Her mother was oblivious to Eve's tone. Eve chuckled to herself. *My momma is still the same. God, I love that about her. She is going to remain consistent.*

"I haven't spoken to her," said Eve.

"Doesn't she live with you?" Her mother asked, annoyed.

"Mom, you know April. She lives with me one month and she's with Daniel the next month and then with Amy the next. She's a nomad."

"I do not know what I'm going to do with you and your sister. You two seemingly try to avoid me at all cost. If I wouldn't have come back, it wouldn't have made a difference, I guess."

Eve groaned. *This woman will guilt a dog into apologizing for barking. Well, you're not getting me today. I'm too tired to deal with guilt of not loving my momma today.* "Mother, please. You know I have a job that takes up a lot of my time. And right now if I don't get off the phone and return a few more phone calls I'm not going to have much going in my social life."

"Well, I don't want to keep you." She sighed.

Eve rolled her eyes.

"I just wanted to talk to you, but if you have something else to do, I will call you later."

This time, it was Eve's turn to exhale noisily. She didn't want to admit, but her mother succeeded in her game plan. She made Eve feel ungrateful for the sacrifices a mother makes. *She only wants to talk a bit. I guess I can do that. She is the woman who gave birth to me.* "Mom before you go, you never told me about the things you bought on your trip," she said.

"Oh Eve, you would not believe the sale they had on shoes." Eve's mother went on for an hour about her trip and everything else. When they finally hung up, her mother was satisfied and Eve had to admit she really enjoyed their conversation. Sometimes, she forgot just how fun and crazy her mother was.

Eve called her sister. April was at her man's house. Eve warned

April of the impending call, but it was too late. April was on the other line with their mother by then. Eve laughed and hung up the phone leaving her sister to her fate.

She tried to call Teresa and Lola, but neither was home. Taking that as a clue, she went into the kitchen and found something to eat. As she pulled things from the refrigerator, she thought about Elijah. Thinking about him made her warm. She began to daydream about all the things he did the last time they were together. Lost in thought, she almost didn't hear the doorbell. Tightening her housecoat, she went to answer the door. Her doorbell rang again. She peeked through the peephole and Elijah stood there poised to ring the bell again. She unlocked and swung open the door.

"What the hell are you doing here?" She snapped.

"Well damn. I just thought I would come by and say hello. If that was a mistake, I apologize."

"Have you heard of a phone? You could have called."

"I did. There was no answer. Then I decided to drive by and see if you were home. Again, I apologize for causing you any inconvenience." He turned to walk away, and Eve felt stupid.

"Elijah, you don't have to leave. I was just...You don't have to go."

"Hey, I really need to apologize. It was wrong for me to come without talking to you. I will call you when I get back to the hotel."

"Elijah, that doesn't make any sense," she reasoned. "You're here now and I don't have anything to do. Come on in."

"I tell you what. Why don't you get dressed and we can go to the café for coffee and conversation?"

Eve pulled at her night coat. *Don't go girl. You're tired and you don't have the energy. You know he'll want to get busy and you can't resist him. Don't go.* Eve sighed.

"Give me 15 minutes."

***

At the café Elijah ordered a big hearty breakfast and Eve ate soup and cornbread then ordered a hot fudge brownie sundae. They talked about their day and how Elijah's contract ended on Friday. He told her how he was still going to be able to see her, if she wanted to because he was going to still be working in the city.

"There is another merger going on in the city?" Eve asked, scooping her ice cream into her mouth.

"Yes. It's a little multimedia firm that's being taken over by E.L. Parkhaven. Ole girl is trying to get into everything. No one really knows what she does any more. Anyway, it's only a three-month project, or so they only anticipate the need for me that long."

"Don't you usually handle big firms like the one my company went through?"

"Generally, but I wanted something a little closer to home. I like being able to see my kids." Sirens went off in Eve's head at the mention of his kids. "And I wanted a little more time with you before we go our separate ways," he added.

"Or, so you'll be free to experience the next woman in the next city that raises an insatiable desire in you to have her?" Eve didn't mean it as a question. She meant it as a dig. She knew she hit below the belt on that one, but didn't feel like being generous.

Elijah took a sip of his coffee and chose not to say anything. They sat in silence for about ten minutes.

Ok now Eve, she thought, *you were just a major bitch. What are you going to say to get out of this one?* He didn't give her a chance.

"You do realize, Eve, that you don't have to be here? I asked and you could have said no. My assumption was that you enjoyed being with me. Is that assumption wrong?"

"No," she answered dejectedly. "I do enjoy our time together."

"And since you have knowledge of my family and where I stand in this, then you know that we are eventually going to part ways?"

"Yes."

"Then let's not spend our limited time playing games with each other. I want to be with you. I like you, I desire you and I want that for as long as we can."

Eve gave a halfhearted smile and stayed silent. Elijah went in his pocket and pulled out his wallet to pay the bill.

"Eve, one more thing, I'd like you to let me know if someone else comes into your life." Eve looked at him confused. Sensing she didn't know what he was getting at, he explained. "I asked that so I can make the decision if I want to share or not."

Sometimes one head is better than two.
Chapter 19

After Eve returned home, she called Teresa and Lola to tell them that she was working from home and that she was cooking breakfast and she expected them to be there. Lola, who never turned down food, was the first one at Eve's door at 7:00 a.m. Since Eve knew Teresa was going to be at least another hour, she took this time to talk to Lola about Elijah.

"Girl, that shit is a trip. What did you say? Your boy is off the hook!" Lola ran and hollered all throughout the house as Eve told her about her conversation with Elijah. "I can't believe he broke it down like that," she continued, "What the hell did you say?"

"I was stunned." Eve sat on her couch with a mimosa in her hand. "The only thing going through my head was 'Damn you really don't give a damn about me and my feelings do you?'"

"Okay. So once he said 'so I can decide if I want to share,' you said..." Lola started anticipating what was to come next.

"I said 'well there isn't anyone right now, but I will let you know'."

"Ah, hell. No, you didn't say that. Oh damn sis, what the hell were you thinking? That shit was corny."

"What the hell was I supposed to say?"

"You could have said fuck you for not giving a shit."

"Okay, Lola, but what was that going to accomplish?" Eve inquired of her friend.

"Well hell, I don't know. I know you would have had the bomb sex though."

Eve looked at her confused. "Please tell me how you got there?"

"Check it, Eve. When two people get really mad at each other and they are sexually attracted to each other too, there are fireworks ma' dear."

"Well, I was a bit peeved, so I guess that's why that shit was so good," Eve confessed.

"You both need to be mad, you slut." Lola smiled and play punched her friend in the arm.

"It takes one to know one." Eve replied with a pillow whack in Lola's face. This started a fifteen-minute pillow fight until they both fell into a fit of laughter.

Eve's doorbell rang.

"Get the door, while I get another glass for Teresa." Eve left Lola to answer the door.

Lola opened the door wide and stood with her hand on her hip. She and Teresa had gotten over the major problems they had, but there was still a certain amount of underlying tension.

"What's up Lola?" Teresa greeted as she walked in the house pulling off her jacket. "What were you two laughing about when I came up to the door?"

Lola closed the door and didn't see Eve walk back into the room. "Oh, Eve was telling me about..."

"Hey Teresa," Eve interrupted. "We were having a good old fashion pillow fight." Eve handed Teresa a glass of the special orange juice.

"Oh goodness, I'm glad I missed that one. I have the worst headache in the world. It's around that time of month and I'm feeling lousy."

"All you need is a good sexing from night to day. That always makes my period blues go away." Lola gave Teresa a high five and screamed, "Ya heard me?" sounding like a Louisiana rapper.

"You two are silly." Eve laughed. "Come on in the kitchen. Breakfast is almost ready." They followed her in the kitchen.

"What did you cook?" Teresa asked.

"I fried some chicken, eggs, grits, and biscuits."

"Okay, what man rang your bell in the last few days? That's the only time when you try to cook," Teresa pointed out.

"Elijah. Who else?" Lola interjected.

Teresa glanced at Eve and then looked at Lola. "It could have been Nathan."

Lola looked at Eve excited. "Girl, did you kick it with Nathan? Was it banging?"

Eve rolled her eyes at Lola. "No, I didn't get busy with Nathan. Dang Lola, we only went on one date."

"If you want to quibble, you technically haven't been on any dates with Elijah," Lola retorted.

"Eve," Teresa asked ignoring Lola's statement, "Are you going to let Elijah go if you and Nathan hit it off?"

"We have hit it off, but I really hadn't thought about not seeing Elijah." His last words flashed through Eve's head. *"If someone is in your life, that doesn't matter to me as long as it doesn't matter to you."*

"Why would you hang on? I mean, Nathan is free, isn't he?" Teresa insisted.

"Yes, he is "free" as you call it."

"Then what is the problem?"

"I know the problem," Lola stated as a matter of fact.

"And what is that?" Teresa asked irritated.

"The sex with Elijah is the bomb and it ain't guaranteed to be with Nathan."

Eve's eyebrows lifted as if she could make that argument.

"Why is this always just about sex?" Teresa asked. She was disgusted with where this conversation was going.

"Because Eve's and Elijah's relationship is just about sex."

"But isn't Nathan's and Eve's relationship about more than sex?" Teresa pointed out.

"I guess you can say that, since they haven't had sex, but..." Lola added as she got up and took a piece of chicken out of oven. "I have a suggestion for Eve. Why don't you just fuck Nathan and see where he stands in the mix."

"Oh, that's brilliant Lola," Teresa snapped sarcastically. "She should make herself vulnerable to two men at one time. Didn't we used to call that a slut?"

"Maybe you did, but I called it fun." Lola stuffed a piece of chicken in her mouth and let crumbs fall on the table in front of her.

"Can you both stop talking about me like I'm not here?" Eve insisted as she sat a plate in front of Lola. "You two have a real bad habit of doing that."

Eve pulled her Teflon pan and scrambled the eggs. The grits were warming on the stove and the chicken was in the oven. When she took the chicken out of the oven and placed it on the table, she also pulled out bowls and filled them with eggs and grits with loads of butter and set them on the table. The biscuits were wrapped in a cloth and had been sitting under her bread warmer.

They sat around the table and held hands. Eve said grace then they dove into their meal. Eve was so relieved they were eating. It took the attention away from her. In addition to the fact that she knew her friends always had a better disposition after they ate. When they were finished, Lola went into Eve's bedroom to make a call to her boss and Teresa and Eve remained in the kitchen.

"Eve, I know I said I didn't want you to talk to me about Elijah, but I have a question."

"Okay ask." Eve muttered as she took a swig of her drink.

"Is this thing with Elijah really just about sex?"

"Why are you asking?" Eve inquired as she looked at Teresa to see if she really wanted to get into it.

"Because I just want you to know what is really going on." Not giving Eve a chance to answer the question at all, Teresa continued. "Did you know that Elijah is a cake man? That's according to an article I read on the Internet."

Eve's eyebrow went up.

"Oh, I know you're thinking that is a little strange to just be reading, but I did some research on affairs right after I found out my father cheated on my mother. I needed to know why. Anyway, online there is a website called The Other Woman or TOW for short. I read this article that said that men like Elijah are cake men."

"Did this article mention Elijah by name, because I don't recall you speaking to him long enough to know what kind of man he is?" Eve responded defensively.

"I know because men who will have a sexual affair with a woman based upon sex and nothing else want to eat his cake and have it too. Therefore, sweetheart, you have a cake man."

"Girl, I know for a fact that psychology was not your major in college, so why are you trying to psycho-analyze my life and relationship?" Eve remonstrated.

"Eve, calm down," Teresa whispered. She looked for Lola to return any minute. "As it looks to me, you don't have a relationship. You have sex. I'm just trying to help you out. I don't want to see my girl with her nose spread wide open behind a man that will go home to another woman at the end of the day."

"Teresa you are right. It *is* just sex." Eve breathed between her teeth. "That is all. You know me? I'm not trying to break up a happy home. I wasn't even looking for this. I fell into it and the sex got good. I had no idea how good it would be. For the first time in my life, I took a chance and did something I knew was wrong. Although I know I probably shouldn't, I pray that however it ends, it won't be too bad." Taking a deep breath, she continued. "Now, I can kick my own ass about this. As a matter of fact, I already have, but damn it, I'm in this now. I have to follow through. I respect your feelings enough not to discuss this with you, so now I'm asking that you respect me enough to get off my fucking back."

Teresa, having never seen Eve in that way, backed up-literally and figuratively. She nodded her head and gave Eve a half smile and headed into the living room. Eve wanted to follow her, but she didn't feel like being giving this time. She stood in the kitchen until she heard the door close. Eve sat at the kitchen table with her hands on her head.

She always was the one who felt the need to comfort others and worry about them. She wouldn't do that now. She wanted to lick her own wounds. She was in a constant struggle about her involvement with Elijah and most of the time she managed to suppress the thoughts and move on. Teresa's attempt to make her see the white elephant standing in the living room wreaked havoc in her denial.

"Hey, where did Teresa go?" Lola asked coming in the kitchen and heading for the fried chicken. "I heard the door close and I hurried off the phone. I didn't want to miss anything, and I wanted to hurry in here and tell you guys what the guy at work..." For the first time, she noticed Eve sitting with her head down.

"Eve, what happened?"

Eve looked up at her friend with dry-eyed suffering. Eve allowed a bittersweet smile to replace her look of misery. Lola moved and put her arms around her best friend. Eve shook her head slightly and closed her eyes harnessing the power from her friend into her own spirit. Lola didn't ask any more questions. She didn't have to. Her friend needed her strength and Lola was always more willing to give it.

In the few hours that Lola stayed, she helped Eve wash the dishes and get the house straightened. Eve told Lola about her date with Nathan and how excited she was about it.

"So Eve, is he all that?" Lola asked nibbling on a biscuit.

"Believe it or not, he is all that. He's a little paranoid. He followed me home after our dinner earlier this week. He wanted to make sure I made it home safely."

"Oh hell, hon." Lola warned. "That sounds like a stalker to me."

Eve laughed. "It's not like that, Lola. It was a genuine concern. Before I got in my car in the parking lot of the store he checked under it and in it to be safe."

"And this doesn't sound fanatical to you?" Lola retorted.

"No. He's in security. That's what he does for a living. If he wasn't concerned about my safety, I would be worried."

"Well, honey bun, if you like him, I love him."

It wasn't too long after that Lola headed for her office. She told Eve that some of the guys at the cultural center were giving one of the newly engaged men a stripper for a present. They asked the women that worked in the office to come in late. Since she was calling to tell them she would be late anyway, it wasn't a problem. When she thought the excitement was over she decided to go and catch up on some work. But Lola didn't leave before she declared, "I'm insulted no one had asked me to strip for them. Hell, I could have used the hundred and fifty dollars plus the tips they paid the stripper," Lola said.

Eve laughed.

Date night.
Chapter 20

Eve spent the rest of the day sitting around her house relaxing. She knew Elijah was in town and briefly toyed with the idea of calling him over, but she quickly squashed the idea. She didn't think it would be a good idea to see both of the men in the same day. Even though she already had, it wasn't the same. When she met Nathan the first night, she didn't have any expectations, so being with Elijah didn't matter. But now she wasn't sure what was about to jump off with Nathan. She didn't want to mix it with thoughts of Elijah.

Eve's doorbell rang at 7:00 p.m. on the dot. Since she had been ready since 6:30, she grabbed her purse and went to the door. Nathan stood dressed in a black pair of jeans and black and cream sweater that laid well across his broad shoulders. Eve smiled at him as she watched his eyes appraise her. She, too, had chosen black jeans with a two-inch boot, her own sweater crimson and cream.

"You look good, girl," he said smiling and taking her hand in his.

"Thank you, kind sir. I must say that I cannot complain about the way you look tonight."

He smiled and kissed her hand. He pulled her out of the house and reached behind the door and locked it. She waited on the steps as he took her key and secured her security screen door. Once everything was protected, he put his arm around her shoulders and walked her to his truck.

"Um Nathan," Eve asked. "Did you have something special planned tonight?"

"I thought we would go to dinner and maybe dancing. Why?" he asked opening the car. "Is there something you would like to do?"

"Well, I was coming home from work this week and noticed a Ferris wheel. The fair is in town. I haven't been since I was fifteen years old. I thought that would be fun."

"That does sound like fun. I'm okay with that."

"Good. I was hoping that you'd be." Eve smiled getting into the front seat. "I'm just thinking about what I'm going to eat first. I think I want a corndog and I can't leave there without a funnel cake."

Nathan walked around the car chuckling to himself. When he got in, he reminded her to set the alarm on the house. Then, he asked about Michael.

"Michael had a concussion and he's doing well, but he's going to drive Teresa crazy."

"Why?"

"He's off work for a week and taking advantage of his situation." Eve told Nathan of the antics that Michael and Teresa had been going through, and Nathan laughed all the way to the fair.

When they arrived, the first thing Eve did was head for the food. She inhaled a corndog and fries and continued to sip on her Pepsi as they walked around. Nathan voiced concern about the rides. He felt anything that was put up in a matter of hours couldn't be that safe. Eve managed to coerce him on a few. After the first few rides, Eve was ready for her funnel cake with strawberries and whip cream. Nathan enjoyed watching Eve eat the sweet treat.

"Would you like to taste some before I eat it all?" she asked.

Nathan leaned over and took a bite from her fork.

She enjoyed watching him. Her heart fluttered at the intimacy they shared.

"That was pretty good."

"Are you going to get you one?" Eve asked diving into her plate.

"You're not sharing anymore?"

Eve stuffed her mouth full of strawberries, smiled and shook her head.

Nathan laughed and guided her toward the games. Being the gentleman that he was, he invested twenty-five dollars in trying to win Eve the giant Pink panther. He got that, along with the fish and the nightglow necklace rings. Eve was literally a kid in a candy store.

As the evening went on, Nathan and Eve strolled down to where the vendors were and watched the man spray names on t-shirts and couples have caricatures made in their likeness. Eve thought about having their picture done, but thought better of it. After all, it was their first real date.

About an hour before the fair was to close for the evening, Eve grabbed Nathan by the hand and headed for the Ferris wheel. She took the tickets out of her pocket and gave it to the attendant. "Nathan, this is the last ride of the night and it's non-threatening. What do you say? Are you going?" Eve smiled up at him like a teenager.

"Yes, but on one condition."

Eve frowned. "What is that?"

"That I can kiss you when we get to the top." Nathan saw the attendant smile out of the corner of his eyes.

Eve smiled broadly and grabbed his hand pulling him toward the Ferris wheel car. They slipped into the seats and the attendant secured it for them. They began to slowly move up. Eve pointed out all the highlights of the fair as the car rose higher and higher. The wheel made a complete rotation and was on its way for a second. Just as they hit the top, the wheel paused. Eve looked down toward the attendant to see what was going on, but he didn't look up once. She turned to Nathan to ask if he thought something was wrong and was met by soft, sensuous lips on her cheek.

Eve allowed her eyes to close as his lips kissed her face, her eyes, her forehead, her chin, her nose, and finally her mouth. There was no pressure in his kiss. His mouth was relaxed and his tongue moved into Eve's mouth searching for hers. When he found it, he flicked it like a mating dance and Eve's tongue responded. She didn't even realize she stopped breathing until he pulled away from her. Her breath was ragged and thoughts were muddled. She didn't even lift her head. She simply rested against his chest and allowed him to stroke her back and neck. The sudden jerk of the Ferris wheel shoved her further into Nathan's chest and his arms tightened around her. When they got off the ride, Nathan let go of her long enough to retrieve the big, pink animal from the attendant. The attendant smiled and Nathan nodded. He grabbed Eve's hand and they headed toward the gate. Right at the exit, Nathan spotted a photo booth.

"Okay Eve, we're going to make this a memorable night. Okay?"

"I thought we did that on the Ferris wheel," she commented, smiling at the thought.

"Well, we need to get it on film." With that, he jumped into the picture booth and pulled her in on his lap.

Eve giggled.

Nathan reached into his pocket and pulled out a dollar.

Eve snatched up the money and proceeded to put it in the machine. As the money slid in, she leaned back on Nathan's chest and smiled. *Snap! Snap! Snap!* The pictures were taken.

"Don't move," Eve instructed Nathan. "We need to get another set, so we can both have a whole set."

"No sweetheart, you don't move." Nathan stilled her hips. "You're the one sitting on my lap."

If Black women blush, Eve did right then. She reached into her jacket pocket and put more money in. This time before the picture was taken she turned and put her arms around Nathan's neck. *Snap!* Then she kissed his cheek. *Snap!* And then he grabbed her head and kissed her on the mouth once again. *Snap!* This time, she had more than a memory of a kiss. They bustled out of the booth, got their pictures and headed out to the parking lot.

When they pulled up in front of her home, Eve invited Nathan in for coffee. He eagerly accepted and got out of the car to open her door for her. Once she was out of the car, he went to the back of the truck to get her stuffed animals and other knick-knacks that she purchased. At the door, he put the pink animal under his arm, and he took her keys from her and opened her front door entering first. He placed the stuffed animal down and walked into the dark house. He disappeared in the house. Eve went in behind him, punching the code into the security system and turning on the living room lights. When he came back into the living room, he informed her that no one was there.

"I didn't think so." She responded putting her purse on the table and heading toward the kitchen.

"You have a nice home. I like the cherry wood theme in your bedroom. That is really nice."

"Thank you," she yelled from the kitchen. "However, I need you to know that I feel weird about having you going through my house."

"Eve, you can never be too careful," he yelled back and moved over to her stereo and flipped through the CDs. "Nice. I love a woman who still has CDs."

"I still have some vinyl too," Eve said as she walked back in the room and plopped on the couch. "The coffee is on. Now, why exactly did you leave the police force?"

"I was forced to when I got shot."

"Oh," Eve said surprised.

Nathan smiled and laughed at her expression. "I'm sorry. I know I shouldn't have just laid it out that way, but that is what happened. I was responding to a call of domestic abuse. I made mention to my partner that I hated these calls because people are so emotionally charged you don't know what is going to happen."

As Nathan talked, he put on a CD. Smooth jazz filled the air.

He came over and sat by her on the couch.

"When we got there, the husband was standing inside the house with a gun to his wife's head. After some negotiations and the call for back up, the husband let her go. She came running out of the house and he pointed the shotgun straight at her and fired. He ended up killing her and wounding me and another officer. It was about six months after that I decided to leave the force. Even though I physically recovered, I couldn't see myself doing that again."

"Damn. That sounds like a Law and Order episode," Eve said not fully believing what she was hearing.

"I wish it were, but I got the bullet hole to prove it." Nathan lifted his shirt over his head and revealed his auburn brown chest and broad shoulders. His chest was well defined and his stomach had the glorious six-pack that makes you drunk just looking at it.

Oh shit! This man is too much. As Eve's eyes traveled over Nathan's body, they were drawn to a puckered indentation right at his ribcage on the right side. She reached out and touched it before she realized what she was doing. Nathan's skin was warm to the touch and smooth. In a rather bold move, she allowed her hand to trace down to his navel where there were fine hairs leading into his jeans.

His growing ragged breath brought Eve back to reality and she pulled away. Extremely embarrassed, she jumped up from the couch avoiding his eyes and escaped to the kitchen to get the coffee. She came back five minutes later with the coffee mugs filled. Although not directly looking at him, she noticed Nathan had put his shirt back on.

Thank God. I temporarily lost my mind. I sure don't want that to happen again. "Did you want some cream and sugar to go with that?" she asked, very conscious that he was looking at her.

"No, I like my coffee black."

"You know my father use to tell me when I was little," she said, searching for conversation. "Coffee makes you black. For the longest time, I wouldn't drink it."

Nathan smiled and reached for his coffee mug. "I think that at one time in every Black child's life they were told that when it came to drinking coffee."

"Or they were told that it would stunt your growth," Eve added.

"My parents and grandparents use to always say some crazy stuff," Nathan said, and the sexual tension began to ease as the conversation changed. "When I used to get in trouble and I was going to get a spanking, not only did they make me go get the switch off the tree, but while spanking me they would tell me 'stop yo' hollarin' or I will really give you something to cry for. I was so confused. What could be worse than a butt full of welts from a switch?'"

"Oh, I got you," Eve said laughing. "My parents used to say a hard head makes a soft behind."

"I got that one too. What about, 'yo' behind don't believe fat meat greasy?'" Nathan sounded just like Eve's grandfather used to. His imitation sent her into fits of laughter.

"I forgot about that one," Eve said trying to recover.

They continued to talk about all the sayings ole black folks would say and things that used to happen when they were little. They talked until Nathan yawned. Eve looked at the clock. It was 2:45 a.m.

"Man, I didn't realize how late it was. I should be going," Nathan announced.

Eve really didn't want the night to end. "Do you have to work tomorrow?"

"No, I just didn't intend on keeping you this late, unless we..." Nathan allowed his words to cease and the deeper meaning to penetrate.

"Oh," Eve said fully understanding. "Well, I guess you'll be leaving then?"

Nathan laughed. "You a cold piece, girl."

Eve smiled seductively and walked Nathan to the door. "Not really, but it's not time to warm up."

Nathan smiled down at her and moved to kiss her. Before their lips met, he hesitated and gestured his head for her approval. She leaned into him and placed her lips on his. His mouth rested lightly on her lips and he breathed in deeply as if taking in her scent. *Is he going to continue this or not?*

Slowly, his lips began to move against hers and she opened her mouth allowing her tongue to escape and explore. Eve felt Nathan take in a breath and increase the pressure of his lips on hers. This kiss was so soft yet so urgent. Their mouths were like whirlpools. One would begin to pull away and the other would suck them back in. Eve's head began to spin, and she felt her body lean into Nathan. It was that movement that unlocked their mouths and allowed oxygen to fill their lungs. Eve laid her head against Nathan's chest trying to catch her breath. She finally stepped away and looked into his dark brown eyes. She barely heard his murmur goodnight. She watched him open the door and walk to his truck. Eve closed the door and locked all the locks and ran to the window to watch him pull away. As soon as his taillights disappeared down the street, she started hopping around her house with excitement. She had just kissed him goodnight with an unforgettable lip lock that promised more at another time. She screamed and ran up the stairs. She ran into her room pulling off her clothes and threw herself on the bed. She climbed into the bed and reached for the phone on her bedside table. She thought to call Teresa, but at three o'clock in the morning Lola was the only one that would wake up for some information like this. She dialed Lola's phone number, and she picked up on the first ring.

"Hello," Lola sounded as if it were three in the afternoon rather than in the morning.

"What are you still doing awake at this hour?" Eve asked.

"Just waiting on your damn call, bitch," Lola quipped sarcastically. "What the hell you want? I'm waiting on my date to get back with the condoms."

"You telling me he came to your house with no condoms?"

"He didn't come with enough condoms," Lola corrected.

"Oh damn. He had no idea who he was messing with."

"Apparently not." Lola laughed. "Well, I think he got a clue 'cause we have already used the ones he had and I'm not wasting mine on him. I have the extra large and that he ain't."

Eve laughed. "OMG, Lola."

"As Popeye would say 'I am what I am.' So what are you doing up this late? Or should I say early?"

"Nathan just left," Eve said modestly.

"Get your freak on, girl," Lola said obviously excited for her. "I guess I ain't the only one tramping tonight. So give me the juice. How was it? As good as Elijah?"

"I didn't have sex with him, Lola Bennett. You know I'm not into sleeping with two men at the same time," Eve said indignantly.

"Don't knock it 'til you try it," Lola muttered.

"Anyway," Eve said ignoring the comment. "He's fine and I rather tell you about our date when we don't have time issues. How long has ole boy been gone?"

"Oh, here he is right now. I'll call you in the morning. Let's go to the mall tomorrow afternoon. We can have an early dinner."

"Okay, I'll call Teresa and let her know what's up."

"If you must," Lola replied. Then she hung up.

Right then, Eve's phone beeped. It was a text. "I'm home. Thank you for a beautiful evening, until next time."

She sent a smile emoji and then she turned over and went to sleep with a smile on her face.

Company picnic.
Chapter 21

Nathan called early the next morning inviting Eve to his company picnic. Eve, half asleep, agreed then fell back to sleep. When Nathan called back and told her he was on his way to pick her up, she hopped up and ran into the shower. She was out the shower and dressed just a few minutes before her doorbell rang. Eve greeted Nathan at the door.

"Well, good morning."

"Good morning yourself." He leaned over and gave her a kiss. "I'm surprised you're ready. I knew when I called you were still asleep."

Eve looked embarrassed. "How did you know?"

"I heard it in your voice. That's why I took the long way over here. I wanted to give you some time."

"Well, if you were being considerate, why did you bust me out like that?"

Nathan laughed. "I'm sorry. I just couldn't help myself."

Eve smiled too. "Let me get my bag."

She walked into her room and came out with a blue canvas bag and a blue windbreaker jacket. Eve noticed Nathan was assessing her attire so she stopped, pretending to look in her bag, giving him the opportunity to check her out. She knew she looked cute in her white pedal pushers and the matching top. She turned around toward her room as if she forgot something so Nathan could get a look at how the top tied in three strands across the back and the rest was open. She could feel his eyes burning into her back. She had to smile to herself. She turned around and went back into the living room.

"Okay, I'm ready to go. Where is the picnic going to be?"

"It's at Howland Park, down by the lake."

Nathan opened the front door and ushered her out to the truck with his hand resting on the small of her back. Getting into the car, Eve smiled and thanked him. *He definitely has man hands. They aren't calloused but rough, thick, hmmmmm. I'm vibin' him.*

"I hope you don't mind," Nathan said as he settled in the driver's seat. "I have to go back to my house. I was in such a hurry to come pick you up that I left the ice chest sitting at the front door."

"No problem, I'd like to see where you live anyway."

"I don't live too far from where the picnic is being held."

"Then I should have driven over to your house," Eve complained. "It didn't make a lot of sense for you to travel twenty minutes away from the park to pick me up."

"No worries, mon," he said in a Jamaican accent. "I wanted to. Plus, if I would have been waiting on you, you would have still been sleep."

Eve chuckled at the truth of the statement.

Twenty minutes later, Nathan pulled up to a black wrought iron gate that he opened with a button from inside his car. They drove up the curved driveway of a ranch style home that overlooked the lake. It was beautiful. His lawn was tacked down by two weeping willows. His flowerbed pushed up gardenia bushes, and Eve noticed a red hummingbird feeder. His home, partially covered by the trees, was white with blue trim. Two huge mahogany doors stood like soldiers barring entrance into his abode.

"Would you like a quick tour?" Nathan asked getting out the truck.

"Sure."

He opened the door. Right in his foyer, he punched a few numbers on a keypad and then turned to smile at her. "Welcome to my humble home."

Eve smiled and walked in. Wood floors spread throughout the foyer and there was no carpet until she walked down three steps into the living room. There, she found a plush white carpet. Nathan had decorated his living room with an oceanic theme. He had two plush turquoise green leather sofas with additional throw pillows of tropical fish colors. Eve gasped at the coffee and end tables. They were bronze sea turtle sculptures that were topped with a glass top. She noticed the afghan thrown across a leather chair and ottoman that had sea turtles designed on it. For all the beauty in the room, the most gorgeous thing was the wall-size aquarium. There were so many fish that Eve couldn't believe her eyes.

"Nathan, this has to be one of the most beautiful living rooms I have seen in my entire life."

"Thank you," he said looking at his watch. "If you don't mind, I will show you the rest of the house later. I promised someone I would meet him at the picnic in ten minutes."

"Sure. I'm positive that I will have another opportunity."

"Yes you will."

***

Nathan and Eve pulled up to the picnic. There were people everywhere. Nathan grabbed the ice chest from the back, and Eve laid the blanket on top of the chest and grabbed the lawn chairs. They headed up toward the main tables of the picnic.

Nathan spoke to everyone they passed.

Damn he knows every damn body, Eve thought.

As if he could read her mind, Nathan said, "I know it seems strange that I'm talking to everyone that we pass, but when you are in security, it's your job to know everyone."

Eve, feeling stupid, nodded and smiled. She noticed he was looking around. "You looking for someone?"

"Not really. I just told one of the new consultants how to get here. I hope he didn't get lost. As a matter of fact, you might know him."

"Who is he?" Eve asked eyeing the table with the food.

"Elijah Mann."

Eve used every muscle in her body to still the physical reaction she was about to have at the mention of Elijah's name. *He better not show up. Oh My God, please don't let him show up.* "Yeah, I know who you're talking about. He was the consultant in our merger." Eve waited for Nathan to say something else, but another employee that worked with Nathan greeted them. Eve smiled, but she, too, began to look around.

Nathan found a spot in the middle of all the action under a tree. About fifty feet in all directions, something was going on; volleyball game, basketball court, and most definitely the eating. He sat the ice chest next to the tree and spread out the blanket. Eve dropped her bag and opened the chair sitting them right next to the ice chest. Just as she was about to pull bottled water from the ice chest, she heard Nathan laugh out loud and a shadow fell over her.

"Hey man. I'm sorry I'm late."

Eve turned to find Nathan hugging a fair-skin, elderly gentleman just as tall as he but not quite as big. Next to him stood a deep chocolate brown woman whose age only showed in silver gray hair. Eve immediately noticed that they were sister locs that made her think of Lola.

"Hello, chocolate," Nathan said to her, reaching over to hug and kiss her as well. Nathan turned and reached for Eve's hand to help her up.

"Donald and Susie Browne, I want you to meet a friend of mine, Eve Newborn."

Eve opened her hand to receive Donald Browne's hand when she felt herself swung up into a broad chest in a big bear hug.

"Donald, put that girl down. She doesn't know you and she may not want you hugging her like that," Susie spoke, punching her husband in the arm.

Donald sat Eve down and Eve lost her balance and fell into Nathan's chest. Eve was smiling.

"Well, hello to you too," said Nathan.

"I must apologize for my husband," Susie said, taking Eve's hand into her own. "He acts like he has no home training sometimes. It's really nice to meet you. Nathan told us a lot about you."

Eve raised an eyebrow and glanced at Nathan. He sat there smiling at her like a boy on his first day of school.

"Nathan and Donald worked together on the force."

"Yes." Nathan cut in, grabbing Donald and Susie's stuff and setting them up by his and Eve's. "Donald was my partner when I was just a rookie. This man was my father when my own father was too far away to help a brotha out."

"Look Nate, I'm not that damn old," Donald interrupted. "I shall only be fifty-four on my next birthday. So why don't you say I was more like an uncle."

"Alright Uncle Don," Nathan mocked. "Are you ready for some basketball?"

"You got it." Donald grabbed his water bottle and turned and kissed Susie. Eve smiled at the older couple. Their affection was so strong.

Nathan leaned over and kissed her lightly on the lips. "I shall return victorious, Eve. And when I do, have my food ready woman!"

"Will do." Eve replied in her most subservient voice going along with Nathan's little joke. "I shall have it all set up for ya. Anything else I can do?"

Nathan laughed and shook his head. "Come on old timer, fifty-four ain't as young as you think it is."

"Nathan, you ain't no spring chicken."

"Old man, my thirty-six years are still younger than your fifty-four."

Donald and Nathan walked toward the basketball court, and Susie and Eve sat in silence watching them go.

"It's nice to see Nathan with someone. I thought he was a

hopeless case." Susie's comment snapped Eve out of her thoughts.

"Why? Nathan is wonderful."

"Because that last woman he was serious about took it out of him. We didn't think he would ever get over it."

"Really? He made it sound like it was a mutual breaking up."

"It was. He didn't mean that he didn't love her. He just realized she couldn't live with him being a cop that wasn't ready to commit."

"Yeah, that's what he said."

"He must really like you," Susie said digging into her picnic basket.

"Why would you say that?"

"He doesn't allow us to meet many of the girls he dates. Actually, the last one we met was by accident. I think we ran into him at the movies. We invited them to dinner, but he declined. Today, he called and told us that he was bringing someone."

"We only had our first date yesterday."

"It must have been a hell of a date." Susie laughed.

"It was nice." Eve smiled.

They sat and talked for the next half hour. They waited until Donald and Nathan came back from playing before they got up to get food. Nathan had hurt his ankle in the game, so Eve offered to fix his plate. Surprised by the offer, he took full advantage of it.

"What do you want on it?"

"Whatever you put on the plate I will eat. I just appreciate the offer."

Eve put her hand on her hip and pursed her lips. "My momma did give me some home training."

"But that ain't all she gave you," Nathan said looking at Eve and licking his lips.

Embarrassed, Eve turned to Susie and asked her if she was ready. Both women went to get plates full of ribs, chicken, potato salad, and beans. Susie piled her plates expertly and had headed back to her husband quickly. Eve found herself running out of room fast and the plates felt weak. She balanced the two plates on both hands and started towards Nathan. When she faltered and almost dropped the plates, Nathan ran over to help.

"Thank you." Eve responded with a big smile. He brushed her hand lightly when he took the plates and Eve's stomach quivered. "I do not know how Susie manages. She got those two plates that had as much food as ours and she was gone."

"It's a lot of practice. They have six kids and the balancing act is her specialty."

"Damn six kids." Eve shook her head at the thought. "I used to want four, but two is looking better and better."

"Why not four? You're still young."

"Well, I'm not getting any younger, so I think I'll keep my goal at two. How long have Susie and Donald been married?" Eve asked as they walked.

"They've been married thirty-two years."

"That's almost as long as my parents," Eve responded.

"Yes. I look at them and I always say to myself that is what I want," Nathan said looking at his two friends laughing and eating on the blanket. "Susie married him as soon as he finished the academy. She has been able to handle his job, their kids, and everything. She is phenomenal."

"I should say so. She makes it hard on us women who can barely make it through a work day and we don't have to come home to anything."

Nathan and Eve made it back to their blanket and sat down to eat. The four of them ate and laughed for hours. When the picnic coordinator began to clean up, Eve and Nathan gathered their things to leave as well. Susie and Donald were still sitting.

"It was nice meeting you," Eve spoke reaching to give both of them a hug.

"Our pleasure, Miss Eve. We hope to see you Sunday."

"What's Sunday?" she asked turning to Nathan.

"Oh Susie and Donald always have a family dinner; I go because I'm like family."

"Yes. And you are now invited," Susie interjected.

"Why thank you. Hopefully, I will be able to make it."

"We will." Nathan answered for the both of them. "And we will get together next week to play golf."

"Be prepared to be beaten young man," Donald challenged with a handshake.

"We shall see."

Nathan grabbed most of their stuff and Eve the rest, and they headed to the car. Placing the things in the truck, Nathan took Eve home. When they pulled up to her house, he shut off the car and walked her to the door. Eve handed her house keys to him and he opened the door. As soon as they walked in the house, Eve found herself in his arms, being kissed passionately.

"I have wanted to do that all day," Nathan said after breaking the kiss.

"I wish you would have done that earlier. I could have used a couple of those today."

"Your wish is my command."

Nathan brought her face up to his and softly laid his lips on hers sucking in her breath. When she gasped, he put his mouth down over hers and allowed his tongue to search her mouth for all its sweetness. He held her face while he worked his lips over hers and her face. When he pulled away, she took a deep breath and smiled.

"Would you like something to drink?" she asked walking in the living room and turning on a lamp.

"Sure. Anything you have is fine."

Eve went into the kitchen to put some coffee on and Nathan went to the stereo and slipped on some jazz. Listening to her rattle pots and pans in the kitchen, he went in to investigate. Eve stood with her back to him. He admired her shape and found that he just couldn't help himself. He slipped his hands around her waist and nuzzled her neck. Eve melted back into his chest and he began to move her to the rhythm of the music.

She closed her eyes and tuned out everything but him. His hands spread across her stomach and moved down to her curvaceous hips. He allowed his hands to flow with her hips as she swung them back and forth with the cadence of the melody. He eventually turned her body to face him and moved his hands to her plump behind and pulled her close to him.

"You are a beautiful woman. I just want to love you tonight. Will you let me?" She could feel the evidence of his need as he kissed her ear, her neck and whispered all the things he wanted to do. She was butter in his hands. *I shouldn't be doing this but he feels so good. I don't want to be one of those women that is sleeping with more than one man.* Nathan began to knead her ample ass like fresh bread dough. With each caress, he pulled her into his groin. He was ready and she knew she didn't want it to stop.

She grabbed his hands and tried to lead him out of the kitchen to her room. He stopped her. Things seemed to move so fast. Eve suddenly found herself lifted in his arms as he assaulted her mouth with feverish kisses. After a moment, he allowed her feet to touch the ground so he could remove her top. She had no recollection of her halter being untied. It slid away like a fresh wave leaving the sand. Stimulating her lace-encased breast through her bra, her nipples were so extended that they almost popped out of her bra on their own. She ran her fingers down his muscled arms, back and chest. *This man is going to burn me alive.*

She didn't realize she was being moved to the kitchen table until the bowl of fruit fell to the floor. Trying to gain her balance, her hands ran across apples and bananas sweeping them to the floor with the rest. Her body rested partially on the table with her legs hanging off and Nathan in between them. He lifted her body off the table with one hand and with the other her pants were pushed down to her ankles and underwear pulled to the side. He continued to kiss her.

"You are so damn sexy." He whispered in a husky voice.

He continued to regale her with wanton thoughts and sexual compliments as his fingers manipulated her womanhood. He pumped his fingers in and out of her sending stimulating sensations. She didn't know if she had ever been that excited. Eve tried to slow everything down by pushing him away, but it was impossible. His mouth continued its assault on her neck and breasts while his hands left her body and unbuckled his pants. He pulled away and let his pants fall.

Eve couldn't believe the thrill that was waiting for her. He was bare under his pants. The sight of this man made her squeal in delight. He let go of a low, sexy chuckle and pulled her to him. He sank himself into her with such urgency that she felt her release almost immediately. His was a few minutes later.

He lay on top of her for a moment with labored breathing. He began to kiss her lightly and moved his weight off of her. "I'm sorry baby. I wanted that to be longer. I just wanted you so badly."

"There is no reason to apologize. You make me weak."

He smiled and leaned to give her another kiss before moving away. The absence of his body sent a shiver through her. She felt cold and moved to stand. When her feet hit the floor, her knees buckled and she caught herself leaning on the table once again. She felt his fingers trace along her face and she closed her eyes.

She wasn't sure if she was ashamed or not. She had just let a man take her on her kitchen table after two official dates. That was something she would have never thought she'd do. She had done so many things in the past months that she would have never done. He lifted her face to him and she opened her eyes. He smiled at her. She gave a tentative smile back.

"Are you going to let me make it up to you?" he asked looking intently in her eyes.

"Sweetheart, I will let you do anything you want to."

He leaned to give her another kiss.

She moved quickly off the table and grabbed his hand to lead him to her bedroom.

This time he followed.

Sunday dinner.
Chapter 22

Eve was getting dressed when the doorbell rang. She glanced at the clock and it flashed 7:30. *Damn Nathan, why do you have to be on time all the dang time?* She grabbed her shoes and headed toward the door when the doorbell rang a second time.

"I'm coming. Give me a second," she yelled.

Sliding to the foyer in her nylon encased feet, she opened the door. Nathan stood dressed in a navy blue suit, white pristine shirt and a silver and navy blue tie. *This man is fine, fine, fine.*

"Good morning, Mr. Garrison. You look good." She reached up and placed a quick kiss on his lips.

"Good morning, Ms. Newborn. Can I return the compliment?" he asked grabbing her hand and swinging her away from him to check her out.

Eve stepped out and modeled her outfit. It was a white blouse that gathered at the waist and lay slightly over her hips. It had an elastic neckline and long sleeves that billowed out at the elbow. The matching skirt hugged her hips until it reached her knees where it followed suit and billowed out around her calves. Her white sandaled heels were hooked to her fingers as she twirled for him.

"Hmmm, a vision in white; my own angel," he muttered while kissing her hand. Letting her go, he commanded her to finish getting ready so they wouldn't be late to the 8:00 service.

When they were out of service, Nathan headed toward his house. Eve had packed a change of clothes. She and Nathan were expected over to Donald and Susie's around eleven. She thought it would be easier to change at Nathan's house. When they pulled up to his house, Eve still was impressed. She never thought a single man would keep flowers in his yard. She was so taken with his house she didn't realize he had gotten out of the car.

"Come on," he said opening her door.

"I'm coming." She gave her bag to Nathan and jumped out with his assistance.

When they got inside, he led her to his spare bedroom where she could change. The room had the same white plush carpet. In the middle of the room was a queen-size bed that was framed by an oak head and footboard. The bed was made up in rich purple and lavender colors with matching curtains. On the wall above the bed was a sunset view done in the same colors of the room with little splashes and specs of gold. Eve didn't realize how long she had been just standing there until Nathan knocked on the door and told her to hurry so he could give her a tour. Coming out of her trance, she slipped out of her clothes and slipped into a pair of white pedal pusher overalls with a white t-shirt and flat white shoes.

Nathan met her outside the door and walked her through the kitchen and den. Every room in his house had its own personality, yet it was him—bold and daring. He saved his bedroom for last. Eve walked into it through double doors and fell in love. The white carpet was throughout his home and his room was no exception. The room itself was huge and the bed was the biggest she had ever seen. It sat high on a platform and was covered with a goose down comforter and various shades of blue and white pillows. Another aquarium was against the far wall. It wasn't as large as the one in the living room, but it seemed to hold just as many fish.

"Nathan, this is beautiful."

"Thank you." He snaked his arms around her waist and kissed her on the neck. "I wanted it to be the last room you saw. That's why I had you change in the spare room."

"Did you decorate your house?" Eve asked, giving him better access.

"Most of it, but I let my sister and my mom do my spare bedrooms. The room you was in had lavender in it. Do I look like a lavender person?"

Eve had to laugh. Lavender was not this man's color, but seeing his house she felt like she saw him more clearly.

Nathan began nuzzling her neck. His hands moved down to her hips. Eve closed her eyes and allowed the sensation of his touch to course through her body. He moved away from her and turned her to face him. He cupped her face and smiled as he placed a soft kiss on her mouth. Eve wrapped her arms around his neck and pressed her body into his. She could feel him responding.

He placed his hands on her bottom and lifted her from her feet to where she had to wrap her legs around his waist. He walked her to his bed and sat her down. Eve ran kisses over his face and neck and stopped only when she needed to scoot back on the bed. Nathan leaned over and unsnapped her overalls and began pulling them off. As he joined her on the bed, the phone rang.

"Are you going to get that?" Eve asked in a whisper against his lips.

"No. Let the machine pick it up," he said while removing her shirt. He began to eagerly kiss her breasts through her bra.

Eve allowed the ringing of the phone to be whisked away by the sensation of his tongue taking her away. The voice on the machine brought them both back.

"Nathan, hon. I know it has been a long time, but I was hoping that you would call me. I need to speak to you. Oh and Susie wants you to bring a bottle of wine to dinner. She is how I got your number."

Nathan was stone still and Eve felt the growing warmth they developed grow cold.

"Who was that?" Eve asked.

"That was Erica," he said gruffly as he got up from the bed. He handed Eve's t-shirt to her and reached down and grabbed her overalls. He waited until she had the shirt on to give her the overalls.

"We'd better get going. I'm going to have to stop at the store and get some wine."

Eve didn't say a word. She just got dressed and followed him to the car.

What the hell was Erica calling for? I thought he said she was long gone? Oh see, I don't need to get involved with no bullshit. Oh, this mofo and I are going to have to talk. I ain't having two Elijahs in my life.

Nathan said very little until they got to Susie and Donald's house. They greeted them at the door with hugs and smiles. Donald and Nathan headed toward the living room and Susie dragged Eve toward the kitchen.

"How was church this morning?" Susie asked as she cut up lettuce.

"It was good. Pastor Gregor is wonderful."

"Yes, I heard. Donald and I go to First Methodist."

"Oh." That was all Eve could say. After a moment passed she asked, "Is there anything you want me to do?"

"Oh no child, just keep me company. I thought my kids would be here today, but one by one they canceled."

"I'm sorry to hear that."

"Don't be; they are here almost all the time, so if they have something to do they know I don't get hurt that easily. Anyway, it gives us time to get to know a little about you and Nathan."

"Well," Eve said. "To be honest there is not a lot to tell, and after today I'm not sure there will be anything to tell."

"Why is that?" Susie asked, putting the knife down.

"Because Erica called him and that didn't sit right with him." *Or me.*

"Oh, Lord. If I would have known he would've been upset, I would have never given that child his number."

Eve sat with nothing to say.

"Oh Eve, that child is married. She just happened to be in town and she was calling to invite him to the reception. Did I mess something up between you and him?"

Eve was so relieved that Erica was married that she forgot

Susie was talking to her. "I'm sorry, Susie. What did you say?"

"I hope I didn't mess anything up between the two of you."

"Oh no, he just got quiet and distant. I guess he'll talk when he's ready."

Susie got up and began removing dishes from the cabinet. "Could you go and get those two while I set the table?"

"Sure." Eve walked toward the sound of the television where the two men were. She found them sitting on the couch with their face glued to the football game. She noticed Nathan looked less pensive than when they arrived. "Susie says for you two to come and eat. Dinner is ready."

Donald hopped up and went toward the kitchen.

Nathan looked at Eve and motioned for her to have a seat. "Eve, I'm sorry about earlier. When Erica called, I just knew there was going to be drama."

"Why?"

"It's like she has a homing device. One of the reasons my relationships never lasted too much longer than a month was that if I really began to like someone, she always called trying to rekindle. It usually has a disastrous effect on my relationships."

"Only if you let it."

"Well, yes and no. I don't have any feelings for her other than the first love feelings we all carry, but she would make it sound so believable and most of the women I dated would believe it all. I never would try to change their minds. But I want you to know the call was about the fact that she got married. Donald just told me that."

"I know. Susie mentioned it to me."

"Did she?" He sounded surprised.

Eve nodded.

"Well, are you alright with everything?" he asked, looking into her eyes.

"Nathan, everyone has a past." *And a present.* "I'm okay as long as you are."

"Good." He leaned over and kissed her. "Then let's go eat."

Dinner with Susie and Donald was great. Susie was a great cook and Eve learned all about Nathan's time on the police force and the antics they pulled on him as a rookie. They were full of non-stop stories and Eve laughed so much her sides ached. Nathan took it all in stride and even told funny anecdotes that occurred with his current job. He mentioned how he accidentally caught some of the big boys and gals in the office participating in some overtime activities. No matter who was talking and what was going on Nathan was attentive and affectionate toward Eve the whole time.

When Susie and Donald asked them to stay and watch a movie, Eve and Nathan agreed. They watched two movies and ate ice cream and popcorn.

"Hanging out with you people will make me fat," Eve commented as she rubbed her full stomach.

"I will still like you," Nathan assured her as he took her ice cream bowl into the kitchen.

Eve smiled and watched him walk through the door. She turned to where Susie and Donald were and they were oblivious to her as they snuggled and smooched on the couch.

Eve didn't hear Nathan come back until he spoke. "In my experience, when they start that it's time to go."

Eve slipped on her sandals and got up from the couch. Nathan announced they were leaving and Susie and Donald got up to see them out. Eve promised to return to meet all of Susie and Donald's children.

Nathan pulled up to Eve's house, got out and opened her door. Checking the house, he came back to the front door where he left her. He leaned down, placing his hands on her hips and kissed it.

Although Eve enjoyed the feeling, she didn't want anything physical right then. "Nathan, I'll see you tomorrow okay?"

Nathan looked hurt. "Okay. Just tell me, does not wanting me to stay have anything to do with Erica?"

"Oh no, it just means I have to get up early and I have some stuff to take care of."

Nathan searched her face for a moment. Eve gave him a smile and traced his lips with her finger. He smiled and took her finger into his mouth. Eve almost changed her mind but then he let go and smiled.

"Alright," Nathan said. He kissed her one more time and left.

When Eve closed the door behind her, she immediately headed toward the shower. After a nice hot shower, she called Nathan to make sure he got home and then called Teresa. When Teresa answered the phone she sounded a bit out of breath.

"Hey girl, what are you doing?"

"Girl nothing, Michael just left and I was cleaning up."

"Why? Did you have sex hanging from the chandelier?" Eve laughed.

"No," Teresa cut her off. "That's Lola's style. Actually, we had a fight."

Eve sobered quickly. "Are you alright? Did he hurt you? I will call Nathan and we will go kick his ass."

"No girl, I'm fine. After I threw my lamp at his head, he decided I was a crazy bitch and he was out."

"Well, what the hell happened?"

"He wanted sex and I didn't want to give him any?" Teresa replied dryly.

"Why?" Eve asked confused.

"Why what?"

"Teresa, it ain't like you two haven't had it before. What was the problem?"

"Lately, he has wanted it all the time. I suggested we wait until we were married. It's only a few weeks away. He got pissed off and then we started fighting. Anyway, why you calling? I thought you were having dinner with Nathan's friends."

"I did. They are so nice, and Nathan's house is gorgeous."

"You went to his house."

"Yeah, I changed my clothes there. Anyway, we started messing around and his phone rings . . ."

"You messing around with him already?"

Damn, I forgot who I was talking to. I show ain't going to tell her I slept with him. "Yes Teresa, but you will be happy to know nothing happened because his telephone rang..."

"Who was it?" Teresa interrupted again.

"Teresa," Eve yelled frustrated. "Let me finish. It was his ex-girlfriend."

"What the hell she calling for?" Teresa yelled in the phone. "He is a lying and cheating bastard, ain't he?"

"Do you want to know the whole story?" Eve asked calmly. She knew she called the wrong person, but she couldn't hang up now.

"Yes. Go ahead."

"Well, she called and that stopped our messing around. He got really pensive and didn't really talk until we got to Susie's. Then he found out that she was just calling to tell him that she got married."

"Oh."

"Yes, but I have to say," Eve said. "I initially thought like you and I didn't want a cheating bastard in my life."

"You mean *another* cheating bastard," Teresa mumbled in the phone.

"Maybe I should have called Lola."

"No, I'm sorry. I'm just being a bitch because I'm mad that Michael left, that's all. Did you work it all out with him?"

"Yeah Teresa, I did. I really like him."

"I can tell," Teresa answered.

Eve heard another voice. "Who is that?" Eve asked.

"Michael just came back. I got to go. Oh Eve. If you like him, don't let him get away."

Eve sat in the bed and thought about her day. *Oh yeah, I like Nathan a lot.*

It's all good!
Chapter 23

Over the next few months, Eve began to see Nathan exclusively with the exception of Elijah. Elijah's contract had ended with her company several months ago, making it easier for Eve. Elijah accepted a semi-permanent contract with Parkhaven and worked in the same building in I-Tech as Nathan. Once, when Nathan and Eve were discussing the merger at Parkhaven, she asked Nathan if he saw Elijah. He said they had very little contact beyond when he first ran the security check. Eve wasn't sure how she was doing it, but she managed to keep up with these two men. She found herself sweet on Nathan and addicted to Elijah. She sat her desk looking out her window thinking it all over.

This is a good combination. I have the best of both worlds. I have a man that wines and dines me every chance he gets. He's fine, sexy, a little paranoid, but all good. Even the sex is bomb! Elijah has something I can't let go of. He has an inexplicable draw. He can look at me or smile and I will do anything he wants me to do. I have done freaky things with him I never thought I'd do and may never do again with anyone else. Believe it or not that kind of binds us together."

Eve's phone rang and snapped her out of her thoughts. "Hello, this is Eve Newborn."

"Eve, hello, Gerald McClintoch." Eve sat up in her chair at the sound of her boss's voice.

"Yes sir, what can I do for you?" she asked in her professional voice. She began to shuffle papers.

"I was wondering do you happen to have Elijah Mann's phone number?" *Why is he asking me for Elijah's phone number?*

As if he were reading her mind, he went on to explain. "I need to get in contact with him about a few of his suggestions. My secretary is out sick and this temp is an idiot. Do you have it?"

Paranoid much, Eve? "Ah, yes sir. I have his cell. Would that be alright?"

"That would be fine. And thank you, Eve. I appreciate this."

Eve rattled the number off by memory and they hung up. She began to look over the papers on her desk, but her mind kept drifting to the two men in her life. She thought back to the first time she slept with Nathan. Eve smiled thinking about that night. Then, her mind shifted to the conversation she had with Lola the day after.

"Girl, was it good?" Lola asked eating a fudge brownie sundae.

"Honey, I thought I was just going to spontaneously combust. That man lit a fire I didn't know I had."

"Really?" Lola asked shocked. "Well, what about Elijah? I thought you said he was the bomb too?"

"He is!" Eve defended quickly. "That's the dilemma. I can't sleep on his skills either. They're just really different. With Nathan it's intense all the time. He seems like he's in a hurry to get to the good part. He doesn't leave anything untouched. It's just that we literally burn each other up. With Elijah, he's seductive and takes his time in loving every part of my body. He gives the best mind fucks that anyone can give. And you know the biggest erogenous zone is supposedly the brain."

"Which one is better?" Lola continued.

"It's not a matter of better; it's a matter of what I'm in the mood for. I have a little craving for Elijah style right now."

"When was the last time you saw Elijah?"

"It has been about two weeks," Eve answered, taking her spoon and scooping some of Lola's sundae. "He has been traveling."

"When do you expect to see him again?"

"Tonight," Eve replied. "He said he has a meeting that will let out late, so he got a room here and will go back home tomorrow.

There was a silence between them. Lola heaped a big bit of the delicious dessert in her mouth.

"Have you noticed we are always eating when we talk?" Eve asked

stealing another scoop of ice cream.

Lola shrugged. "Are you going to have sex with him tonight?"

Eve looked unsure. "Probably. Why else would I meet him? It's not like we have a real relationship."

Lola observed Eve and was worried about her friend. "But Eve I know you. Sexin' two men is not your style. That is my style, except I like it at the same time."

"Oh shut up!" Eve said laughing.

"Girl, you are already walking around in unfamiliar territory. You don't need to make your journey that much more difficult."

"You're beginning to sound like Teresa," Eve teased, trying to avoid the truth of Lola's words.

"As much as it pains me to admit it, she may have been right." Lola shook her head and shushed Eve when she tried to speak. "I'm still an advocate of letting grown folk do what they are going to do," she continued. "But girl, I'm sure you didn't see any of this coming. And me, with all my experience, didn't see it coming neither. You need to make some quick fast decisions."

"I know," Eve answered.

"What about this Erica. Is she a problem?"

"No."

"Well cool."

Eve did see Elijah that evening and they did have sex. Although it was good, as it always was, she was a bit preoccupied with the changes in her life in the last few months. When she left his hotel that night, she didn't go home and immediately drop off like she usually did. She sat up, listened to her CD collections and began to try and figure out what she was going to do.

After she dragged herself out of bed and to work the following morning, Pat walked in and put more paperwork on her desk. "Eve, your mother called and she wants you to call her back."

"When did she call?" Eve asked looking through the new files placed on her desk.

"When you were on the line with Mr. McClintoch. I'm just giving you the message when I realized you didn't pick it up off my desk."

"Where were you?" Eve snapped, irritated for losing time like that.

"I went on a break." Pat replied a bit perturbed.

"I'm sorry Pat. I'm just stressed," Eve said leaning back in her chair and rubbing her eyes. "Did the copy man call? He was supposed to come and fix the copier this morning."

"Yes. He'll be here in the next twenty minutes." Eve looked at the clock and it read 11:10 a.m. *Damn, I need to talk to my momma!* Eve picked up the phone dialed her mother. "Hey Mom."

"Hi sweetheart, I called to see if you can make it for lunch."

"Yes, that'll be fine, Mom. I'll come and pick you up at 12:30."

"Okay, but we don't have to go out. I made some homemade stew and cornbread."

Eve stomach growled. She loved her momma's cooking. "Okay I will be there around 12:30 then."

At 12:30 on the dot, Eve was pulling up in front of her mother's home. It was a ranch style brick home with green trim. Her mother and stepfather bought it right before they were married. Eve's biological father died right after she was born and her mother married again when she was two. Although her dad was technically her stepfather, Seth Newborn had been the only daddy she had known and he treated her like his own. Eve remembered she and her mother lived in the house about a month before the wedding. She was a flower girl in her mother's wedding, and she was so happy that her mother was giving her another daddy. Even when her little sister came, she never felt misplaced.

"Hi Mommy."

Eve's mother met her at the door. Judith Newborn stood all of five feet three inches and was a petite woman. She had cocoa colored skin and the most beautiful expressive hazel eyes. Eve used to envy her mother's beauty. Everyone had told her she took after her natural father. A few folks, who didn't know Seth wasn't her biological father, commented that she looked a lot like him.

"Hey babe, Come on in. I got to pull the cornbread out of the oven."

Eve walked into the familiar living room. She looked around and smiled. It always brought memories back of her little sister and her running through the house and playing hide and go seek. She made her way through the living room into the kitchen. The aroma of freshly baked cornbread was in the air. Eve saw a big stockpot on the stove that held her mother's awesome stew. Eve walked over to the cabinet and pulled out two bowls while her mother pulled the cornbread out of the oven and began to melt butter on it.

"Thanks for calling me, Momma," she said, filling the bowls. "I have been meaning to call and talk to you."

"Well, how is that boyfriend of yours? I heard he's something special."

"How did you know about him?" Eve asked setting the bowls of stew on the table.

"Your sister told me. You know she can't hold water in a water bucket." She laughed placing fresh cut hunks of cornbread in front of Eve and taking a seat herself.

"Well, Momma that's what I was going to talk to you about," Eve said. She waited a minute and said her grace. Then she continued. "His name is Nathan Garrison. He's head of security in one of the buildings downtown."

"Does he look good?" her mother asked, scooping stew from her bowl.

"Of course, do I ever go out with ugly men?"

"There was that boy Damian in high school. Oh child, that boy was ugly."

"No he wasn't," Eve laughingly protested.

"Yes, he was. That boy was in bad need of a dentist *and* a

dermatologist." Both Eve and her mother laughed.

"That's wrong, Momma. That is so wrong."

"I'm being truthful. Anyway, so how serious is it with you and this Nathan?"

"We've just started dating. He's a really nice guy. I think you and Daddy will like him."

"When do we get to meet him?"

"I'm not sure. I want to see where we are going before I bring him to the family."

"I understand." She was satisfied with what she heard. "Did I tell you what happened with your father?"

"No, what happened?"

"His boss at work walked off the job and left all responsibility in your father's lap."

"Well, it's not like Dad can't handle it."

"Yes, I know he can..." Eve let her mother go on about her father, but was only half listening. She was curious how to bring up her situation. She could always talk to her mother about things. Then she thought better of it. She didn't want to bring her into this mess.

I got it bad and that ain't good!
Chapter 24

Eve sat on the couch watching television. It was a Friday night and Nathan was out of town. Teresa called and tried to get her to go and taste the food for the reception with her and Michael. Eve didn't feel like being with the couple of the year. Lola had tried to get her to go to the club, but Eve had decided she was going to stay in tonight.

Eve jumped in the shower and decided to shave. As she ran the razor up her leg she imagined what it would look like if she shaved her public hair off. Having never done it before, she decided to do something a little different and daring. *Hell, it's not like life isn't daring for me right now.* After she showered and shaved she looked at herself in the mirror. She didn't know what all the hype was about. *This shit looks weird, but I don't have to worry about my bikini lines. They're taken care of.*

After the shower adventure, Eve put on her pajamas, snuggled up with her blanket and a bowl of popcorn ready to watch her favorite classic movie, *All About Eve*. The movie just started when the phone rang.

"Hello."

"Hey, what are you doing?"

Eve sat up at the sound of Nathan's voice and turned the volume down on the television. "I'm watching a movie. What are you doing? Are you in your room?"

"No, I'm back in town. My family is a mess, but I love them."

"How was your sister? "

"She is fine. She is heartbroken over some guy she was seeing. My mother made it sound as if she was suicidal, but she's okay."

"I'm glad." Eve glanced at the television and saw Betty Davis.

"I just wanted to let you know I'm home. Can I come over?"

"Sure, if you want." Eve was in the mood for some good loving and that's typically what she got with Nathan. *I wonder if Nathan is capable of getting a little freaky,* she thought as she heard him yawn. "You sound tired. You need a back massage?"

"Actually..."

Eve's phone clicked signifying there was another call.

"Hold on Nathan. My phone is ringing." She clicked over. "Hello."

"Hmmm, do you know what I'm craving?" Eve's stomach contracted. It was Elijah.

"What exactly is that?"

"Your punany."

"Is that right?" She said coyly.

"Can I have a lick?"

"Will that be enough? Just one lick?"

"Not nearly, can you meet me?"

"Where?" Eve asked too quickly. She was craving some Elijah.

"I'm in room 233 at the Airport Hotel."

"Give me thirty minutes."

"Okay."

Eve hopped up off the couch and hung up the phone. It immediately rang again. *Oh shit! I left Nathan on hold. Think, think, think. Okay, calm down and just flow.* She answered the phone. "Hey, I'm sorry. That was my mother." She lied. "She called to tell me my sister was at it again with her boyfriend. I'm going over there now."

"You shouldn't go over there alone. I will meet you," Nathan offered.

"That's not necessary. My sister is at my parents, and so I won't be in danger. Plus, I can hear it in your voice, you're tired. Go on to sleep and I'll talk with you later."

"Baby, I will be there in fifteen minutes to take you to your mother's," he insisted.

"No! That's okay. Please stay home and get some rest."

Nathan yawned again. "Alright, call me in the morning to let me know what happened."

"I will, Nathan. Take care, baby."

When Eve hung up the phone, she ran to her room to change clothes. The drive over, she wondered what was wrong with her. The greatest guy she ever met was into her and she was headed for Elijah. She debated about turning around and going back home. Then she thought maybe she should call Nathan from her cell and head to his house. She had been there twice and she thought she could find it. Eve couldn't make up her mind until she found herself pulling into the airport hotel.

When Elijah opened his door, he looked as good as always. He leaned over and gave her a kiss on the cheek and a small squeeze. Eve moved in and took off her coat. She was wearing a green pullover jumper and black flats. He looked at her and smiled. She went and sat on the couch in the room. She sat there anticipating what was to come and confused at the same time. He leaned on the door and stared at her. It was at that moment she began to feel cheap.

"Would you like something to drink?"

"No, thank you."

He walked over and pulled a soda from the refrigerator and handed it to her as he sat on the other end of the couch.

"What happen to the coy lady that I spoke to on the phone?"

Eve took a sip and looked up at him. "She is really trying to figure out if she should be here."

"Why?"

"Because I feel like a dog." She got up and moved across the room. "You call and bark and I came wagging."

Elijah chuckled to himself. "I don't think of you that way. I was thinking of you in some certain ways, but that was not one of them." He stressed his words to make his meaning evident. "Although that dog reference does conjure up some images."

At that time, there was a knock at the door that startled Eve.

"Don't worry. It's just room service." Elijah got up and answered the door. After paying a tip, he pushed in a tray of fruit: chocolate dipped strawberries, strawberries with whipped creamed cheese, honey glazed bananas, sliced kiwi and grapes. On the other platter were different cheeses and in the big silver bucket a bottle of wine.

"Well damn!" Eve said walking over to get a good look. She reached down and picked up one of the strawberries. She could never resist strawberries. She took her first bite with her eyes closed and savored the juices of the fruit. Her groaning made evident her enjoyment. When she opened her eyes, Elijah sat there staring at her.

He grabbed her hand that held the berry and brought it to his own mouth. He took a bite and the juice ran down her fingers. Eve found herself watching his mouth as he chewed. He never took his eyes off of her. He ran the tip of his tongue over her fingers catching the juice into his mouth. His tongue encircled her tasty digits and began a sensuous assault.

Eve felt her being quiver. *Well, I will be damned. This man is licking me.*

"Is that your one lick?" she asked a bit huskier. The coy girl was back.

"Not in the least. This is only the beginning." Elijah pulled her to him and began kissing around her mouth. His hands dipped down into the tray again and grabbed more fruit, which he shared with her between kisses.

It was one of the most sensual moments that Eve experienced in her life. Her nerves were on end and the hair on her body rose. She felt his breath on her neck and face smelling of chocolate and fruit.

Placing the fruit back on the table, Elijah moved her to the bed. She sat facing him. He was on one knee in front of her. Slowly, he began stroking her thighs. The green jumper found its way past her waist on the floor in what seemed to be a matter of seconds. Eve wore a green satin bra and matching panties. Her heart fluttered when he gave her a look of admiration. Having taken his hands away for a moment, they returned to her thighs although they moved from the outside to the inside. He gently parted her legs and continued to rub. Eve was so turned on, if he would have asked her to bark like a dog, she would have howled at the moon. His hands made their way to her underwear and slipped over her womanhood. Eve let out a moan she didn't know she was holding.

"It seems as if you have a surprise for me," he said smiling. Eve was confused for a moment and then remembered she had shaved. "Do you trust me?" he asked.

Eve nodded.

"Answer me. Do you trust me?" Elijah allowed his finger to slip inside her.

"Yes," she said breathlessly.

"Good." Elijah got up and walked over and picked something up off the dresser. Walking back, he sat on the bed and brought up a scarf to cover her eyes.

Eve resisted.

"I thought you said that you trusted me?"

Eve looked at him. She moved her hand and allowed him to tie the scarf around her eyes so she couldn't see.

"Unsnap your bra for me," he whispered.

Eve almost didn't hear him. With shaking hands, she reached up and unsnapped it from the front. Her breasts were released and she sensed Elijah's smile. He reached up to tweak both her nipples. Another moan escaped her.

He then moved away from her, and she listened trying to locate him in the room. After a few moments, she felt his breath on her face. Then she felt his hands touch her breasts with a silk cloth and her nipples were buzzing. He stretched it across her chest and allowed both of his hands to follow the length of her arms. When his hands reached hers, he grasped them tightly and brought her hands over her head causing her back to arch and breasts to rise toward the ceiling. He held her hands over her head with one hand and brought the other down to knead her bosom and used the scarf to further agitate her hard buds.

The sensation of the silk and his hand caused Eve to stir and arch her back even more. It was then she noticed that he took the silk cloth and wrapped both of her hands over her head and tied them to the headboard. She allowed her fear to creep back up.

"What are you doing?"

"Trust me," he insisted. "Lift up so I can remove your underwear."

Eve lifted her body. Elijah grabbed the thin sides and moved the lacy green panties over her hips and down her legs. When they were off, he smiled and stuck them in his pocket. Eve felt his weight leave the bed and, unsure what he was going to do, she waited. Eve lay before him in all her glory. She heard the intake of his breath. She felt him come over and kiss her bare mound.

"Damn baby, that is some powerful shit you are doing to me. You are trying to kill me with your bare baby girl, aren't you?"

Eve smiled wishing she could see his expression.

"I want to make a fruit dessert with cream and eat it and then I want to get drunk tonight. Is that alright?"

Eve didn't know how to answer that. She couldn't imagine why he would want to do that.

"Is that alright?" he asked again, smiling at her.

"I guess," she whispered.

It was then that Elijah went back to the fruit tray and got the whipped cream cheese. He dipped his finger in the cream and smeared it on Eve areoles. The chill of the cream caused her distended nipples to harden even more. He then began to smear it all over her breasts, stomach and her bare baby girl.

"Hmmm, I love whipped cream cheese." He stuck his finger in the bowl to get the last little bit out. As he traced her mouth with the cream-covered finger, he whispered, "That is almost the best part of this dessert."

Next, he held a grape bunch over her mouth and allowed her to eat the grapes from the vine. The juice began to slide down her face and he would lean over and lick it off her. After feeding her a few grapes, he plucked them off the vine and strategically placed them all over her body. Then he fed her strawberries and did the same thing, and the same with the kiwi. Eve was excited. The rich tangy flavors of the fruit and Elijahs touch almost sent her over the edge.

She felt him change positions to where he was straddled over her. She began to feel his tongue nip and lick at her neck. He licked her body clean. Whenever he encountered a piece of fruit, his teeth would barely scrape her skin sending chills through her body. His teeth grazing against her nipples as he plucked a grape off them sent an orgasm so strong through her that she jerked lifting him off her body. Not even allowing her climax to pass, he continued. With every lick, he sent a message down to her waiting pussy that he was coming.

When he was finished, he announced he needed a drink. "Would you like something to drink Eve?" he asked.

Eve nodded, still dealing with phantom licks like the ones that assaulted her before. He brought a glass of wine over to the bed and helped her sit up a little to drink. He took the blindfold off and she looked at him. He sat and smiled. She tried to loosen her hand, but he stayed her.

"Eve, I'm not finished." He walked over grabbed the wine from the table and sat back down. He leaned over and kissed her gently on the mouth. She tasted the cream and fruit that were laid on her body. He tasted the wine she consumed. "Evie, it's time to get drunk."

"I don't want to get drunk. I just want to be untied."

"Evie, I want to get drunk," he said as he leaned in to kiss her. It was an open-mouth kiss, slow and deliberate. She almost didn't notice Elijah pouring the wine on her body. "I need to wash down my dessert with wine." He whispered against her lips. "The wine and your body intoxicate me. I want to get drunk."

He continued to pour the wine over her body and then he moved away from her and slurped the wine from her skin. This new sensation sent her pulses into overdrive. He poured a little at a time and licked it off.

"I want to get drunk, okay?" Elijah kept repeating himself as he poured and licked.

And with every lick Eve would answer "okay." All night long Elijah tasted her with his tongue and body, and Eve drank as much as he thinking *this is a hangover that I will gladly endure.*

<u>Twisted.</u>
Chapter 25

Eve was digging around in her closet for the mate to her shoe when there was a knock on the door. She rushed to the door and swung it open to reveal her chocolate Adonis. Nathan stood smiling at her.

"You miss me?" he asked, slipping his arms around her waist.

"You know it." Eve strained her neck to taste those delectable lips.

"Good. You ready?"

"Not quite," she said looking at him from head to toe. He wore beige linen pants and a button down cream silk shirt. "I think I might need to take it up a notch. Come on in." She moved away from the door motioning for him to close the door.

As Eve strolled to her room, Nathan noticed her yellow pedal pushers and matching crop blouse. "What you have on looks good to me." He yelled after her. "But if you want to change that will be fine because we got a little time." Nathan plopped down on the couch and turned the television on. He scanned her digital cable for a minute or so and settled on watching videos.

Eve had just finished buttoning her linen pantsuit when Nathan's yelled to her from the living room. "Hey Eve, Erica called me again today."

Eve stopped in her tracks and sat on the bed. *I wonder what this will mean.* "What did she want?"

"Nothing really. She was calling to tell me she heard I was with someone special and she wanted to invite me to her second wedding. She told me to bring you with me."

By this time, Eve had made her way to the living room. Unaware that Eve had come out of her room, Nathan was startled when she spoke. "Are you going to the wedding?"

"I hadn't really thought about. One of the reasons I brought it up was that I wanted to talk to you about it. "

"What is the other reason you brought it up?" she inquired suspiciously.

"I don't want any secrets between us," Nathan answered, getting up from the couch, turning off the television and walking around to her. He lifted her chin so that she was looking him in the eyes. "I want to be straight with you and let you know what is going on in my life at all times and on all levels."

Eve just stared back and kept silent. *On all levels, huh?* Her mind flashed on Elijah. *I'm not sure Sir Nathan if that will be reciprocated.* Eve finally smiled. "You ready?"

"I am. Let's go woman." Nathan grabbed her hand and led her out the door.

Nathan took Eve to a local playhouse. When Eve found out where they were going, she was so excited. It was a new play with an all African American cast and it had been receiving great reviews.

As they walked into the lobby, Eve saw a lot of people she knew and worked with. As she conversed, Nathan stood patiently by and scanned the sea of faces. When he came across one that was familiar to him, Eve noticed his body stiffen. When she realized he wasn't looking or listening to her, she followed his gaze. There was a beautiful, tall, brown-skinned sista that reminded Eve of the model Beverly Johnson. The girl had it going on and she knew it.

"Who is that?" Eve whispered to Nathan.

"That's Erica." He replied through tight lips. As he spoke Erica's eyes caught his and smiled. Nathan's eyes narrowed.

If there's nothing there, what is his problem? Eve watched Erica make her way toward them.

Nathan's hand tightened in Eve's.

"Hello Nathan." She greeted him with a kiss on the cheek. "It has been a long time since I have seen you."

"Hello Erica." Turning to Eve, Nathan introduced them and Eve spoke and smiled. Erica gave a perfunctory smile and turned her attention back to Nathan.

Well damn!

"Nathan." She gushed with a genuine smile. "Are you going to come to my wedding reception? You know Robert and I already married in Europe, but we're having the reception here."

"Yes. I know. That is the message you left on my machine," Nathan answered stiltedly.

"Well, you never responded. Are you coming?" Erica asked as if she might pout if he said no. She placed her arm on Nathan's and moved into his personal space.

Eve, caught off guard, found herself moved away from Nathan, although he never let go of her hand. *I don't believe this bitch. Does she not see me standing here while she's trying to drape her ass over Nathan?*

"I just brought it up to Eve today," Nathan responded, backing away from Erica and pulling Eve back to his side. Eve linked her arm in his. Reaching down, he grabbed Eve's hand and kissed it before he continued to address Erica. "We haven't had a chance to discuss it."

It was at that moment Erica took the time to give Eve the look over. Eve noticed a look of curiosity. "Eve, have we met before?" Erica asked staring at her. "You look familiar to me."

"I don't believe so," Eve replied offering a weak smile.

"May I ask what it is you do? Maybe I have seen you in business circles."

Eve cleared her throat and tried not to look irritated. "I'm an office manager."

"Oh," was all Erica said, but she looked at Eve with a look of uncertainty. "Well, I'm sure we haven't run into each other. My husband owns numerous hotels, and when he is out of town I take care of business here."

"Oh." Eve was unimpressed. She thought Erica very shallow

and she couldn't see how Nathan had been with her.

The lights began to flicker in the building signifying the play was going to start. A handsome older man walked up behind Erica and touched her arm.

"Erica, Sweetheart, we need to find our seats."

"Oh, Robert, this is Nathan." If Eve hadn't seen it with her own eyes, she wouldn't have believed that someone could have transferred all her charm and energy that was focused on Nathan to the man standing beside her. "Nathan, this is my husband, Robert."

Nathan shook hands with the man and introduced him to Eve.

"Your wife is lovely," the man said.

Eve blushed and then realized what he said. *Oh wow, he thinks we are married.*

Erica buzzed in quickly, "Uh, they're not married."

All three standing there looked surprised at her outburst. Robert was humble enough to give an apologetic nod and smile. There was an awkward silence. "Well, I can hear the orchestra," Robert spoke loudly enough for his voice to cover the silence that loomed. "The play must be starting. It was nice meeting you both." Robert grabbed Erica by the arm and they left Nathan and Eve staring after them.

After the play, Nathan and Eve went to dinner raving what a great play it was and reliving the scenes. After they finished eating, they decided to go to the lake where the company picnic had been and walk along the banks. As they walked, Nathan grabbed Eve's hand and brought it to his mouth.

"You did that when Erica was talking to us earlier," Eve mentioned.

Nathan sighed, knowing they would have to discuss her sooner or later. "I just wanted her to know I'm fully occupied with you."

"Why would that be necessary for you to do, when she should be purely occupied with Robert?"

"I cannot even imagine what Erica is thinking." He sighed. "I'm more curious to know what you are thinking."

Eve paused for a moment. "I'm thinking that Erica wants you still."

"Well, she can't have me. I want you to have me." He reached down and placed a soft kiss on her mouth.

"But you had an extreme reaction to her. I was looking at your face when you saw her. You were so tense."

"She makes me that way," Nathan said leading Eve to an empty bench. "I made it sound like there was no beef between us when we broke up, but the fact is she has always been a bitch. I didn't recognize it until she left me for another man that had more money."

"Yeah, I can see the bitch thing," Eve mumbled.

Nathan laughed. "So you can see that I'm still very much angry with her but mostly with myself for being a sucker."

"You're not a sucker, Nathan. You're a lifesaver. Cherry flavored and all." They both laughed.

"Girl, you are too much," he said kissing her hand again.

"What?" Eve asked with her eyes growing wide and a huge smile. "I was just agreeing with you." Nathan chuckled a moment then he grew serious.

"Eve, you got my headed swimming."

"Well, let me throw you a life jacket," Eve said, leaning over and giving Nathan a long, sensuous kiss. Nathan chuckled when she pulled away.

"I'm sure with that you just threw water on a drowning man," he said.

Eve smiled, wiping the lipstick off his lips. His eyes eventually caught hers and she could feel his intensity in her soul.

"Eve baby," he said with a sense of urgency. He reached for her and pulled her into his chest. "Girl, you got me so twisted. You are everything I have ever wanted in a woman."

Eve allowed her head to continue to lie on his chest. His

muscular arms wrapped around her frame giving her much comfort. *He feels so damn good!*

"Eve, can I be with you tonight?"

She almost didn't hear him over his rapidly beating heart.

"Yes," she said, figuring that they could about Erica another time.

When they arrived back at the house, no words were spoken. Nathan took the key from her and opened the door. His usual method was to make her wait outside as he checked her house. This time, he grabbed her hand and she followed him through the procedure until they ended up in her bedroom. He turned to look at her and Eve pushed him back until he fell on the bed. She began to disrobe and his eyes never left her face. Even as her shirt gave way and her pants dropped, he held her eyes. It wasn't until she began removing her under garments that he allowed his eyes to wonder over her body.

Completely nude, Eve walked between Nathan's parted legs and pushed his chest so that he would lie back on the bed. She climbed atop him and began to unbutton his shirt. When she reached for his belt, she leaned over and licked his hardened nipples. His moan was full and robust. She knew he wanted her and that turned her on even more. As she loosened his pants, Nathan arched his pelvis, also lifting her on him like she was riding a horse, in order to move his pants down his legs. Once he got them past his narrow hips, he brought his body back down and Eve was able to pull his pants and underwear completely off. Nathan reached for her and Eve willing climbed aboard and road the train to the Promised Land.

Hours later, Eve lay on Nathan's chest exhausted. Their love session was intense and their energy was spent.

"Eve, you might be the death of me. Where did you learn those tricks?"

You don't even want to know. "You didn't know?" Eve said lifting her body up on her arms. "I'm an around the way girl."

"I'm glad you came around my way."

"So am I." Eve sat and ran her fingers over Nathan's face as he lay with his eyes closed. "Nathan, do you think you're going to Erica's reception?"

Nathan's eyes popped open, but he didn't move. "Where did that come from?"

"I was thinking about our encounter with her and how you said you feel about her."

"You don't have to worry about Erica," Nathan said, moving to his side and resting his head in hand.

"I wasn't worried," Eve countered quickly.

"Baby, I told you she's not an issue."

"I know," Eve said, leaning back in the bed as Nathan moved to get out of the bed. "Are you leaving?" Eve asked alarmed.

"No. I'm going to the restroom."

"Oh."

Nathan ran back to the bed and jumped on causing Eve to roll toward him. He leaned over and whispered in her ear. "It's all about you. You have me wrapped around your finger," he declared. Kissing her on the forehead, he hopped off the bed and ran into the restroom.

Nathan, my dear, I'm much more twisted than you.

<u>Relax, relate . . . what the hell?</u>
Chapter 26

Eve went to work early on Monday morning. Even though she had spent Friday evening with Elijah, she spent most of her Saturday and Sunday with Nathan. She and Nathan agreed on Sunday that they would make it an early evening because they both had to be in the office early. She had so much paperwork that she was occupied most of Monday morning. It wasn't until Pat peeked in the door that Eve ever looked up from her computer.

"Yes Pat, what's up?"

"The copier went down again and the paper wasn't delivered yet."

Eve sighed. "And exactly why are you telling me?" Eve was so frustrated with the fact that her employees didn't seem to be doing their jobs. Where was the department head?

"Well, Angela called in sick today. No one else seems to know who she talked to or what is going on. I came to ask you what you wanted me to tell them because you were the one that handled this stuff the other day."

Running her hands through her hair, she picked up the phone. "Yes, I need to talk to Thomas Green." A few moments passed. Eve motioned for Pat to sit down. "Ah yes, Mr. Green. This is Eve Newborn over at Clearview/Oxford." She motioned for Pat to give her the notes about the copier. "You sent a maintenance man out to service our copier just a few days ago." Glancing down at the notes, she clarified, "Tuesday to be exact. This machine has since broken down a third time." Eve speech paused indicating the man on the line was speaking.

"You want to know my title? I'm the director of operations. I'm the one they come through to get approval to use your company. Now, what I would like you to do is send over a loaner and take this one into the factory for repair. I know this will not be a problem because this was a negotiation in our contract. If it is a problem, we will have to review the contract and see what the stipulation for termination of the contract is. Am I making myself clear?" Eve listened and nodded her head as Pat sat patiently. Finally, Eve spoke again. "Thank you Mr. Green. My assistant will be taking over this call to get some more information and she will be expecting you later this afternoon." She pressed hold and hung up the phone.

"Okay Patricia, about the paper, I think that was brought in after hours yesterday. I saw a truck down there unloading when I went out. It may be down in the storage room. Have someone from Angela's area check. If not, make the phone call to the company and tell them we will need the paper today or we will need to get it from another source here on out. I think our contract with them is almost up. Is there anything else?"

"You got a call from your friend, Teresa. She asked that you call her at the office."

"Got it, thanks Patricia. Go ahead and take the call. Get on that other stuff as soon as possible?" Pat nodded and left the room. Eve called Teresa's direct line.

"This is Teresa Charles. How can I help you?"

"Hey girl, what you want?" Eve asked sitting back in her chair.

"Hey, I want to remind you that we're supposed to be having a spa time today." This was a treat Teresa and Eve were giving Lola in celebration of Lola being named director of the cultural center.

"Oh yeah, let me get off the phone, so I can be on time."

"Ok. See you then."

It was about an hour later that Patricia knocked and entered Eve's office again.

"Well," Patricia began. "I guess now is the time to remind you that you are meeting both Teresa and Lola at the Green Mint Spa at noon."

"Yes. Thank you," Eve said taking a deep breath and filing papers away. "I need that right now more than you know. You are a lifesaver. Cherry flavored most definitely."

Patricia smiled. "Is there anything else?" she asked before she left.

"Just tell me that after the spa I don't have to come back."

"Your calendar is clear."

"Great."

Eve met up with Lola and Teresa outside of the spa. They all went in, were greeted and taken into separate rooms. They removed their clothes and put on club robes. They were in for a treat. Teresa, Lola and Eve were carted off in three different directions to get their body wraps and massages. They didn't meet up again until about an hour later in the steam room.

"Teresa, girl, I owe you my life for this treat. I have not felt this way since my very first multiple orgasm," Lola exclaimed causing some of the other women in the room to snicker.

"Shut up Lola! I can't take you anywhere," Eve scolded, embarrassed enough for everyone.

Teresa laughed. "I'm happy that you enjoyed it. I was told when we leave here, we all go to the same room to get our facials, manicures and pedicures."

"Are my acrylics going to be a problem?" Lola asked raising her hand and showing off her beautifully manicured claws.

"No they shouldn't," Teresa answered, closing her eyes and laying her head against the wall.

"Lola, didn't you say you were thinking about taking them off?" Eve asked, going over to put more water on the steam rocks.

"Yeah, but it just wouldn't be me."

"I need to be going to get this hair done," Eve added, tightening the bun she made at the nape of her neck.

"I know what you mean," Lola agreed and reached through her locked mane. "I need to get relocked, so I will be looking good for my date. This man is all of that. I met him at the center. He's an artist that is showing his work there. He is fine. He looks like Terrance Howard and I'm trying to build an *Empire*."

"Damn Lola. He must look good," Teresa said, adjusting the towel around her breast. "Does he have a friend that looks like Morris Chestnut, then maybe I can have a thing going with *The Best Man*. If he does I will be at the opening of his show at the center."

"I hear ya girl, because that man is fine too." Lola gave Teresa a high five.

Eve sat back laughing and thinking to herself, neither one of those men had anything on Nathan or on Elijah for that matter.

"You shall be happy to know that we're going to the hair dresser when we leave here," Teresa announced.

"I'm not about to let these White folk up in my locks," Lola announced with certainty. "That's not going to happen."

"Girl, you think I'm going to let them touch mine?" Teresa asked insulted. "Our appointment at Regency Tough Cuts is at 2:00 p.m."

"How did you get us all in at Re Re's?" Eve asked excited about getting her hair done.

"I reserved Regency herself, Sabrina, and Vincent to do all of our hair," said Teresa.

"I know I'm sitting in Vincent's chair," Lola insisted. "That man can do some locs. He's not going to have time to lock them all up, but he can wash and have them looking like something."

"That's the way I planned it." Teresa went on. "Eve will sit in Sabrina's chair and I will sit with ReRe."

Eve was cool with that because she liked Sabrina. She was good peoples and good at what she did. "As long as I look good for tonight. I'm seeing Elijah," Eve said moving back against the wall.

"Where is Nathan?" Teresa inquired obviously trying to get Eve focused on someone other than Elijah.

"He promised the young men he mentors that they would hang out tonight. I try not to interfere with that."

"That's cool. I really like Nathan."

"So do I. Did I tell you all that we ran into his ex, Erica?"

"What!?" Lola and Teresa screamed at the same time.

"Yes, we went to that play the other weekend and she was there with her new husband."

"Well, what happened?" Lola asked. "Dish hon, dish."

"What it comes down to is that Nathan and she had a bitter break up. She acts as though she still wants him, but he ain't trying to get with her."

"How you know for sure?" Teresa asked.

"Because he told me that I was what he wanted in a woman."

"Well, alright diva, you go!" Lola exclaimed giving Eve a high five.

"I hear you, but I'm still, you know, trying to take it slow." *Yeah right, that is why you and Nathan have been going at it like bunnies.*

"Well good. It is about time we stop thinking about unavailable men and concentrate on those who are available," Teresa said.

"Speaking of unavailable what is Elijah doing here? Has he moved here?" Lola asked.

"I'm not sure." Eve shrugged. "I'm not worried about it." Eve tightened her towel and leaned back against the wall with her eyes closed. *I can't worry about it, because if I do I will get caught up.*

"Eve, I heard that his wife is white," Teresa spoke quietly.

"What the hell? That was some random shit," Lola screamed. "Where in the hell did you hear that from?"

Eve was quiet.

Teresa looked at Lola and then looked at Eve. She moved next to Eve. "I was talking to a lady at the planning office. She was bringing in paperwork on some land that she and her husband had bought. There was something wrong with the zoning and she was submitting the paperwork to change the land from industrial to residential. She told me she and her husband planned to build on the land. As I processed the paperwork, I noticed the name Elijah Mann on it. I asked her if that was her husband's signature and she told me yes. She told me that her husband was a merger consultant that landed the job of a lifetime here. I asked her if he worked in this area on any recent mergers and she mentioned the Clearview/Oxford merger."

"That's interesting," Eve said calmly. "I would have never guessed."

"Me either. Does it make a difference to you Eve?" Lola asked.

"No. Not really. We ain't living in the 1950s."

"I thought maybe that would be enough to get you to let go," Teresa said quietly.

"Oh, that was bitch move." Lola laughed.

"T. Let's just go back to not talking about Elijah." Eve stood up and put some more water on the steam rock and sat back against the wall.

<u>Black or white?</u>
Chapter 27

Eve left Teresa and Lola at the shop. The disadvantage of having the hairdressers they had was the wait time. Sabrina had Eve in and out and looking good. During her drive home, she thought about what Teresa had revealed.

Entering into her home, she headed straight for the kitchen, poured a glass of wine and sat at the kitchen table. This little bit of knowledge of Elijah's wife was uncomfortable. There was some of the angst that a lot of Black women feel about men who date and marry White women, but it wasn't really that strong. On one level, it mattered to Eve's ego and social awareness, but, on the other levels, it didn't supersede the fact that he was married to this woman and he was just having sex with her. That knowledge was more unsettling in the fact that Teresa had given the woman some humanity. It was easier to think of her as a figment of her imagination, but now this figment is being filled in to a real person.

She got up from the table and noticed an apple on the floor. Bending to pick it up, her mind flashed to Nathan and their exercise on the table. She blushed despite the fact that she was alone. *What I need to do is sever ties with Elijah. Nathan could be the one.* Still smiling, Eve threw the apple away, walked into the living room and put on some music. She was going to her room when the doorbell rang.

"I wonder who this is?" she muttered to herself as she went and peeked through the peephole. It was Elijah.

Damn, I forgot just that easy. I don't really want to be bothered. Eve thought for a moment about how to get out of seeing him. The doorbell rang again. She opened the door. Elijah smiled that devilish smile and leaned against the doorpost. *This man looks so good. So much for trying to get rid of him.*

"What's going on, Momma?" he asked, looking her over. "Your hair looks good." He reached over and ran his fingers through it.

"Thank you. You don't look so bad yourself." He had on a pair of blue baggy jeans and a black sweater. On his feet he wore a pair of black leather sandals. He continued to stand and stare at her.

"You think you might let me in? We don't want the frogs out here to jump in while you are standing with the door open."

Eve jumped back searching for the bullfrogs that hung out on her lawn. It was after a thorough search that she moved to the side to let him in.

"What was that about?" he asked walking into her living room. This was the first time he had ever entered into her house. All but a few of the stipulations they had agreed on had been broken. It was the second time they were together that they stopped using condoms, and now she allowed him in her home. If she ever called him at home, she would have proven herself a liar. At this point, she was only a half-truth speaker.

"What?" she asked. She walked to the stereo and turned it down, grabbed her wine glass from the table and settled herself on the couch.

"Why was I standing at the door so long?" Elijah removed his jacket and laid it across the back of the couch.

"Tell me about your wife." Eve spoke before she thought.

"What do you want to know?" he asked, as if she asked him the time. He sat on the couch and looked at her.

"I want to know what she looks like, how did you meet, etc."

"Well, I think she's a beautiful woman. I met her when I was a consultant on a merger. We decided to live together. We had children together and then we got married."

It's convenient that he left out the fact that she was white. I guess that doesn't matter.

"Why?" he asked cocking his head to the side.

"I was curious."

"Well, now I want to ask you a question."

"Go ahead."

"I know that you are seeing someone else. Why didn't you tell me?"

"What do you mean seeing someone else?" Eve asked, nervously taking a sip of her wine.

Elijah cocked his head to the side and let an easy smile slide up his face. "I overheard some people at work mention your name. I then found out that you were associated with Nathan Garrison, the guy over security. He's a nice guy."

Eve was dumfounded. *Was my business all in the street like that?* "He is a nice man and I have only gone out with him a few times." *Why am I acting like I owe him an explanation? I don't owe him shit.*

"Oh. Well, have you fucked him?"

Is this jealousy? Why would he care? This man cannot be jealous. I wonder what he would say if I answered truthfully? Eve cocked her head to the side looked at Elijah with pursed lips. The smirk she gave was more than enough to reveal the truth, but Elijah waited for a verbal response.

"Yes." She answered regarding him closely.

"Did you enjoy it?"

"Yes."

"As much as you enjoy me?"

Eve hesitated. What if she answered truthfully? Does that mean Elijah is gone? She decided to play a dangerous game.

"About as much as you enjoy your White wife." *Eve, what the hell?*

Elijah literally sat back and stared at her. There was no quick wit response, simply a long moment of silence. When he finally spoke, it was not what Eve expected.

"I find that it is interesting that our conversation was about you and Nathan Garrison and it was switched back to me and my wife again. By the way, she is not white. Tell me, how did we end up there?"

Eve didn't answer. She was so embarrassed. She didn't know why she said it. She was clueless as to what she wanted to accomplish by saying it.

"My wife is very fair, but she is as black as we are," he explained, as if he read her mind. "Although I'm not sure why I'm explaining this all to you, I have nothing to hide, so I will. Her grandparents were both mixed." Elijah sat back and allowed that easy smile slip onto his face. "And so now you know my dearly beloved is not White. If she had been, would that have changed anything we've been doing?" He let the sarcasm seep out of his mouth. "Maybe it makes it a little easier to swallow the fact that you have been with a married man if it's not a sista?" He mocked in a falsetto voice, "then you don't feel as bad?"

Elijah picked lint off the end of his pants in a manner of a man unconcerned with what was going on. Eve just sat and watched him. What could she say?

"Eve, when are you going to realize that what we have going has nothing to do with my wife? It is about you and me."

"If that is the case, Elijah, why are you concerned about Nathan?" Eve retorted.

"Touché." He smiled. "However, I asked you to tell me when you were seeing someone, so I could decide if I wanted to continue. Now, I look at you, sitting here on your couch looking sexy as hell, and all I can think of doing is taking you on this couch. I thought Nathan might be in the way, but it is obvious that he's not. If he were, you wouldn't have let me in."

Eve knew in some ways the cocky son of bitch was right, but he didn't have a clue how deeply Nathan touched her. But then why should he? The only thing he had to know was what he did to her, and that he did know.

After Elijah left, Eve sat in her robe in the living room. She had just taken a shower and had picked up a novel that she had been trying to finish. As she settled the doorbell rang. Glancing at the clock, she frowned. *It is past midnight who could this be? Elijah called me when he was in the car, so I know it's not him.* She moved to the door when the knocking came.

"Who is it?"

"It's me."

Eve smiled. "Who is me?"

Nathan stood on the other side of the door a bit irritated. "Girl, let me in. You know the police patrol your neighborhood regularly. If they see a big black man standing out here, you know I would be heading downtown. And you got frogs out here, and I like them as much as you."

Eve opened the door and Nathan stepped in. As she closed the door behind him, she was swept up into his arms and carried to the couch. He plopped down on the couch with her in his lap.

"How is my baby doing?" he asked kissing her face.

"I'm doing better as the kisses increase."

Nathan chuckled. "Did you have a busy night?"

"No, I just sat around the house and tried to finish up the novel." Eve snuggled against him and leaned her head back on his chest. "I thought you were out with your protégés and they were supposed to spend the night with you."

"I was, but one of the boys' mother was being crazy. She blew up my cell and told me to bring her son home because he didn't take care of his chores. Jamal told me she was tripping because his daddy got engaged to someone else." Nathan sighed and shook his head. "It was a mess. I took them all home right after the game."

As Nathan talked, his hands moved up and down Eve's thigh. She had been with him long enough to recognize the signs that he wanted a bit more than conversation.

Lord knows I'm tired and just want to go to sleep. Elijah wore me out. I don't think I have anything left for Nathan.

Nathan hands continued to run the full length of her thigh. He began to place soft kisses on Eve's neck. That always sent chills down Eve spine, and she responded with a shudder. As one hand inched its way to her honey pot, the other moved to the swell of her breast and cupped it firmly. Eve began to squirm as her arousal began to increase. She was relieved that even though she was tired she still responded to Nathan's manipulations.

Am I really about to go out like that? Elijah just got through giving my body the thorough treatment and now I'm trying to get a second opinion with Nathan? But I think I'm in love with Nathan. How can I deny my body to a man that essentially has my heart? But then again how could I give my body to one man whose heart I'll never have? Oh my! I think I'm about to play myself.

Nathan's hands managed to bring Eve consciousness back. He teased her nipples and kissed her neck. Eve soon found herself turning in his lap facing him and giving him full access to her breasts. Nathan grabbed them and ravished them like a man that hadn't eaten for days. She held his head to her, lost herself, and took comfort in their passion. She wasn't aware when Nathan picked her up and moved her into her bedroom until he sat her on the bed.

He removed her robe and stared at her body as if he had never seen it before. He pulled her toward him and kissed her on the top of her head. Eve was puzzled. This was not what she was used to with Nathan. Elijah was the type that paid attention to detail. Nathan and Eve usually burned each other quickly but satisfying. Tonight it was different.

"Eve baby," Nathan whispered pulling her closely. Eve buried her face into his massive chest and began kissing and sucking on his nipples. His breath caught and he pushed her slightly away. Eve sat back and smiled at him. He returned it and leaned to place his lips on hers.

"Eve," he said again. She looked into his eyes. "I love you, Eve."

If Nathan had not been holding her, she might have fallen on the floor. Although she had admitted to herself that she was in love with him and she believed he felt the same way, he was the first to speak it out loud. For him to say it took her by surprise.

"Eve, you don't need to say it to me until you are ready, but I already know that you do. I think I have since we were on the Ferris wheel. This just feels so right. Holding you in my arms lets me know that I'm home, baby. I love you."

Not saying anything Eve moved to wrap her arms around Nathan and kiss him with all the love she had in her. She loved this man, but there was no way she could tell him until she was done with Elijah.

Nathan lay Eve across her bed. She lay naked and wanton for him. He grabbed hold of her ankles and placed her feet upon his chest. His hands roamed up and down her legs sending shivers to every pore of her body. Eve almost came undone when he slipped her toes into his mouth. The whole time he watched her every reaction. Eve felt herself release twice before he let her foot go and leaned over her on the bed.

"Tell me what you want," he whispered as he kissed her stomach.

"I...I...I—" her breath was caught when his tongue circled her belly button and traced the path made by baby-fine hair towards her core. When he reached his destiny, he was rewarded with more honey. Nathan's tongue tasted every part of Eve's womanhood and then some. His tongue flicked her button while his fingers manipulated her opening. Eve could not remember when they became one. She only had memories of extreme shock and pleasure but most of all love.

Eve watched Nathan as he slept. *This man is everything I want and I love him more than he even thinks that I do. I'm getting rid of Elijah. I cannot risk losing Nathan. I don't think my heart can handle that.*

<u>You play with fire; you get burned.</u>
Chapter 28

Eve didn't talk to Teresa until the following Saturday. Eve called her girls and invited them over for breakfast. As they sat around the table talking, Eve shared with them that Nathan told her he was in love with her. Teresa shrieked, jumped up and ran over to hug Eve.

"Girl, when did this man tell you that he loved you?" she asked swinging Eve around like two little girls playing ring around the roses.

"Last week. And can I tell you he was something else? I have made love before, but that man took me to the moon and back."

"I'm so excited for you," Teresa exclaimed and hugged Eve again. Eve pushed her away laughing.

Lola sat at the table drinking coffee. She already had this conversation with Eve and she was really excited for her, but since then she had a lot of time to think. Lola thought Eve and Nathan in love was a good thing, but she wondered about Elijah. Lola decided to speak.

"Where does Elijah fit in this love thing?" Lola asked getting up from the table and walking across the kitchen to pour herself some more coffee.

Teresa grew quiet and looked at Eve. Eve stared at Lola. Lola looked at them both and sipped the coffee from her cup.

"What do you mean?" Eve finally asked.

"I mean, are you still screwing him?"

"Damn, Lola." Teresa intervened. "Of course not, she is in love."

"I simply asked a question."

"Well, damn. You ain't ever been one to shy away from being a wet rag," Teresa muttered and plopped herself in the empty chair next to the table.

Eve smiled and shook her head. She walked over to the coffee pot to fill her cup. She didn't want to get into this now. She especially didn't want to speak about Elijah. *Damn Lola.*

After Eve took a couple of sips of her coffee she turned to Lola. "Let's just say, Lola, that's all good. I have that under control."

"So much control that you fuck one man and have barely enough time to shower before you fuck the one you love?" Lola pulled no punches.

"What?" Teresa questioned. She was confused as to what they are talking about.

"Nothing, just Lola's active imagination at work."

"Oh, now I'm imaginative?" Lola retorted. "Girl, please. You're playing yourself. I know you don't want Teresa knowing that you been ho'ing but get over your damn self. You got yourself in some shit you thought you could handle. Now, all I'm asking is how you're going to get the situation handled?"

"I got it handled!" Eve yelled.

All three sat in silence. Lola stirred her coffee, Eve picked at a muffin, and Teresa sat trying to figure out what was going on.

"Eve, are you sleeping with both of them?" Teresa asked quietly breaking the silence. Eve never responded. "What exactly is being handled?" Teresa insisted tired of being ignored.

Eve's face hardened into a stone mask. She gave Lola a look that said tread lightly. Lola ignored it and continued on.

"Evie, I don't want to hurt you, but I think you're in over your head. This is not you. This is not what you do. Hell, this is what I do, not you."

"I'm not...I just want to understand," Teresa blustered frustrated that she wasn't getting any answers.

"There is no reason to be confused," Eve spoke quietly. "I'm in love with Nathan and I have an unexplainable attraction to Elijah. I know Nathan should be enough...in fact, he is enough. It's just that

Elijah does something to me that makes me want him despite my love for Nathan and despite his wife."

"Eve," Teresa commented. "I thought it was over between you and Elijah. I mean, most women who fall in love aren't sleeping with another man."

"Don't bring your self-righteous bullshit up in here," Lola warned. "This is not the time or the place."

"Excuse me; I was not the one who busted her out. I didn't even know this was going on," Teresa retorted.

"Of course you wouldn't. You've been planning a wedding and not paying attention." Lola dismissed Teresa's claim. "I didn't bring it up to bash on Eve. I brought up so she could take a look at herself." Lola turned to Eve. "You didn't intend to end up here, but here you are. I just want you to look at it, so we can figure how to get you out of this."

"I don't need or want your help," Eve spat out, breaking her silence. "I don't want your fucking judgment and I don't want your fucked-up help. All I really want is for both of you to get out of my house."

"You ain't got to tell me twice," Lola said, moving to grab her purse.

"Eve I..." Teresa started.

"Get out!" she yelled. "Get the fuck out." Eve sat in her kitchen as her two best friends headed for the door. When she heard the door close, she ran her hands in her hair and screamed. *What the fuck am I doing? How the hell did I get myself into this mess? How could I just kick out the two people in the world that I know would help me? I know what I need to do.*

***

When Eve spoke with Nathan earlier, he told her he was going out with the boys from the center again and would call when he got home. Since she was in for the evening, she decided to check her email. Logging in, she immediately started deleting all the unimportant emails. As she sat at her computer, her phone rang. She didn't want to talk, so she sent it to voicemail. After emptying her inbox, she picked up her phone to listen to her message.

"Well Momma, I guess you're not at home. I thought maybe we would be able to get together tonight. Are you out with Mr. Garrison? I guess it's my loss then, right?"

Elijah's voice appealed to all of her base senses. Eve moved quickly to push the call back button. "Elijah?"

"Oh, so screening your calls? Or was Mr. Garrison there and he just left?"

"Neither. I just didn't hear my phone. Anyway, what's up?"

"I just got out of a late meeting and I was hoping that we could get together."

"Where is your wife?" Eve curiously asked. She heard a small chuckle before he answered.

"She's visiting her mother."

"Oh wow. Does this not sound like a bad movie? The husband calls his mistress when his wife is out of town."

"The x-rated kind," he said chuckling again.

Eve thought for a moment. "Elijah I don't think I want to go out this evening."

"That's alright, sweetheart. I'm on my way." With that, he hung up the phone. She didn't have the opportunity to tell him she didn't want him to come either.

It was about thirty minutes later when there was a knock on Eve's front door. She checked the peephole and it was Elijah. When he declared he was coming, she didn't bother to change from her sweats, style her hair, or put on makeup with an exception of lip balm. Elijah had never seen her this way. She opened the door and he stood there in his Black sweater and blue jeans looking as delicious as ever. He gave her the once over and smiled.

"I hope you like Chinese. I was hungry and I brought enough

for both of us." He walked in moving around her and setting the bags on the table. Eve sighed and went into the kitchen for plates.

I really don't want him here. I need to think of a way to get him out of here. She came back into the living room and Elijah had spread the food on the coffee table and kicked his shoes off. Eve sat the plates on the edge of the table and then plopped down on the sofa.

"So how is everything going over at Clearview/Oxford?" he asked.

"It's fine. There are some minor adjustments that need to be made before everything is going completely smooth."

"Like what?" he asked dishing the food onto the plates.

"Well, Angel, one of my department heads, was out today. The way she handles business makes it virtually impossible for her assistants and those who do her work to do anything when she is absent. It is so damned annoying. I had to make a couple of calls that were not mine to make. I have too much on my plate to do her job."

"Yeah, I think I remember her," Elijah said handing her a plate. "What was she out for?"

"I don't know," Eve replied, irritated by the questions. She stuffed her mouth full of food.

"Are you okay?"

"I'm just tired."

"You want a massage? I know you can't reciprocate, but I'm willing to give one."

Elijah moved behind her and began massaging her shoulders. She wanted to tell him to stop, but his hands felt too good. His hands moved up and down her back until they worked her shirt up. His hands on her flesh felt so wonderful that she had to put her plate down so she wouldn't drop it. With her eyes closed, Eve sat and enjoyed his manipulating her muscles. His hands began to take a detour from her neck and back to her breasts. Eve stiffened. Elijah's hands paused for a moment and then continued to massage her breasts. Eve then opened her eyes and sighed as she moved away from him completely.

"What's wrong?"

"Nothing," she replied. "I'm just not in the mood."

"Well, if you sit back down I can get you in the mood," Elijah coaxed.

"Elijah, you need to go. I'm not feeling well."

Elijah moved over and stood directly in front of her. Eve had her head lowered and arms wrapped around her waist. He lifted her chin until their eyes met. She was so easily lost in his dark sensuous looks.

"Let me make you feel better," Elijah whispered as he began to kiss her eyelids. "I can, you know. I can make you feel better than you ever thought."

Eve closed her eyes and received his kisses. She didn't want to, but she felt helpless whenever she was with him. He stood with his hands on her waist and just kissed her. He moved from her eyelids, to her nose, her cheeks, her ears, and finally to her mouth. When he tasted her mouth, all thoughts of Elijah leaving disappeared. His lips danced so softly across hers. His tongue lovingly caressed her mouth and he caught her bottom lip between his teeth. He sucked it a little and let go.

He began to rub his face against hers and allowed their noses to touch, and then moved from cheek to cheek. The feeling of heat from his breath caused her to warm from the inside out. He spoke softly of how beautiful and sexy she was. He told her the things he wanted to do and some things he dreamed about. Still, his hands stayed on her waist.

Eve's hands slid up his arm and snaked around his neck. She tried to move in, but he stayed her. He continued to kiss her and rub his face against hers. And his words never stopped. This man knew just what to do to excite her. She felt no boundaries with him and it scared her. Elijah eventually pulled Eve into his arms and they spent the whole night doing all the things he wanted to do and then some. She didn't hear her phone ring when Nathan called.

<u>Visions of white.</u>
Chapter 29

Eve waited for Teresa outside the bridal shop. Teresa showed up late in typical Teresa fashion.

"Girl, I'm so sorry I'm late. Michael wouldn't let me go, if you know what I mean."

Eve rolled her eyes. "I see your idea of abstinence is working."

Teresa smiled.

"Look before we go into this store. I need to apologize to you. My going off on you the other day was so uncalled for. I need you in my life and I don't want you to worry about me. I'm going to handle this," Eve said, sincerely.

"All is forgiven, but I have to tell you I never thought you would hurt me like that." Teresa kissed her friend on the cheek.

Tears escaped Eve's eyes. "I will do whatever it takes to avoid hurting you like that again." Eve hugged Teresa. "Well, rather than standing out here hugging, come on in here girl and let's find your dress," Eve said opening the door to the shop.

When they walked in, they were immediately greeted. Once Teresa was announced as the bride, they bombarded her with questions. When they discovered her wedding was in a few weeks and she didn't have a dress, the women began to freak out. Eve laughed and began walking around the shop looking for her bridesmaid dresses when the sexy lingerie in the back caught her attention. She was drawn to the black leather bustier and thong. *Damn! This is right up Elijah's alley.*

"Hey girl."

Eve jumped out of her skin. She turned and saw Lola standing there.

"Girl, what the hell? You scared the shit out of me."

"I'm sorry, Pookie. I didn't mean to mess up your little fantasy involving the leather thong," Lola cajoled, fingering the lingerie. "By the way, I have this thong and it's not comfortable."

"Leave it to you, Lola, to have this. You're such a tramp."

"Takes one to know one."

"Anyway," Eve said, excusing Lola's childish comment. "I want to apologize to you for going off on you the other day."

"Hell bitch, I know what's up. You're forgiven."

"Thanks Lola." Eve moved to hug her friend and Lola moved away. Eve knowing Lola doesn't like showing her affections decided to change the subject.

"Have you made the plans for the bridal shower?" Eve asked. She put Lola in charge of this long before the fight. "Teresa said she doesn't want a stripper."

"Yeah, I made the plans," Lola whispered, looking around to make sure Teresa wasn't within earshot. "I have a friend from work that hooked me up with a bomb stripper."

"Lola, Teresa said she didn't want a stripper," Eve scolded, raising her voice.

"Shhhh," Lola whispered, grabbing Eve by the arm and leading her more toward the back. "Girl, Teresa don't know what she wants."

"I don't know, Lola. I don't want Teresa upset at her own shower. You know how she is."

"Damn Eve, you make it sound like Teresa is a prude. We did all go to college and you know she was always down for whatever."

"Yeah, but some of us grew up."

Lola's eyes narrowed. Just as she was about to spit fire, the sales lady came and informed them that Teresa had on the first of the wedding dresses.

"We shall discuss this later," Eve said following the sales lady.

"Oh, we sho' in the hell will," Lola answered confidently.

The first dress Teresa tried on was full of lace and had big sleeves that looked like she should have been floating the Pacific

Ocean waiting to be rescued. Eve and Lola didn't even let the sales lady get through her spill about the dress. They immediately sent Teresa back. The phone in the store rang and the lady helping Teresa went to answer it leaving Teresa by herself.

"Hey you guys?" she called out. "I need some help in here."

Eve and Lola both walked behind the curtain to see Teresa standing in a strapless satin dress. It was cute except for one thing; the dress wouldn't zip.

"I need you to help me zip the dress," Teresa said, twisting her arms and body to hold the zipper together.

Eve moved over to help her. "Teresa, baby maybe you need another size," Eve said struggling with the zipper.

"Ya think?" Lola asked sarcastically. "Those tatas are not going to allow that dress to close. And even if it did, you all know that her bosom is going to be bubbling out the top."

"Look Lola, if you ain't going to help, then get out," Teresa snapped at Lola.

"Sweetheart, I'm helping. The dress doesn't fit. I don't know why you waited until the last minute to buy your dress," Lola said leaning against the wall watching the two struggle.

After about five minutes, Eve acquiesced. "Teresa, I'm going to have to agree with Lola. This is not going to work."

Teresa's face looked stricken. "Look Eve, this dress is a size nine. I'm only a seven. You can't expect me to believe that my wedding dress is going to be one that can fit a cow. Maybe I can have gussets put in?"

"Oh no!" The gasp came from behind them. All three women turned at the voice of the sales lady standing there appalled.

"Gussets won't work with this style and that fabric." She moved quickly to Teresa's side. The two tried to pull the zipper up. It would not budge.

"You must take this off now," the sales lady insisted. "If you bust the zipper, you will have to pay for it."

Lola and Eve turned and looked at Teresa. Teresa's eyes narrowed and her lips poked out.

"Com'on Teresa," Eve intervened. "Why don't you try on the other million dresses in this store?"

"Yes. I have just the dress that will work for you," the sales lady insisted.

As Teresa modeled the different dresses, Eve and Lola would critique and send her back. Eve allowed herself to daydream during her wait time. She dreamed about her wedding day. She knew it would be beautiful and small. Her husband would be standing in a suit with no tie and his shirt open. She would be walking toward him in a straight gown with spaghetti straps and bare feet. Nathan would be standing at the altar waiting for her. They'd declare undying love for each other. She would have an early morning wedding, so she c ould serve brunch at the reception. And she and Nathan would dance all day. However, when she pictured her wedding night, Elijah's face met her in the bedroom. He was ready to do deliciously decadent things to her. Eve began to savor his touch as it moved down her back...

"Earth to Eve...Earth to Eve. Honey, we need you back here to help with a decision-making process." Lola was waving her hands and snapping her fingers in Eve's face. "What's going on?"

"Nothing girl; I'm just zoning."

"Yeah right. You were thinking about your own wedding, huh?"

"How did you know?" Eve asked surprised.

"I could see it all over your face." Lola laughed. "You had that "I wish I were a bride look."

"Oh wow." Eve laughed. "If you say so."

"So who was it?" Lola asked, pulling a lipstick and a compact from her purse.

"Who was what?"

"Which guy was in the day dream? Was it Nathan or Elijah?"

Eve looked away embarrassed that Lola was so on target.

"Eve darlin', can you stop acting like I don't know you? I know it was one of them."

"Actually, it was both."

Lola stopped the lipstick on her lips and looked at Eve.

"What a ménage a trois?"

"Girl, no, dang! I dreamed that Nathan was the one I married and Elijah was the one I honeymooned with."

"I thought you said that sex with Nathan was the bomb!"

"I did."

"Then why is Elijah on the honeymoon?"

"I don't know. I guess it's like Elijah is excitement in bed and Nathan is comfort. I have always dreamed my honeymoon to be buck wild."

"You have also dreamed your tail being a virgin too," Lola said finishing her touch up.

"Yeah well, the best laid plans have gone awry."

Lola looked at Eve and smiled. It took Eve a moment to realize her pun. They both laughed.

"Okay ladies, I think we have found a winner," Teresa announced as she came from behind the curtain.

She looked beautiful. Eve found herself tearing up and had to reach for a Kleenex. Lola wore a big grin and kept saying, "that's it" over and over. Teresa posed in the dress looking at herself in the mirror for about fifteen minutes. Other brides came in the store and made remarks on how her dress looked as if it were made specifically for her. Finally, Eve convinced her to let the seamstress do her job so they could go to lunch. As the seamstress pinned the dress, Teresa talked to Eve.

"Eve, if you and Nathan keep going, you will be the one standing here."

"Don't rush me. We haven't been together that long."

"Girl, please. Don't be like me and Michael. We almost waited too long to be married."

"What do you mean?"

"My momma used to always tell me that a man knows his wife the first time he meets her. It shouldn't take years unless he is not ready. When I met Michael, we were in college but that was a while ago. We have been together on and off since then. But now, he's ready and told me he knew it was me."

"He also knew you were getting ready to kick him to the curb permanently," Lola added.

"That is true, girlfriend," Teresa said, winking at Lola. "I was about to give him the heave ho until he put this here rock on my finger." Teresa flashed her left hand.

"Well ladies, don't buy bridesmaid dresses for my wedding just yet," Eve interrupted. "It ain't that kind of party just yet."

"He told you he loved you. What kind of party is it if it ain't that kind of party? Girl, don't let that man get away."

"You just want everyone to get married because you're getting married," Eve said and slouched against the back cushions.

The seamstress was finished putting the pins in. She led Teresa behind the curtain to help her remove the dress. Eve and Lola sat on the couch in silence. Lola finally spoke.

"Have you told Nathan you loved him yet?"

"No."

"Is that why you're not seriously thinking about marriage? Is it that you don't love him?"

"I do love him," Eve whined. "I need to get rid of Elijah."

"It's just sex, right?" Lola asked in a forced whisper.

"Yes!" Eve threw up her hands in frustration. She moved to get up from the couch when her cell phone rang. "Hello."

"Can you meet me?" It was Elijah.

"Sure," Eve said in a casual tone, avoiding Lola's glare.

"Ok. Meet me at the hotel, the usual room. I'm going to order some fruit. Do you need anything?" Elijah asked.

Eve's mind flashed to the last time they had fruit. She was the platter. "No that's fine. I have to stop by the office and pick up the file and then I will head on over."

"Oh, someone is there?" Elijah asked, lowering his voice to a seductive tone.

"Yes."

"Well then, I shall see you soon."

Eve hung up the phone. At the same time, Teresa came out of the room and joined her and Lola.

"You guys ready for lunch? My treat," Teresa offered.

"I can't go. My boss just called and he needs me to pick up a file and take it to him."

"Eve, it's Saturday," Teresa whined. "You promised you would spend the day with us."

"I know, Teresa, but I have to take care of this." Eve's eyes shifted to Lola who raised her eyebrows and twisted her lips in doubt. "How about I take this file and I'll catch up with you?"

"Okay, but hurry up. I want you to see what you and Lola are going to wear."

"I thought you said we got to choose our own," Lola whined.

"I did. I just saw these dresses and I hoped you guys would like them." Teresa smiled.

All three walked to the counter and Teresa wrote out the deposit check. After making arrangements for another fitting, they all walked out.

"Alright, I'll see you later," Eve said walking toward her car.

"O.K. hon. Don't forget."

"I'll try not to," Eve said getting in her car. Eve saw Lola and Teresa in the rearview mirror. Teresa was waving fanatically and Lola shook her head. Eve headed straight home to shower. Knowing Elijah like she did, she knew she wouldn't catch up with them. She promised she would make it up to Teresa later.

Bridal shower.
Chapter 30

Eve didn't see Teresa before the bridal shower, but she had talked to Lola on the phone. Teresa had emailed the particulars to Eve about the shower a few weeks ago. She wanted the bridal shower a month before the wedding, so she wouldn't be stressed about the final details of the wedding. She wanted to be free to enjoy herself. Teresa gave specific instructions that she wanted this shower to be a classy affair. That was one of the reasons it was agreed to be at Lola's home. Lola's place was extremely modern, right down to her white tiled floors. Her home was done in primary colors and on every wall there were African American prints. Her home could have easily been an art museum. Teresa was convinced it would impress her mother and her future mother in law.

Eve arrived at Lola's house before any of the others so she could help set up. When Lola answered the door, she gave Eve the once over and moved aside so she could enter.

"Hey," Lola said as she closed the door. "I didn't think you were coming."

"Why?" Eve asked and handed Lola her coat and purse.

"Because you didn't make it back to our lunch," Lola said, hanging Eve's things in the closet.

"It was business," Eve lied.

"You can tell Teresa's naïve ass all the lies in the world, but I know it was Elijah."

"No, it *was* work," Eve insisted.

"Whatever," Lola said dismissing her. Lola walked into the kitchen. "Did you get the picture of the bridesmaid outfits?" Lola asked from the kitchen.

"Yes, I did."

Teresa sent Eve a picture of her bridesmaid dress and told her where she should go and get fitted. Since Teresa was choosing the dresses, she paid for all of the bridesmaid's dresses and shoes. Eve and Lola had decided that part of their wedding gift was to replace some of that money.

"What did you think?" Lola asked coming out of the kitchen and sitting the food trays on the table.

"I liked them," Eve said sampling the food.

"I was trying to let us get this little sexy number, but you know Teresa. "This will be a classy affair," Lola imitated in a squeaky voice that was supposed to be Teresa.

"Well, it's her wedding. If she wanted us to wear parkas and hold an umbrella that is exactly what we would be doing."

"Girl, bite your tongue. I wouldn't be doing that," Lola said and headed back to the kitchen.

"Did you cancel the stripper?" Eve asked, elevating her voice so Lola could hear.

"Nope, Teresa will just have to get over it."

"Lola, I don't think that's a good idea."

"Too late now."

Eve piddled around the living room for a few minutes before going over to the stereo. She pulled out the Jill Scott CD and set the tone for the shower. About an hour after Eve got there, the first of the guests arrived. Greeting them as they came in, she took their things and hung them in the same closet she saw Lola hang hers. There was a total of twenty guests invited ranging from ages twenty-one to sixty-two. Teresa's mother, aunt and future mother were among them and all of them showed before Teresa. When the doorbell rang and Lola answered it, Teresa stood there smiling.

"I'm sorry I'm late. I got tied up."

"Is that to be taken literally?" One of the guests asked. Everyone laughed and the party started.

Between Eve, responsible for the games, and Lola, responsible for the food and extra entertainment, the shower was a hit. Food and fun permeated the house and people were having a good time. At 8:00 PM the real fun came with the knock on the front door.

With the music playing and Teresa in a full conversation, no one noticed Lola go to the door except Eve. When Lola stepped outside, Eve knew she was leading the stripper around through the back. Eve moved over to the stereo searching for a CD. She waited for Lola to reappear with the go ahead for the music.

"Alright ladies, one more game to play before the night is over," Lola announced. "Sit in the chair in the middle of the room, Teresa."

Lola brought over the chair and Teresa sat down. A few of the women grabbed their purses and pulled out money, while others wondered what the game was.

Eve at the stereo put on Prince's "International Lover." And Lola dimmed the lights. All of a sudden, a figure moved out from the hallway with a white mask, bare chest that was dark chocolate and red pants that left nothing to the imagination. Teresa's mouth dropped open in shock and a full blush crept up her face. Eve looked at Teresa's mother in law, and her expression was just like Teresa's. However, her mother and aunt smiled and grabbed their purses looking for dollar bills.

As the stripper began to dance around and grind on the Teresa, the woman let out howls and calls. When the stripper picked Teresa up with the chair over his head emulated oral sex, Teresa's mother in law excused herself and walked out of the room into the kitchen. Eve motioned for Lola to go see about her. Hesitating, Lola reluctantly went into the kitchen. Eve was glad that Teresa's mother in law was gone because the next thing the stripper did was too much.

He laid Teresa down on the floor. Teresa hands were covering her face the whole time. He gyrated his hips above her pelvic area causing almost every woman in the room to lose her mind. He spread her legs far apart and moved his near naked body all over her. The women were yelling for Teresa to take her hands away from her face and watch, but she wouldn't. Teresa's mother even tried to pull her hands away, but Teresa was too strong.

Eve noticed a flash and realized it was Teresa's aunt was taking pictures. She laughed to herself. *With the money we are spending, I'm glad someone is getting the money's worth.* Turning her attention back to Teresa, she noticed the stripper taking a Suzie Q dessert snack out of his bag. He carefully removed the two chocolate cakes pieces with cream in middle from the wrapper and placed it on Saran Wrap. He then moved back between Teresa's legs. He placed the tasty treat between Teresa's legs and then proceeded to lick the cream from between the brown chocolaty cake. Even Eve had to take a breath on that one. It was one of the most of erotic things she had ever seen and, of course, she flashed on Elijah. *I wonder if Elijah has done anything like that. The next time I see him, I'm going to have him add that to his repertoire.*

The women in the party were now sticking dollar bills in the stripper's g-string and he turned his attention to them. Teresa managed to get off the floor and ease into the kitchen unnoticed by the group. Eve saw her leave and followed her.

"Lola, I told you no strippers." Teresa laughed.

"The stripper wasn't for you. It was for all those hollarin' women out there."

"Where is Michael's mother?" Teresa asked, looking around the kitchen.

"She said that she didn't want to spoil it for you. She left out the back."

"Damn. I didn't want that shit to happen," Teresa said frustrated and cutting her eyes at Eve.

"I told you no strippers. You knew my mother-in-law was coming and I wanted it to be decent and respectable. I knew Lola wouldn't adhere, but I thought you would."

"Look Teresa, Lola is a grown woman. I told her no strippers, but she had already gone and paid for them," Eve argued. "What was I supposed to do?"

"Convince her otherwise. Now, I got to hear about this for the rest of my life. And you know she's going to tell Michael he's marrying a worthless gutter tramp," Teresa said to no one in particular.

"Teresa, it's not that bad. Your aunt and your mother are having a great time," Eve said, trying to show the lighter side of an awkward situation.

"I noticed. One more thing Michael's mother will throw in my face. I told you how high and mighty she is."

"Oh Teresa, get over it. It's done. Your mother-in-law will get over it too." Lola dismissed the subject as if that were all was to be said about it. She walked over to the refrigerator and pulled a bottle of wine out.

"That's your problem, Lola. You never regard anyone but your damn self."

"I threw this shower for you!" Lola retorted.

"And neglected my wishes, too," Teresa shouted angrily.

"Who are you hollering at? This is my fuckin' house and you ain't about to get crazy up in here." Lola slammed the wine bottle into a bucket of ice.

"I'm grown and can get crazy anywhere I stand."

"Ladies come on," Eve said trying to diffuse the situation. It was already too late.

"Oh no, Bitch, you gonna to have to get the hell out of here with that shit."

"I think I will." Teresa headed toward the living room.

Eve looked at Lola who poured herself a glass of wine.

"Lola, I told you this would be a disaster. You need to apologize."

"I ain't apologizing to her tight ass."

Eve shook her head and ran after Teresa. Teresa had just

reached her car. "Teresa, you can't go. All the people in there are here for you."

"The last time I looked they were preoccupied with a stripper."

"Teresa, is it really that bad?"

"That's not the point, Eve. I wanted something classy. Now, it's right there in the gutter with everything else that Lola does."

"That's not fair. You know Lola was doing what she thought would be fun."

Teresa looked at Eve confused. "Who are you? Why are you making excuses for Lola not paying attention to my wishes?"

"I'm not making excuses I just..."

"Ever since you let your morality hit the window and started fucking Elijah, everything is acceptable to you. Even abandoning me on our girls' day out to get your freak on."

Eve looked as if she had been suckered punched in the stomach. She hadn't told Teresa she was with Elijah that day.

"Yeah, your girl, who you are trying to excuse, sold your ass to me," Teresa scoffed. "I know you met with him. I hope it was good enough to diss your girl for."

Eve didn't say anything. She watched Teresa get in her car and drive away. When the rear lights turned the corner, she went into the house. By the time she made it back in, the stripper was leaving and Lola had announced that Teresa went to see about her mother-in-law. The ladies began to gather their things and left one by one. When everyone left, Eve picked up the trash can and silently began to clean. Lola looked at her to see if she would speak, but Eve ignored her.

"Okay Evie. I will call Teresa tomorrow and apologize. Although you know she was wrong for stepping to me in my house."

Eve stopped and looked at Lola. They stared at each other for about thirty seconds, but it was long enough to make Lola uncomfortable.

"What?" Lola finally asked. "What more can I do?"

"Why did you tell Teresa that I went to see Elijah?"

Lola fell silent.

"Why would you do that?"

"Eve, it wasn't like that. I didn't mean to tell her..."

"What? You tripped and the words tumbled out of your mouth?" Eve began throwing things in the trash can. Every time a piece of trash would go in some seemed to dribble out. "First, you disregard Teresa's request and then you tell her my business."

"You told me you didn't go with him. You told me it was business," Lola countered smugly.

"That would have made what you said even worse, because you would have been lying. Just so you know, it was business. My business!"

"You know what, Eve? I'm tired of you and Teresa's bullshit. Just get out."

"That won't be a problem for me either." Eve dropped the trash can in the middle of the floor. She walked to the closet and grabbed her things and was out of the house in a flash. On her way home, she thought about the evening. It didn't go at all how she planned. When she reached her home, she noticed Nathan's car in the driveway. When she pulled up, he got out of the truck.

"Hey baby," he said as she got out of the car.

"Hey Nathan, what are you doing here? I thought you were out doing your big brother thing."

"I was, but they were working my nerves, so it was an early evening."

"Oh. How long have you been waiting?"

"Not long. I called Lola's house to see if you were still there. She said you were on your way home."

"How did she sound?"

"She sounded pissed off. What happened?"

"I'll tell you inside."

Eve and Nathan walked to the door and, as usual, Nathan went in first. She sighed as she waited right outside the door until he was convinced it was safe. She then went in, put her things in the chair next to the door and walked toward the kitchen to make coffee. As she made their coffee, she gave Nathan the low down on what happened, of course editing the Elijah part.

"Teresa was really mad. And when she left I was mad at Lola and then she got mad at me. It was a mess."

"Oh baby, I'm sorry you had to deal with that." Nathan pulled her close to him and she nestled herself against his chest. "But you know you should have stopped Lola."

"How the hell was I going to stop a grown ass woman?" She jerked away from him.

"I don't know, baby. Maybe you should have been more insistent."

"You want to know why I wasn't more insistent? I didn't see what the problem was. So what! A stripper! Big deal!" She rationalized.

"Obviously, it was a big deal," Nathan said, treading lightly.

"You know what, Nathan? I think you need to go home. I'm not good company tonight," she said, getting increasingly annoyed.

Nathan sighed and reached to massage her shoulders. "Oh baby. Let me help you get rid of some of that tension."

Eve shrugged away from him. "Go on home. I will call you later," she insisted.

"Eve, I don't think we should be fighting because of Lola and Teresa."

"Neither do I, which is why I think you need to go so we won't end up fighting."

Nathan kissed her on the forehead and walked to the door. "If you need to talk, call me," he said, opening the door.

"I will, Nathan. Call me when you get home. My cell is dead so call me on the house phone. If I don't answer, I'm in the shower.

Leave a message and I will call you back."

"Okay Eve. I love you." And Nathan left.

Eve plopped down on the sofa and began rolling her neck to get the kink out. *I need to get up and take a shower.* After a few moments of silence, Eve regretted sending Nathan home. *I should have let Nathan stay and work out the stress, but his siding with Teresa was irritating. To shut him up, all I has to do was whip it on him. That would have definitely taken my stress. When he calls me to let me know he made it home, I think I'm going to ask him to come back. I know that shit is fickle, but if he loves me he has to love all of me, fickle and all.* Eve got up from the couch and headed to her room. When she passed the phone, it rang. She picked up quickly thinking it was Nathan.

"Hello."

"What are you doing?" It was Elijah. *Damn this man's timing is impeccable,* she thought. *Does he have radar when I need sex?*

"I'm about to take a shower."

"You need help scrubbing your back?"

Eve thought for a moment. *Maybe I don't really need Nathan. I don't want anything but the sex, and I know that sex with Elijah will indeed relieve my stress. Damn, good timing!*

"Be here in ten."

"I can do even better. I'm pulling up now."

"What the hell? Why would you do that? I could have had company."

"That is why I called, sweetheart. Now open the door."

Eve opened the door and Elijah was standing there in all his beautiful glory. She didn't even give him time to speak; she pulled him in, jumped on him and began kissing him. When they came up for air, she ripped open his shirt and kissed him down the chest. As she moved up his neck, he grabbed her behind and lifted her where her legs were wrapped around his waist. He walked her to the bedroom and dumped her on the floor. As they came out of their clothes, Eve barely heard the phone ring.

"You gonna get that?" Elijah asked, kissing her throat.

"Let the machine get it."

Nathan's voice was clear. When she heard it, she tensed. Elijah, by this time, had worked his way down between her legs. One touch of his tongue and she no longer heard anything but the pleasure waves in her ears. For the next two hours, Eve and Elijah hit every stop of the sexual exchange highway and were exhausted from the trip. Elijah left early in the morning and Eve locked the door behind him, went and played her messages.

"Hey Baby. I made it home. I wish I could have been more comfort to you. If you want me to come back, I will. Call me if you want that. I love you."

Eve erased the message and went and got into her bed. She laid there, sleep evading her like a cheating husband, wishing that she hadn't let Nathan leave.

The reception before the wedding.
Chapter 31

Nathan picked Eve up late for Erica's reception. They had long since made up for the night of the bridal shower. Eve apologized the next day and Nathan, being the understanding man that he was, just kissed her with forgiveness. It was the very same day that they decided they would go to Erica's reception. It was at Eve's insistence.

"Eve, we don't have to go. We could paint the town red," Nathan suggested as he put Eve in the car.

"Nathan, I think we need to go. She has been calling you and Susie, worrying you two about your presence at the reception. I think we need to go as a show to her that you have moved on and so should she." Nathan sighed as he drove. "Plus, I look damned good in this dress and I want her to be jealous. Not only do I look good, but I'm on your arm."

Nathan glanced at Eve with a grin. She did in fact look good in her backless fitted black evening dress. It fell right above her ankle and had a slight fishtail giving her room to walk.

"Well Momma, since you put it like that. I say let's do this."

Eve wrinkled her nose. She hated when he called her Momma. It always reminded her of Elijah. She didn't want to think about him. She wanted it to be just her and Nathan.

As they pulled up to the hotel, Nathan leaned over and kissed Eve on the lips. "I love you," he said and moved to get out of the truck.

"I love you too…" *Oh shit, did I just say that out loud?* Eve looked at Nathan's back and saw that he paused. Then he continued to get out and come around to her door. When he opened her door, his smile was blinding. *I did say it out loud. Oh well, just roll with it Evie. Just roll with it.*

As they entered into the ballroom, Eve had to admit that it was a fabulous reception and as much as she didn't want to admit it, Erica looked phenomenal. She stood by her husband greeting their guests with a raw silk strapless fitted gown that was embroidered from the top to the train tip behind her. Eve and Nathan made their way to their host.

"Welcome. Thank you for coming," Robert greeted them.

"Thank you for the invitation," Eve responded.

"Nathan, you look quite dashing tonight," Erica commented, looking at him from head to toe. Nathan wore a black suit and white shirt and tie. His suit fit like a glove and he did look good.

"Thank you. Eve picked it out," he said.

Eve smiled and slightly elbowed him in the ribs.

"Oh," Erica responded glancing at Eve. "Well, enjoy yourselves. Your name is on one of the tables, so just look for it."

"Thank you."

Eve and Nathan moved further into the ballroom and began to mingle with the other guests. Eve was surprised she knew some of the people at the reception. When they found their table, she was surprised to see Teresa and Michael.

"What are you doing here?" Eve asked.

Teresa gave her a deadpan look. The tension between them could be cut with a knife. "Michael came home and said he ran into an old friend and we were invited to a wedding reception. I didn't know it was Erica."

"Hey man, I'm Nathan." Nathan reached over and shook Michael's hand.

"Are you the same Nathan that was at the hospital?" Michael asked.

"Yes."

"Thank you for being there. It meant a lot to my fiancé and I appreciate it."

"It was no problem. So are you two ready for the big day?"

"Yeah, we're ready," Michael answered. Teresa sat and drank her wine silently. "You are coming with Eve right? You know she's in the wedding?" Michael asked.

Eve looked at Teresa and Teresa still didn't say anything.

"Yeah man, I know. That has been all she has been talking about for the last few weeks. I'm not sure if I can make the wedding, but I'm going to try to make it to the reception."

"Excuse me." Teresa got up from her seat. "Michael, baby, I'll be back." She went toward the ladies' room.

"Eve, go after her. I told her what happened at the shower was no big deal and my mother would get over it."

"I know Michael, but she was really mad," Eve answered realizing that she must not have told him the whole story.

"She wants to make up, but you're going to have to go to her."

Eve looked at Michael and Nathan squeezed her hand. With that bit of encouragement, she followed after Teresa. When she walked into the ladies' room, Teresa was applying her lipstick in the mirror.

"Teresa I'm sorry, about everything that went down."

"You sure have been saying that a lot lately," Teresa said, placing her lipstick in her purse. "And I guess I will have to say I agree."

"Teresa, I..."

"What? What could you say to me that would help me understand how my best friend in the world would start screwing a married man, meet a great guy who is in love with her and not give up the married man? And on top of that, you have cursed at me, kicked me out of your house, ditched me to go be with the married man and then allow my wedding shower party to be ruined by Lola." Teresa took a breath. "Wow, did I leave anything out?"

"I don't have any excuses, Teresa. I know I've fucked up, but I'm getting it together now. I just told Nathan I love him and I'm ending everything with Elijah. I just want us to be back as we were, and I just want to stand for you in your wedding."

"You know, Eve. Even after all that we have been through in these last few months, it never dawned on me that you wouldn't stand for me, but I want *you* to stand, not this fucked up person you have been over the last few months."

Eve allowed the tears she had been holding to escape. Teresa watched them roll down her cheek and land on Eve's dress. "You're going to have to redo the make-up, sis," Teresa said handing Eve a compact.

"Thank you, Teresa. Thank you for keeping on forgiving me."

"Honey, if I can deal with Lola and all her madness, I can forgive you."

Returning from the ladies' room, the two walked back to their table smiling. Nathan and Michael were already eating when Eve and Teresa joined them. After the toast and cutting of the cake, they moved to the dance floor. The DJ was playing all the old school grooves and Nathan, Eve, Michael and Teresa were all cutting a rug. Just as they were about to leave the floor, the DJ played "Always and Forever." Nathan grinned at Eve pulling her into his arms and began rocking her in a slow groove. Eve melted into his arm. *I feel so safe in his arms. It's like nothing can touch me.*

Nathan began singing in Eve's ear. "Always and Forever...Each moment with you...Everyday love me your own special way...Take time to tell me you really care..." Eve danced listening to husky, slightly off key, baritone voice and knew Nathan was all she ever really wanted in a man. When the song ended, Nathan kissed Eve in the middle of the dance floor. So lost in their kiss, Eve barely felt Teresa tapping on her shoulder.

"Excuse me. You all need to move. You're messing up the soul train line."

Nathan lifted his lips away from Eve's. They noticed they stood right in the middle of the dance line and Atomic Dog was blaring through the speakers. Both laughing, they danced the rest of the way through the line followed by Teresa and Michael and then they all returned to their seat. Michael broke away to talk to the DJ. Nathan walked to the men's room leaving Eve and Teresa sipping on their drinks and watching everyone groove through the line.

They sat at the table and talked about the decorations for Teresa's big day and what was left to do. Soon Michael came and grabbed Teresa's hand to dance. Smiling at the engaged couple, Eve realized that Nathan had been gone a while. She got up and went looking for him. As she walked past the double doors entering into the ballroom, she saw him standing in the lobby of the hotel with Erica.

Take a deep breath, girl. You don't trust Erica, but you trust Nathan. Give him the benefit of the doubt before you go off. Eve looked around and noticed a partition that was high enough to keep her hidden but was close enough to them to hear what they were saying.

"Look Nathan. You can keep Eve as your little prize, but you know you still want me," Erica said in a soft purr. Her hands slid along the lapels of Nathan's jacket.

"No, I don't Erica." Nathan shook his head. "If this were a few years ago with a different woman, you might succeed. But I love Eve. More than I ever loved you and you seem to be forgetting that you just got married."

"Well, are you sure you can trust her?" Erica spat back obviously affected by his words.

"What is that supposed to mean?" Nathan exhaled noisily.

"I saw her in this hotel with a man not too long ago."

"Oh really?" Nathan responded with bored disbelief.

"Yes. I was here making the last of the arrangements for our reception and Robert and I saw them. Robert mentioned his name was Elijah Mann."

Eve's heart began to race hearing that she and Elijah could have been seen together. Damn! Could she have seen her and Elijah? They were usually very careful.

"Don't lose sleep over it, Erica. They used to work together. Anyway, this isn't about her. This about you. Stop calling me and move on with Robert. He seems like a good man. Stop trying to play him like you played me."

"Robert is good for one thing, money. I need a little extra attention." Erica purred and moved in closer to Nathan.

Eve bit her lip.

"I'm not interested. Eve is all I want and all I will ever need. I plan to spend the rest of my life with her." Nathan turned away from Erica and began walking toward the ballroom.

Eve noticed Nathan walking her way and she looked for a place to hide, so he wouldn't know she was listening. She stood right by the door of the restroom and slipped right in. When she figured he already walked past, she came out. She ended up running into him. "Hey," she said as he grabbed her around the waist to keep her from falling. "I was looking for you."

"I just had to step out and get some fresh air. When I did, Erica followed me out."

"You want to talk about it?" Eve asked impressed that he admitted to it.

"There is nothing to talk about. I told her I didn't want her and that I wanted you." With that, he kissed her on the forehead. It lacked some details, but that was in essence what Eve had heard and she was satisfied with that.

"Since that's taken care of, why don't you take me home and take care of me," Eve suggested slipping her arms around his neck

"That will not be a problem.

I feel a change coming.
Chapter 32

Eve worked long hours the next few weeks and spent very little time with Nathan. Her schedule was so busy and her guilt was so enormous. She hadn't had a chance to break it off with Elijah and the situation was really beginning to take a toll on her. Eve starting having bouts with insomnia at night. When she could sleep, her dreams would remind her of the love she felt in Nathan's arms and the heat she felt in Elijah's. Elijah made it no better with nightly calls of pleasure, unspeakable words whispered into the phone encouraging her to touch herself and tell him what she felt. Sometimes, Eve wouldn't answer the phone and he would leave suggestive messages on her machine. She found herself playing the messages over and over to hear what he said. He left messages on her cell phone even more wicked than those at home. She found herself being aroused listening to her messages at work. On more than one occasion, she had to go to the restroom and clean herself. Elijah would often come by unannounced, sometimes even after Nathan had left. No matter how Eve told him no, she found herself turned inside out before the night was through. She couldn't say no to him. Why wasn't she this excited about sex with Nathan? She enjoyed him, didn't she? He was a good lover. The problem was that she was scared and she still hadn't figured out why.

Eve had just arrived home from work. She kicked off her shoes by the garage door and went to the kitchen to get a soda. She didn't bother to pour it from the two-liter bottle into a cup, she just swigged from the bottle and walked back into the living room and plopped down on the couch. She reached over the back of her couch and pressed the answer machine to retrieve her messages.

"Hey girl, it has been a minute since I heard from you. Give me a call." It was Lola. Eve had been avoiding her since Lola kicked her out of her house. Although she and Teresa came to an understanding, Eve still felt so stupid. Teresa was the next voice on the machine.

"Hey Eve, I wanted to let you know I'm not mad that you didn't say bye to me at the reception. When I got home, I thought about our conversation and I realized that we have been friends too long to let bullshit get between us. And it's all bullshit, but the forgiveness is real. I also wanted to make sure that you didn't forget about the dress rehearsal for the wedding on Friday. Your suits are in and they look good. If I don't hear from you before then, I will check with you on Friday."

Eve took another drink from her soda. *I can't believe she still wants me to stand for her. I thought she would have found my replacement by now. Replace me with a relative that's already married or maybe with at least someone not sleeping with a married man. I'm not sure if I should stand for her. How could I stand there as a witness and a vow taker to uphold the sanctity of marriage and I'm fucking a married man? That shit doesn't even make sense.* Eve's thoughts were interrupted with the last voice on the phone.

"Evie, baby I ran into Teresa today and she invited me to come to your rehearsal dinner on Friday. I hope that is ok. Call me when you get in. I miss talking to you Miss Workaholic. I hope you slow down when we get married." Nathan's very clear and very distinct voice faded the instant he spoke of marriage to Eve.

Did he say marriage? He couldn't have said that. I'm hearing things. Oh my God, did he say marriage? Eve reached over and hit the rewind button on the answering machine. She paused before she hit play. If he did say marriage, she didn't think she wanted to hear it again. She erased her messages and got up to take the bottle back into the kitchen. Just as she placed the bottle back in the refrigerator, her phone rang.

"Hello."

"Well Bitch, you still mad?" It was Lola.

"No, I'm not mad, but you didn't have to bust me out like that with Teresa."

"I'm no buster, I'm a truth teller," Lola responded. Eve sat down at her kitchen table and Lola went on. "Evie, have you talked to Teresa?"

"No, not since the reception. I just got a message from her a minute ago. Why? What's up?"

"What reception?"

Eve told Lola about Erica's reception, leaving out the part about Nathan and Erica.

"Oh cool. I'm happy you two were able to get things right. Anyway, Teresa is in a panic about the wedding."

"She must just be having last minute panic attacks with irrational thoughts," Eve said trying to be convincing. "Although I have to tell you I'm surprised she still wants me in the wedding. You know how much she talks about the importance of standing up at a wedding and how you are vowing to uphold her in her marriage, blah, blah, blah."

"Yeah, but Eve you're her best friend. I'm not sure if she could do it without you. Now me," she continued. "She could marry without me there."

"You're one of her best friends, too," Eve said.

"Does a best friend sleep with her best friend's man?"

There was silence on the phone. Eve looked at the phone as if she was trying to see Lola through it. Eve finally spoke. "What did you just say?"

"Eve, I have been carrying this around with me for a good little while. You know when Teresa was dating that guy Phillip? It was one of the long periods of time she and Michael broke up."

"Lola, please tell me you lying. Tell me you are lying. They were apart for about six months, right?"

"Yes. I didn't mean for it to happen. I was out one night and I saw him. I had been drinking and you know I have always been attracted to the same kind of men as Teresa."

"Good God! How did it start?"

"It was one day that Teresa and I had one of our typical run-ins and I was pissed, so I decided to just flirt with him. I went over to him and bought him a drink. I was all over him and he didn't seem to mind. I took him back to a friend's apartment that night and the sex was off the hook. I thought it would be that one time, but he kept coming back for more, and I have always had a weakness for some good dick."

"How long did this last?" Eve asked, still very much surprised.

"It was only a few times. As soon as Teresa became suspect, we began to feel guilty. We stopped seeing each other and I found out that I was pregnant."

"Oh stop now! This shit is too much like a damn soap opera."

"I didn't say it was his, but I didn't know if it wasn't. So I made a deposit at the clinic and swore I would never tell."

"So why didn't you keep that promise," Eve asked disgusted. "This was some shit I didn't need to know."

"Well, I was going to ask you, do you think I should stand for her?"

"You know that was years ago? You haven't slept with Michael, have you?"

"No! Oh no, girl. I can be a trifling bitch sometimes, but I'm not that trifling. Although I'm attracted to Michael, and I know he has in the past been to me, I couldn't do that to her again. I'm a lot older and wiser."

"Are you sure you and Michael never crossed the line?" Eve asked warily.

"No. Hell, he won't even stay in the same room with me. I'm sure you have noticed that."

Eve thought about it. Michael never stayed long with Lola around. Eve had always thought it was because he didn't like the way Teresa and Lola went at it. She, on many occasions, had heard him tell Teresa that Lola wasn't a real friend because real friends don't treat each other that way.

Eve thought for a moment before she spoke. "Lola, I think you need to stand for her. It happened a long time ago, and her current relationship won't be affected. Plus, she would really want a good reason why you backed out. Just don't tell anyone else."

"Who else am I going to tell?

"I'm just saying, if she ever found...Now on that note I gotta go. I'll talk with you later." Eve hung up the phone. She reached back into the refrigerator and pulled out her soda. She went to the cabinet and pulled out the brown liquor that Nathan kept there. As she mixed the two, she shook her head in disbelief. When it rains it pours. *I will be glad when this wedding is over because everything else will be over and Nathan and I will live happily ever after. I hope.*

Nice day for a wedding.
Chapter 33

Teresa looked happier than either Eve or Lola had ever seen her. The church was decorated with coral and white flowers. Down the aisles the flowers were as extravagant as the bouquets Eve and Lola were carrying. Rehearsal flew by and the rehearsal dinner was so much fun. Afterward, Eve and Lola took Teresa out on the town for her last night as a single woman. They mended a lot of their broken fences. Then, Lola convinced them to go to a strip bar. The irony was not lost, but Teresa was down. She didn't have a problem with strippers; she just didn't want them there with her mother-in-law. They hit every strip bar for women that Lola knew about. Teresa was treated like royalty and got in a couple of dances with Crossing Midnight and Mr. Long. After Teresa was thoroughly embarrassed, they headed back to the hotel where they were all staying.

Teresa's glow on Friday night was only a preview of the radiant expression of Saturday, her wedding day. The day was beautiful. The sun was shining and the birds were singing. It was a perfect day for a wedding. Eve and Lola both dressed in coral linen pants suits with the fitted duster that buttoned to the waist and hung open to the floor. Their coral fabric pumps were dyed to match perfectly, and both had their hair pinned up with waterfall effect. They looked beautiful, but never more beautiful than the bride.

Teresa was absolutely stunning. Her red hair was perfectly pinned up with cascading curls falling around her face. Her headpiece was a rhinestone tiara that caught most of the curls. She wore a raw silk dress with a square cut neckline and fitted bodice. Out from the bodice, her dress flowed out and was encased with hand-sewn pearls from the waist to the tip of her three-foot train.

Her shoes had the same embroidered design as her dress. She looked like she had just stepped out of the pages of a bridal magazine.

When Eve saw her best friend walking down the aisle with her father, tears began to build up in her eyes. She was so beautiful and looked so happy. The tears actually managed to fall when her father lifted her veil and gave her a kiss. Eve allowed her eyes go to Teresa's mother and she beamed with pride at both her husband and her daughter.

When there came a point in the ceremony for a song, Eve took that opportunity to look out at the crowd. She smiled when she saw Nathan. He smiled at her and blew her a kiss. She turned to give her attention back to the ceremony when she caught Elijah's face in the back of the church. *What in the hell is he doing here?*

It was at this time that the vows were being given.

"Teresa, will you take Michael to be your lawfully wedded husband, to love, honor, and seek his counsel in all matters. To stay faithful, and true, to be his help mate, and his leaning post, to be the mother to his children, and to support him in his endeavors, forsaking all others until you leave this earth?"

Teresa responded with a loud and resounding "I do."

"Michael, will you take Teresa to be your lawfully wedded wife, to love, honor, and seek her counsel in all matters. To stay faithful, and true, to be her protector, progenitor, priest, to be her leaning post, to be the father to her children, and to support her in her endeavors, forsaking all others until you leave this earth?"

"I do."

"Ladies and gentleman let us be mindful that we are not witnessing a game. This marriage is a creation by God. It is in this relationship that we are to populate the earth. It is in this relationship that intimate love is to be shown to the world. And in this relationship, God's glory should be evident. Those of you who sit and bear witness that this man and woman have come together as man and wife also have a responsibility. Those who are under the presence of my voice I ask that you repeat after me. I as a witness of this marriage . . ."

"*I, as a witness of this marriage . . .*"

"Will support what God has put together . . ."

"*Will support what God has put together . . .*"

"Will honor the vows spoken here as they are my own . . ."

"*Will honor the vows spoken here as they are my own . . .*"

After the witness vows were given, Pastor Gregor pronounced them man and wife. The whole church erupted in applause and the exit music began to play. Since most of the pictures were taken before the wedding, the wedding party went immediately to the reception. Teresa wanted the rest of the bridal pictures to be taken over there.

The reception was nice and the food was great. Teresa and Michael worked the room and managed to greet every table that was there. When they cut the cake and had their first dance, Eve was relieved that her official duties were pretty much over. She found a seat by the back wall and waited for Nathan. Nathan had told her the night before the wedding that right after the wedding he had to take one of the boys he was mentoring to a game. He promised to make it to the reception by the time everyone was getting ready to get their boogie on. Eve leaned her head against the wall and watched Lola dance with two men. *That girl did not even care that we had Teresa's grandmother here. She is a mess.*

"You look beautiful today." Eve recognized his voice immediately.

"Thank you. So what in the hell are you doing here?"

Elijah moved a chair away from the table and took a seat. He smelled so good that Eve didn't want to look. She knew he looked as good as he smelled, if not better. "Michael and I go to the same gym. I saw him there with Teresa. I spoke and Teresa introduced us. Every time I went to the gym after that Michael and I spoke and he invited me to the wedding."

"Where is your wife?" Eve asked looking around.

"She had other plans this evening so I came by myself," he said smiling.

Don't smile at me fucker. Do not smile at me. I can never resist your smile.

"Why aren't you out there dancing?" he asked, sipping his champagne.

"I'm waiting on Nathan to get here," she said smugly, thinking Nathan's name alone would keep him away from her.

"Where *is* my boy Nathan? I spoke to him briefly before the wedding."

"Why would you speak to Nathan?" Eve asked defensively.

"We work in the same building remember?" Elijah sat back in his seat and continued smiling at her.

"Oh. Well, he took some kids to the basketball game."

"Hmmm, I just heard the game went to a second overtime. It must be a good one," he remarked, gazing out into the dance floor.

Damn it! That means Nathan is going to be even later. If I know Nathan, he is going to take that boy to get ice cream too. Eve's cell phone rang. "Excuse me." She got up and walked toward the exit with her phone. "Hello."

"Hey baby. I was calling to tell you I will be there as soon as I can. We just got out of the game and I'm going to take little man here to get a cone and then run him home. If traffic is kind, I will be there in about forty-five minutes."

"Ok. Take care. Love you."

"I love you too baby. Bye"

Eve hung up the phone and looked to see if she had any messages displayed.

"Oh, you two are in love?"

Eve spun around at the sound of Elijahs voice. In the reception, she didn't too much pay attention to what he had on, but she could see him clearly now. He stood before her in a black suit and emerald green shirt and matching tie. His coat was open and the tie was loosened around his neck. He stood there with two glasses of champagne.

"You scared the hell out of me."

"I'm sorry. I didn't intend to."

"I'm okay. I'm just going to go back in the reception."

"I brought you a glass of champagne. And you didn't answer my question. You're in love now?"

"Look Elijah, just let it go," Eve said. She was at the point that she realized she was tired of all the games they played. She craved the sex, but it wasn't worth what it was doing to her life. "You know what? Let it all go. Don't call me anymore. Don't leave any more messages on my machine or my voicemail. What went on between us is over. There is nowhere else we can go. We've had sex every way I know how and some ways I didn't know existed. We have exhausted the possibilities."

"Oh Eve." He chuckled with his usual cockiness, moved toward her, grabbed her arm, and began walking her further down the dark hall. "We have only touched the tip. There are so many other places I would like to take you. And I know you want to go."

"Oh see, that's where you are wrong." Eve pulled her arm from his grasp. "I'm sure there are places you could take me and I would like seeing, but I don't want to go with you. You could convince me, but I don't want to be convinced. I'm tired of being guilty."

"Guilt is a useless emotion. There's nothing you can do about what's already done," he stated, leaning against the wall between two large pillars.

Eve looked him as if he had two heads. She downed the champagne in the glass she had and set it on the table. "Well, I'm tired of lying. To answer your question Elijah, yes I love Nathan. I don't want to lie to him anymore."

"I can respect that. I will honor your wishes until you change your mind again." Elijah reached for her hand and began to massage her palm.

"Thank you, and I'm not going to change my mind."

"Okay." He brought her hand to his lips and kissed it. He looked into her eyes and she stared back. "Eve," he said in barely a whisper. "One more taste before I let you go?"

Eve shook her head no and tried to pull her hand away. He tightened his grip and pulled her toward him. He began to nuzzle her neck. She pushed, trying to get away, when she felt his tongue slide down the side of her neck and slip into her ear. Her heart fluttered and her knees grew weak. She stopped struggling and grabbed his shoulders.

Elijah turned Eve so that she was against the wall and began kissing down her neck toward her breasts. His hands began to unbutton her jacket.

Eve heard the DJ put on Marvin Gaye's "Sexual Healing." *Damn, I get theme music too? I'm going to let him get a little suckle and then I'll stop.*

Elijah's lips ran over her lace bra and her nipples hardened immediately.

When I get that feeling, I want sexual healing...ah baby. Make me feel so fine...sexual healing.

Elijah had managed to get her breast out of the bra and was licking and sucking like a wild man.

Come on, come on, come on, come on, let's make love tonight. Wake up, wake up, wakeup, wake up, 'cause you do it right...

She began to feel his hands unzipping her pants and sneaking his hands into her panties. The champagne she drank earlier took its effect and her head began spinning. Between the champagne and Elijah, she didn't know if she was coming or going. Elijah's head jerked away from her and that was when Eve heard a voice.

"Ah, my bad Elijah. I was just looking for my lady. I'm sorry to disturb the two of you."

"No problem," Elijah said, smiling.

Eve couldn't see who it was, but she recognized his voice.

"Have you seen Eve Newborn? She was the maid of honor today?" Nathan asked.

"No, man I haven't..."

Eve couldn't remember if she walked out or if Nathan walked closer, but she remembered vividly the expression on his face when he saw her with her breast hanging out the front of her jacket and her pants undone. Nathan looked at her from her head to her feet. She saw all the emotions from shock, to hurt, to rage. Nathan's hands balled into a fist and then unclenched. His mouth pinned together and his eyes grew hard and then they went dead. He said nothing. Eve wasn't going to even pretend that she could explain. Elijah looked at Eve and began trying to help her get dressed. Nathan stood and watched them until Eve was fully dressed again.

"Nathan, I'm so sorry," Eve said walking toward him.

Elijah slipped on down the dark hall and went out the exit at the opposite end of the hall.

"You sure are," Nathan said with a look that stopped her in dead in her tracks. "But who is sorrier, you or me? Erica was right. I'm still a big fool." He then took a box from his pocket and flipped it to her. He turned and walked out the closest exit.

Eve stood too stunned to move. *I know he's coming back. He will need to cool off, but he will be back in a moment. I know he will. It's not like Nathan to walk away and not talk things over. He will be back.*

Eve waited right where she was for a half an hour for Nathan to walk back in. It wasn't until one of the other bridesmaids came out to look for her that she returned to reality. Eve reached down and picked up the box he left and managed to get back into the reception smiling and greeting people. She was thankful that most people were full of champagne and didn't notice the distress on her face.

As she moved into the reception she looked for Teresa and Michael. She overheard one of the guests say they had left for their honeymoon. Eve was relieved. She didn't want to ruin Teresa's day. She moved through the reception until she managed to get Lola's attention. When she told Lola what happened, Lola cursed, got their purses, called a taxi, and took Eve home.

Do I even deserve a second chance?
Chapter 34

Eve found that work was impossible, so she put in for a week's vacation. Elijah hadn't called and had left no messages. Nathan refused her phone calls, blocked social media and sent back letters, cards, and gifts. The only thing he didn't send back was the box he threw at her before he left her at the reception. It was a ring that they had seen on a shopping trip they had. It was a beautiful triangle shaped diamond ring with diamonds circling it. Lola tried to convince Eve to keep it, but she couldn't. She didn't deserve it, but she wanted to earn it back if he'd let her.

Since her last day at work, she had not bothered changing clothes. She had convinced everyone at work and her family that she was going on a getaway. Everyone assumed she was going with Nathan and so most didn't question it. The only one that knew she was at home alone was Lola and that was by accident. Lola had come by to pick up the mail and caught Eve walking from her door to pick up her newspaper. Eve swore her to secrecy and Lola promised. Eve knew Lola would tell Teresa when she came back from her honeymoon. She also knew that once Teresa knew she and Lola would be coming by.

The day after Teresa got back, she and Lola were standing at her front door. Teresa walked in and grabbed Eve as soon as she had answered the door. Lola stepped inside and closed the door behind her. Walking toward the kitchen, Lola asked Eve if she had some coffee.

"Yeah, it's in the usual place," Eve answered as she and Teresa walked to the couch arm in arm.

"Teresa, how was the honeymoon?" Eve asked trying to keep the subject light.

"It was full of fucking and tourist attractions," Teresa answered curtly. "Now, what is going on with you?"

"I fucked up." Eve leaned into the couch, pulling her robe tightly around her. "I fucked up and there is no way back. You warned me, but I just knew what I was doing, didn't I?"

"I didn't come over here for I told you so's," Teresa expressed earnestly. "I was just coming to see about a friend that made some fucked up decisions and has to pay a fucked up price. I told you I never wanted to be involved, but when it was all over I would be here. So here I'm."

As Teresa reached over and hugged Eve, Lola came back in on the last comment. "Big fuckin' deal! You should have been involved all along," she said glibly putting the tray of coffee and muffins down on the table.

"Shut up, Lola," Teresa said, rising to help Lola with the tray.

"Anyway," Lola said, rolling her eyes. "Evie girl, what you gonna do now?"

"I have no idea. Nathan won't take my phone calls. He is sending my letters back. I have no clue what to do. I love that man."

"You want me to talk to him? You want me to see where he is in his thinking?" Teresa volunteered.

"Too late," Lola interrupted with a mouthful of muffin. "I have already talked to brother man and he ain't having it. That man was hurt. He didn't want to even hear Eve's name."

"Damn, Lola, be a little more sensitive to our sista here."

"Eve knows what's up. I'm sorry I keep it real. There is no need in sitting here pretending that Nathan is going to change his mind. That man is closed. He is hurt."

"Yeah, I know," Eve added with her hurt evident. "What do you expect when your man finds you with your titties out, pants undone, with a man you both know is married, and you both have some form of a working relationship with? Shit. My ass would be pissed."

"I understand Eve, but it has been a couple of weeks. He should just want to talk to you and give you a chance to explain."

"What the hell could I say?" Eve asked sarcastically. "Oh, I'm sorry... My bad, I thought he was you?"

All three sat in silence for a minute. Finally, Lola spoke. "I know one thing. You're not spending another day wrapped in your old bathrobe and have your hair slung back in the ponytail. Yeah damn it, it hurts right now, but you can't sit in it. It won't get better that way."

"Lola, I can't do anything else." Eve tried to hold back tears that had been present when she woke this morning. "I can't...I don't know how..." The dam broke and the new tears of the day moistened the dry tear stained roads left from yesterday.

I do love you.
Chapter 35

A month passed and Eve had since gone back to work. She wasn't over Nathan, but it had become a bit more bearable. She still found herself crying at night, but she wasn't having crying fits at work and she counted that as all good. Elijah had made himself scarce, as well. She heard through the grapevine that he was on a six-week consultation assignment for the new company he worked for. Eve had finished up the last of her work when Pat buzzed in a call for her.

"Eve Newborn," she responded automatically as she shoveled papers.

"Hello Eve." Her hands stilled at his voice.

"Hello, Nathan. How have you been?"

"I have been better, but I have been worse." There was silence. "I'm calling to see if you would meet me for dinner?"

Eve didn't know what to say. She had been hoping for this for so long and now he called. "Ah sure, that wouldn't be a problem. When?"

"Are you free this evening?"

"Yeah...yes. I'm free. Where would you like to meet?"

"Where we met the first time. I'll see you around 6:00."

With that Eve hung up the phone. She couldn't work. She picked up the phone and called Lola at the center.

"This is Lola. How can I help you?"

"Girl, he called me. I going to have dinner with him and I don't know what to say. I don't have an excuse. I don't have a reason. I..."

"Hello?" Lola yelled to get Eve's attention. "First of all, you going to slow your ass down and tell me who you are talking about."

Eve took a deep breath and told Lola about her phone call with

Nathan.

"Well, are you going to go?"

"Hell yeah, I'm going to go. I just don't know what to say?"

"Well, if you don't know what to say, what are you going to do?"

"I don't know." Eve sounded annoyed. "I didn't call you for you to ask questions. I called to get some advice on what I should say."

"Hold on. Let me conference call Teresa."

Eve waited as Lola placed her on hold. A few minutes later, both Teresa and Lola were on the phone. "So Evie, he called?" Teresa asked. Eve assumed Lola had filled her in before they clicked back over to her.

"Yeah, so what would you tell him?"

"I would tell him the truth," Teresa said as if there was no other answer.

"Okay, how much of the truth?"

"None of it!" Lola interrupted. "Look, tell him it was the champagne and you let yourself get away from you."

"And she will be lying." Teresa was quick to point out. "Look Eve, you just need to be honest. You haven't been honest since this whole thing started."

"I still think if you want him back you are going to have to lie," Lola added.

"Maybe I don't deserve to have him?"

"I don't think it's an issue of deserve," Teresa insisted. "It's an issue of broken trust. He may never trust you. And you need to be prepared for that."

"Hey, have you heard from Elijah?" Lola abruptly asked.

"No."

"Well damn. He didn't say anything to you at all? I mean, he was there and he knows Nathan."

"I don't know if I'm upset with him," Eve exhale noisily. "Or glad that he did what I asked him to do and not call."

"Yeah, but he should have called to check on you." Lola insisted. "I mean, he just left you there with Nathan. He didn't know if Nathan would beat you or not."

"Oh Lord, Lola," Teresa interrupted. "Can we just deal with one thing at a time? We have to figure out what Eve is going to say to Nathan."

"I'm going to tell him the truth," she decided and ended the call with her friends.

Eve's boss called for a meeting with all managers. By the time she made it back to her desk, it was five o'clock and she was going to have to meet with Nathan. Her nerves began to jump and her hands grew sweaty. She said she was going to tell the truth, but she had no idea how she was going to do it and how much she was going to tell. She figured if he asked she'd tell all.

When she walked into the restaurant, the host smiled at her and nodded for her to follow. She and Nathan had been there so many times he assumed she was there for Nathan. In this case, he was correct. She walked slowly behind the host until she saw Nathan. He was looking at the menu and she took the opportunity to stare at him. He looked good. As a matter of fact, he looked way better than she felt. He was dressed in a pair of jeans and a polo shirt. His jacket was slung over the chair that was next to him. She could tell he just came from the barbershop by the slightly raised and red skin along his edges. His barber always cut too closely and had stray hairs not completely swept from his shoulders. When the host was standing by the table, Nathan looked up at her. His usual warm smile and inviting eyes gave no indication of warmth. Although his stare wasn't cold, there was a bit of indifference in them. The smile Eve had for him fell slightly.

"Hello," Eve greeted as she placed her stuff in the chair next to her.

"Hello."

They sat there in silence. Eve was looking at him to speak and

Nathan was again looking at the menu. Finally, the waitress came to the table and asked if they were ready.

He looked up at Eve in a questioning glance and she nodded and ordered the Chinese chicken salad and ice tea. She didn't think she could keep any more than that down. Nathan ordered the steak and stuffed baked potato with broccoli and cheese.

Eve smiled to herself. This was exactly what they ordered the first time they had dinner together. To break the silence, she decided to share that with him. "You know, we ordered the same thing the first time I met you here."

"I hadn't realized," he answered, sitting back looking at her. "I guess it's fitting that we did it again."

"What do you mean?"

"Well, since this will be the last time we sit here together for dinner," he answered calmly.

Eve's last bit of hope dashed in one sentence. It was over. She already knew it was, but she had kept one fire burning for the mere chance he would be forgiving. Not knowing how to respond to that, she took a sip of water. They sat in silence for a few minutes before Eve spoke again. "How have you been?"

Nathan looked at her as if she were crazy for asking. Eve thought he wasn't going to answer as she watched him take a drink of his water. Finally, he spoke. "I'm as well as any man could be after seeing the woman he loves up against a wall with a known married man sucking on her breasts."

Eve winced at the words and sat quietly. Nathan just stared at her.

I should just leave. I should just get up, grab my stuff, and head for my car. This man doesn't have forgiveness for me, so I'm not even sure why I'm here. I just need to get up. Get up Eve. Get Up!

She didn't.

The waitress brought the food and they began to eat in continuous silence. Eve watched Nathan cut his steak meticulously like he always did. She was more aware of what he was eating than her own food. That didn't surprise her. She kept waiting for him to offer her some of his food off his fork as he always did. It never happened. She watched him devour his food while only moving her salad around her plate. He never looked up at her the whole time he ate. When he finished, he sat back in his chair, drank more from his water glass and finally looked at her. He caught her staring.

"Why am I here?" Eve asked. "I know you haven't forgiven me. If you can't forgive me, then I know that you don't want me. So why am I here? Why did you call me? I got the picture that you didn't want anything to do with me when you didn't call."

"Eve." Nathan spoke her name so intensely that Eve sat back in her chair. He ran his hands over his head and let out a deep breath. Then he slammed the table. "Damn it Eve, why?"

Eve looked around and noticed some of the people at the surrounding table were looking at them. She didn't know how to react. She had never seen Nathan this way.

"Why would you do that to us? Why?" he asked, shaking his head completely confused. "I thought we were so good together. I thought we loved each other. I was going to ask you to marry me that damned night. Why the fuck would you do this to me? On second thought," the conversation switched quickly, "Never mind. I don't want to know."

Nathan got up and placed some money on the table and grabbed his coat. He walked toward the exit and left Eve sitting there stunned. She didn't know whether she was coming or going. One second he was in her face wanting to know why and the next he was gone. When she came to herself, she grabbed her coat and headed for the door. Eve didn't remember actually walking through the restaurant to leave until the cool night air hit her face and she had to put her coat on. She walked to her car and put the key in her car door.

"Eve, I do want to know."

Eve whirled around at the sound of Nathan's voice behind her. "My God, Nathan, you scared me," she said leaning against the car trying to recover her breath.

"Why Eve? Why?" The hurt in his voice penetrated Eve's heart like a jagged knife. When he moved into the light where she could see him, the knife turned. His eyes were wide and glossy and his mouth held grim.

"I...I don't." Eve dropped her head and closed her eyes to hold back tears. She thought she was all cried out. She finally looked at him in his face and said, "I don't have an answer for you."

Nathan moved closer to her and stared in her eyes. "How long were you with him? I mean, was it just that night? Had you been drinking? Tell me something, Eve, so this shit can make sense to me. I have spent the last weeks just trying to make it make sense. Did he force you and I overreacted? Tell me something." The hurt in his voice was almost more than Eve could bear.

Eve allowed her head to drop back and took a deep breath. Avoiding his face, she looked at the other cars around her and licked her lips. She didn't have a clue how to tell this man that Elijah was there before him. *Would he understand that Elijah was an infatuation and that what I had with him he was just physical? How do I get him to understand I never loved Elijah and I have always loved him? I'm going to do what Teresa said and just tell him the truth.*

"Nathan, it wasn't all of what you think. I started seeing Elijah a few months before I met you. At first, I didn't know he was married, but when I found out he was I didn't care. I was alone for so long that I needed someone to make me feel like I was something. And admittedly I was physically attracted to him. So I decided I would just do this thing, keep it to myself because I knew it would be temporary. Soon, I found myself becoming more involved, but it wasn't love. It was like a drug. I thought I needed him even though when I was with him I still felt lonely. I was never under any illusion that I was in love, but I was jealous of his wife.

She had someone to call hers and I didn't. So I allowed myself to be involved with him. I was okay until I met you. You brought sunshine into my life. I was no longer lonely. I was so excited that you came into my life that I was determined to let Elijah go, but I found that I couldn't. He was in my head. He knew all the buttons to push and when he found out about you and he didn't care...He made me think...no let me change that. I fooled myself into thinking I could have my cake and eat it too. I thought I could have whatever it was I thought I needed from him and have your love too."

Nathan stared at Eve in disbelief. "Eve, did you think I would never find out?"

Eve looked down at her hands and took a deep breath. "To be honest, no. I never thought you'd find out. Ironically, you found out when I was trying to end it all. I wanted it to be just us, so I told him that night I wouldn't see him anymore. And while he told me that he accepted that, he began to push my buttons..."

"My God, Eve," Nathan interrupted. "Have you no shame? Are you that weak? Elijah Mann is married with children. Even if you didn't think about me, did you ever think about that?"

Eve had no answer to that. Of course she had thought about his wife and kids, but apparently she thought more of herself. "Nathan, this isn't about Elijah or his family. This is about me and you. The only thing Elijah has to do with this is that I allowed him to get in my head. I allowed him to get to know what buttons to push. Before you came into the hallway, I was telling him it was over. I would like to believe that I would have stopped him before anything more happened."

"But you can't tell me that you actually would have, can you?" he challenged.

"No," Eve whispered. "But seeing you that night released me from this madness."

"Oh really?" he asked sarcastically. "It released a little more if I recall." Nathan's hands brushed across her breasts. Her nipples tightened at the sensation. Nathan smirked when he saw her reaction. "I never realized how easy it really was to 'push your buttons'."

Embarrassed, Eve wrapped her coat around her.

Nathan leaned up against the car and they stood in silence.

Eve didn't know what to think or say. She wanted to tell him how much she loved him and that Elijah was a part of her past and they could work through it, but as she looked in his face she wasn't sure if that was what he wanted to hear. In the restaurant, she was so sure that this was it. This expression wasn't saying the same thing.

Nathan looked at Eve and moved to stand directly in front of her. He stood close enough for her to feel the heat of his breath on her face. With one finger, he lifted her chin and looked directly in her eyes. "I have loved you from the moment I laid eyes on you," he spoke quietly, but with great conviction.

"I love you, too," Eve whispered back.

Nathan bent his head down so that his lips could touch hers. It was one of the softest sweetest kisses that Eve had ever experienced in her life. She felt all the love he had for her and she wanted to give to him everything she had in her. When he pulled away, she stared at his face in awe.

"Eve, I don't know you and I don't trust you." Her awe turned to confusion then pain. He leaned down and kissed her again, this time very hard and quick. "Goodbye."

With that, Nathan turned around and walked away. It only took a few seconds for Eve to realize he was gone for good. The best thing that ever happened to her had just walked out of her life.

A hard head makes a soft behind.
Chapter 36

It had been so hard when Nathan left her in the parking lot that night. She had no idea what to do or who to talk to. She went the only place she knew to go and that was home. When she walked into her mother's house and saw her parents, Judith and Seth, sitting in the living room she just broke down in tears. Her father, never one to be able to handle tears, after discerning that she was not harmed, left her to speak to her mother. She broke down and told her mother everything. About Elijah, Nathan and even being caught. She ended up spending a few days over to her mother's house praying for Nathan to forgive her, but she knew it would be a while before she was able to forgive herself for the whole mess.

A few weeks after her dinner with Nathan, Eve was sitting at home watching television with her sister, April, when the phone rang. April jumped up to answer it. She was expecting an apology call from her on and off again boyfriend.

"Eve, it's for you."

"Who is it?" Eve asked.

April shrugged her shoulders and handed her the phone.

"Hello."

"Hello Momma, long time, no hear." It was Elijah.

What the hell? Why is he calling me now? Okay. Okay. Calm yourself, Eve.

"Hello Elijah," she replied coolly. "Is there something I can help you with?"

"Damn, that was kind of chilly. I was calling to ask you to meet me for coffee or ice cream."

"I have to tell you Elijah, the last time I met you for coffee I ended up in something that completely changed my life. I don't think I can go through another life changing experience. So I'm going to say no."

"Please Eve? Just meet me. I promise it will be okay."

Eve sat on the phone for a few minutes not saying anything. *I so not need to be getting myself in any more shit. If I had the sense God gave a mongoose, I would hang up the phone.*

"Come on, Eve. Just give me an hour," Elijah begged.

Without a hope or a prayer that Nathan would ever forgive her, Eve finally gave in to Elijah's pleading. "Ok. I will meet you at the same place in thirty minutes."

Eve had convinced herself that she was over Elijah. After repeated conversations with Teresa, and Lola, and even her mother, she felt that she had worked this "addiction" she had to him. She still longed for intimacy, but she found herself longing more for Nathan's companionship than anything else. She was feeling lonely again, but she vowed that the way to resolve that was not with Elijah. She convinced herself that seeing Elijah this last time was about closure.

When she walked in, he was already sitting at the table. He had a cup of coffee in his hand and was reading the menu. She watched him a little before she made herself known. His hands were strong and she could see the veins running through them as he gripped his coffee mug. His mouth was inviting as she watched him put the cup to his lips for a sip. He spotted her. An easy smiled slipped on his face and his eyes seemed to twinkle.

That is the look that got me in trouble in the first place. Just play it cool, Eve. Just play it cool. But I have to admit, he is still the sexiest man I have ever had the privilege of knowing. And he seemingly has the knack of catching me at a lonely low point. I'm not going to do this shit again. The first time I can call a mistake. The second time I got to be a fool.

As she walked toward the table he stood. "Well, hello Momma. You are looking too fine," he said with a cheesy looking grin.

"Thank you," Eve replied with a smirk.

He pulled the chair out for her and they both sat down. The

waitress came over and set two glasses of water on the table. Pulling her pencil and paper out of her apron, she asked if they were ready.

"Yes," Eve answered. "I will have the grilled cheese sandwich with French fries. Make sure the edges of the sandwich are crisp but not burnt. And I would like lemonade with my meal." The waitress wrote it all down and with a nod turned to Elijah.

"I want a hamburger...no wait. I want a cheeseburger with everything on it."

"Including onions?" the waitress asked. Elijah looked at Eve. Eve gave him a look as if to say what are you looking at me for? "Everything! I want French fries and I want them crisp. And can I have a soda with my meal? For right now I will drink my water and I'm finished with my coffee." The waitress picked up the menus and Elijah's coffee mug and went to put in the order.

"What did you need to see me about?" Eve asked not pulling any punches.

"Well, damn!" Elijah laughed. He leaned back into his chair and folded his arms. Eve looked at him patiently waiting. Elijah chuckled to himself and shook his head. He then moved so that his elbows were touching the table.

"I just wanted to make sure that you were alright. You know it has been a while and..."

"You are checking on me now?" she interrupted him. "You left me there with a buzz on and angry man and you are checking on me months later? That is real rich, Elijah."

"Look Eve, contrary to popular belief, I'm not an asshole. I never really left. I didn't think Nathan was the kind of guy that was violent towards women, but I wasn't sure." He took a sip of water. "After I walked out the door, I went around the back and came in from the other side with Nathan's back to me. I couldn't hear what you were saying, but I was there in case he got crazy."

"Well, I sure in the hell didn't see you," Eve added weakly. She was relieved to find this out. She had often replayed that night in her head and in conversation with her friends. She often thought what would have happened if Nathan had been the violent type. She knew he was mad enough to do damage.

"Well. Did you two make up?" Elijah asked with such casualness.

"I would think that you would know that." Eve played with her water glass. "I wouldn't be here with you?"

Elijah nodded. "Look," he interjected. "I was just asking. You two could have been trying to work it out."

"Well no, we didn't. So how's your wife?"

"We're separated."

"Oh, she found out that you were fucking other people?" Eve asked directly. She really had no sympathy for him.

"Something like that," he replied coolly. He picked up his water glass and drank allowing ice to tumbling into his mouth.

"So is this why you called? 'Cause now we can sex each other guilt-free?" Eve asked searching for the ice cubes in her glass.

"I never had guilt. That was you. And if I said yes, would you consider it?" Elijah asked, crunching on his ice.

Eve lifted her eyes and found the challenge in his... "Are you asking?" she challenged back.

He smiled. It was then the waitress came bringing the food to the table. She had the order wrong, so Eve and Elijah spent the next ten minutes arguing about their food. Finally, the manager came over and settled matters and their order was corrected and didn't cost them a thing. Through all the turmoil, Eve made a conscious effort to stay away from the dangerous games Elijah knew how to play.

"So Elijah, how long have you been on your own?" Eve ask sipping her lemonade and eating her French fries.

"Not too long after I last saw you. We had been on that path a long while. It just came to a head and exploded all over us."

"Did she find out about us?" Eve asked really concerned. She had always felt bad for his wife and she'd feel worst if it was because of her.

"No. Actually, I saw her having lunch with another man. I didn't much like it. I told her so, she confronted me with my dirt and the rest is history."

"Damn!" Eve said with an ironic smile. "Ain't that some shit. I can recall a time when I mentioned her with another man and you nearly bit my head off."

"Yeah, well. C'est la Vie!"

"I guess it is. I guess the chicken came home to roost."

Eve and Elijah sat in silence for a moment. They were both were going over the last year in their head. It was unbelievable. As they both searched their memories, their eyes met.

"Eve. Are you interested in coming back to my place with me for a drink?"

Hell no! Do not go! Do not go! Are you gonna to be the same fool twice? Eve you know it is not a good idea. But think what it would be like to not have to be bogged down with the idea that he has a wife in kids at home waiting. Gurl, you could get your freak on for real. You know where that path ends. Don't go!

"Yeah, Elijah, I will."

Eve followed Elijah back to his apartment. Since she had only ever been with him at her house or his hotel room, she didn't know what to expect. She was pleasantly surprised. His living room was decorated in black and white and she soon found out that just about every room was. The only splashes of color could be found in the African American prints framed on his walls. Walking over to the stereo, he put in a Maxwell CD and led Eve to the couch. Going into the kitchen, he came back out with two glasses of wine and handed one to her.

"Elijah, isn't this whole scene a bit of a cliché?"

"What do you mean?" he asked, putting his drink on the table and moving closer to her.

"The whole turn on the music, drink a glass a wine to get me in the mood, seduction scene that you got going on here. Isn't this what extremely sappy romantic comedies do? I'm not in the movies. We both know what we came here for, so let's not do this."

Elijah responded by grabbing the back of her head while his lips found hers. His tongue wandered into her mouth, slipping in quietly almost unnoticeably. His hands moved to the buttons on her shirt and bra, removing them within seconds. Her breasts moved freely and he moved his lips to her breasts immediately. He suckled like a babe lapping her hardened nipple with his tongue. Eve made great efforts to grip his shirt to bring it over his head. Every time she grabbed the ends, his mouth would send a sensation through her until her hands grew weak.

Elijah moved away from her and stood up from the couch. He removed his shirt and she allowed her eyes to roam over his honey gold chest. She stood up and brought her hands to his chest. She led her hand down the center of his chest and her fingers got caught in the hair leading to his pants. She heard him emit a low growl and he picked her up carrying her into his bedroom for a night of signature Elijah Mann passion.

Morning came and Eve awoke with a start not sure where she was. It took her a moment to process what had occurred the night before. She looked over at Elijah. He was sleeping peacefully with just a little slobber in the corner of his mouth. She smiled to herself.

Damn it. This man ain't perfect after all. As if I didn't already know that.

As she watched Elijah sleep, it came to her. She didn't want this. This was not what she wanted or deserved in her life. She didn't have to settle for Elijah because he's available now. Well, kind of anyway. She didn't want a man like him. As her mother would say, "If he cheated with you, he will cheat on you."

Eve slipped out of the bed and hurried around the room

gathering her clothes. She went into the bathroom in the hallway and washed up a little. Putting her clothes on, she snuck back in the room to make sure Elijah was still asleep.

"Bye Elijah," she whispered. "You've taught me more than I ever thought imaginable and I ain't talking about sex." Eve giggled to herself and covered her mouth when he moved in the bed. "I wish I could say call me when you want to get down, but that's not how I'm rollin' from here on out. I wish you nothing but the best."

Eve blew a kiss at the sleeping man in the bed and left his apartment. That was the last time she saw him until two years later.

Epilogue

Eve walked down the street with her shopping bags in both hands. Her big white floppy hat sat cocked on the right side of her face dipping over her black Donna Karen sunglasses. Her sandy hair lay across her shoulders. Her navy jacket extended down to her knees and was set off by the matching skirt that didn't dip much further.

Stopping to admire a red chiffon evening dress displayed in the window of one of the exclusive boutiques downtown, she checked her watch. She had time. She was meeting Lola and Teresa for lunch and she knew only Lola would be on time, Teresa was notorious for being late. Luckily, the restaurant where they were meeting was just up the street.

Strolling down the avenue looking at the newest designs, Eve knew she shouldn't have walked from her office to the restaurant. Shopping was her weakness and she always gave in to temptation. Her impulsiveness got her in more trouble than debt and she promised she would make wiser decisions. Two pair of shoes later, she was now looking at this dress in the window. Looking longingly at the beautiful scarlet dress, she exercised her discipline and made the decision to walk past the entrance of the store.

"You know you would look too good in that dress." That unforgettable voice sent chills up and down her back causing Eve to stop in her tracks. She hadn't heard that voice in two years and she couldn't believe she was hearing it now. She took a moment and gathered herself before she responded.

"Well, I'm teaching myself to resist temptations, no matter how enticing they can be." She turned to face her past.

"Well, resisting is overrated," he said, smiling that easy smile. "I say go for it."

"Well, Elijah," she said offering a sad smile. "I did that before and it didn't quite work out like I wanted." *Damn, I remember that smile.*

"Ah, you remembered my name," he answered with mock surprise. "Two years is a long time." His smile broadened. "Well, can I tell you that you look better than ever."

"I could never forget your name," she said, taking off her glasses and revealing deep brown soulful eyes. "And I have more scars from you than even I will admit to and some that will never let me," she whispered to address the latter comment.

He cocked his head questioning. She took in Elijah's handsome face. *Damn, this man will forever be fine.* They stared in awkward silence. Elijah finally spoke.

"I'm still working here in the city, although I do have another offer on the table. Some would say that it's an offer that I can't refuse."

That was such a random thing to say. I have never experienced him seemingly so uncomfortable. "You know those offers you can't refuse sometimes are not what they promise." She paused letting her words stand between them, and then she looked down at her watch again. "I have to go. I hope that all your endeavors work for your good."

"I do too," Elijah answered with a suggestive meaning.

Eve started adjusting the bags in her hands. "It was nice seeing you Elijah. Take care." Eve turned around and began to walk away. She didn't hear him behind her so when he touched her chills skipped along her spine and somehow settled in her stomach. His touch had that everlasting affect. She turned and looked up into his eyes.

"Eve, I was thinking..."

Eve smiled removing his hand from her arm and placing her shades on her face. "No Elijah, don't think. That is what got us here."

"Eve, it's been a while. You don't have a little time for me?"

Elijah asked, grabbing her arms. Eve removed her glasses again and smiled.

"What is it that you need, Elijah?" she asked as if she were pacifying a child.

"That's a loaded question, you know?" He lifted his eyebrows and slipped into an easy smile.

"Not really." Eve tried to sound unaffected when in actuality her stomach fluttered giving into a flurry of butterflies. "I'm meeting people for lunch so what do you need?"

"Can we have a seat for a moment?" Eve turned around and noticed the outside café a few feet away.

"Sure, but only a minute." They both walked over and he pulled her chair out for her. "I could say a lot of things about you, Elijah, and one will always be that you are a gentleman."

"Thank you. I would like to say that you," he said, placing a great emphasis on the latter word, "have always been considerate of me, but I can't do that, can I?"

Eve just smiled and waited knowing that he would bring up the last time they had seen each other.

"Why did you leave?" he asked.

Although Eve was expecting that question, she wasn't expecting the sense of urgency that was there.

"I woke up and you were gone." He went on. "I thought maybe you'd left a note, but there was nothing. And when I called you, your number had been changed. It didn't take me long to figure you didn't want to see me so I avoided Clearview. When I found that I had business there, I looked for you, but by then you had resigned. What happened?"

"Well Elijah, I got a life. I was tired of borrowing other people's life because I didn't like mine. I went back to school and got a degree in social work and now I'm working for a private adoption agency. Two years ago, when I left your apartment, I also left a lot of things that I just didn't like any more."

"Are you saying you didn't like me?"

"It's not that simple, but if that is how you want to take it...that's okay." Eve looked at her watch and realized she was going to be late. She slipped on her shades once more. She leaned over the table and placed her hand on Elijah's. *His hands are so strong.* "I have to go Elijah. It was nice seeing you. Take care." Eve scooted her chair out and rose from her seat. She nodded at him and turned to walk away.

"Eve, this is the last time I'm going to see you, isn't it?"

Eve smiled the brightest smile she had. "A man once told me that it's inevitable that when playing with fire you are going to get burned. I've been there and done that and this is where it ends."

My Dearest Reader,

Thank you for taking the time to read *Inevitable*. This novel was inspired by a time in my life when only married men seemed to be attracted to me and I decided to write about what would happen if someone allowed themselves to get caught up. The relationship between Eve and Elijah was built on pure lust and the ride can be great but like fireworks it eventually burns out. The relationship between Eve and Nathan represents what many women want and how we can easily sabotage ourselves. The friendship between Eve, Teresa, and Lola was intended to play the angel on one shoulder and devil on the other.

When I started writing this story with all these things in mind I found that the characters took on a life of their own and they decided what they wanted to do. We saw Eve move from someone who was reliable, responsible and cautious and into a lying deceitful person of whom she didn't recognize. It was inevitable that this story would end without the typical happy ending that most look for, but Eve received her own kind of happy ending in learning who she did and did not want to be. Now that she seems to have come back to reality don't count her out on getting the love that she deserves.

Best,
Kolene